Knowsley Council

Knowsley Library Service
Please return this book on or
before the date shown below

-9 JUN 2023

You may return this book to any Knowsley Library
For renewal please telephone:

Halewood 443 2086; Home Delivery Service 443 4202;
Huyton 443 3734; Kirkby 443 4289; Prescot 443 5101;
School Library Service 443 2670·
Stock'

Visit us at:
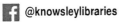 @knowsleylibraries

/lib

D1333669

BOOKS BY ANGELA MARSONS

DETECTIVE KIM STONE PREQUEL

First Blood

DETECTIVE KIM STONE SERIES

Angela MARSONS
HIDDEN SCARS

bookouture

Published by Bookouture in 2022

An imprint of Storyfire Ltd.
Carmelite House
50 Victoria Embankment
London EC4Y 0DZ

www.bookouture.com

ISBN: 978-1-80314-772-7
eBook ISBN: 978-1-80314-771-0

This book is dedicated to Elaine Tasker of the Equine Market Watch horse sanctuary. Without fail, twice a day, every day, this incredible lady drives past our house to care for the ten horses in her charitable care. With only a small team of fantastic volunteers, this lady offers previously neglected and mistreated animals the best quality of life for however long they need it.

Her energy and passion is truly inspirational.

PROLOGUE

I stare through the living-room window. She is napping. This has become her nightly routine. She dozes off around ten, trying to fight the end-of-day fatigue.

She could switch off the lamp and haul herself up the stairs to the larger of the two bedrooms, collapse on the bed and let deep sleep claim her. But she won't because I'm not home yet. She can't sleep until I'm home.

Normally I'd walk in the door, remove my boots and she'd sit up straight, widen her eyes and pretend she hadn't been softly snoring. But not tonight.

'You ready?' the voice beside me hisses.

For just a few short seconds I had forgotten what we were here to do. A pang of regret shoots through me but it's the only way. We have agreed.

I open the door, gently, my jaw clenching with tension at the prospect of even the tiniest noise. I don't want her to wake up and see me. That would ruin everything.

I move further into the hallway, one deliberate, calculated step at a time.

I try to hear past my own breathing, which I'm sure must be echoing around the house. It will wake her. I know it will.

Just above the gentle hum of the fridge to my left, in the kitchen, I hear the soft snoring coming from the sofa. I inexplicably feel both relief and dismay. Does some part of me want her to wake up and ask what the hell we're doing?

I push the thought away. If that were to happen, nothing would change. She would still ruin my life and force me to let go of the thing I love with every ounce of my being.

My jaw clenches in anger. Just the thought sends a wave of rage ripping through my body. She will not separate us. No one will ever pull us apart. A love like ours is unique, forever and I have known it from the moment we met. No one understands that this relationship means more to me than breathing. Without it I might as well be dead.

There is no time for second thoughts. We have a plan, and if we don't carry it out, the alternative doesn't bear thinking about. We will not be parted.

I step silently, slowly into the lounge. I beckon behind me to indicate that the coast is clear.

No words are exchanged. There is no need. We both know the plan.

We stand behind the sofa.

The orange lamp lights up the area around the three of us as though we are the final act of a stage play, the rest of the room bathed in darkness.

Every second counts.

She could wake up.

The hammer rises in the air.

It falls with unflinching certainty.

The sound of bone cracking fills the silence. Then a moan, a gurgle as blood begins to pour from the hole in her head. In this light it appears black. The glistening richness of the liquid is caught in the lamplight as it escapes like lava from a volcano and runs down the line of her hair.

I am horrified by what I see and yet liberated too. There is no more indecision. No more doubt. We are beyond the point of return. It cannot be undone.

The conversations, the wishes, the plans are now real life. We will be together forever. This binds us like nothing else ever could.

The hammer appears before my face. Drops of blood fall onto the throw that's draped over the back of the sofa.

'Your turn.'

I take it, surprised by the weight of it in my hand. My palm closes tightly around the rubber handle.

'Do it.'

I lift the hammer and hesitate as another soft moan escapes from her mouth.

'If you love me, you'll do it.'

Of that there is no doubt. Has never been any doubt. I would do anything to prove my love.

Swiftly and decisively, I bring the hammer down.

ONE

'You sure you're ready for this?' Woody asked, peering over his glasses.

Her back was ramrod straight and her hands rested in her lap. She was the picture of control, and in the last two months she'd learned that appearances were everything.

'Sir, my psych eval—'

'I'm not talking about your meetings with the force psychologist. I have their report and you wouldn't be sitting in my office if they hadn't deemed you fit for duty. I'm asking you.'

'I'm good, sir. Keen and eager to return to my duties.'

He peered at her for another few seconds. She held his gaze.

Was he wondering how she had passed the psych evaluation?

It hadn't been hard.

Kim had known from the minute she walked away from the cemetery after apprehending Symes that it would be far harder to repair her mind than her body. Being beaten to a pulp by one of her old enemies had left deeper scars on her psyche than it had on her flesh. She had known that the physical part of her recovery would take at least eight weeks. The broken bones had mended and most of the pins had been removed, all but one in her right hip that was now with her for life. There had been nothing easy about her rehabilitation, but the focus on mending her body had distracted her from the thoughts in her mind.

She had planned her psychological recovery with the same diligence and had divided her recovery up into four two-week periods, to successfully stage her psychological recovery.

At two psych appointments per week she'd spent the first four appointments talking about the nightmares that plagued her. She'd done her research and offered variations on typical PTSD after-effects. Not once had she divulged the true nature of the night terrors.

The second quarter she'd spent telling the therapist what she'd wanted to hear about how frightened she'd been. By the third quarter, the nightmares were lessening and she was seeing family and friends again. She was walking Barney almost daily and chatting with other dog walkers. By the fourth quarter, the nightmares were rare and she was feeling like her old self much of the time.

It was complete bullshit, but the therapist had swallowed it and patted himself on the back for a job well done.

She was signed out of therapy two days before the medical doctor declared her physically fit enough to return to work.

The nightmares were still there, and the truth about her well-being would never leave the inside of her mouth. It was her battle to fight and no one else could help her. She'd always sorted her problems on her own and in her own time.

'Have you been in touch with anybody?' Woody asked.

She shook her head.

The messages from her team had gone unanswered. Bryant had been more persistent; knocking on her door at least once a week, with some home-cooked offering from Jenny. She'd simply turned up the music and ignored him until he went away.

She'd felt a twinge of guilt watching him walk down the path, but she didn't have the energy to spend assuring people she was okay, especially the people who knew her best.

'I assume you know who has been running the team in your absence?'

Her jaw clenched in response.

'Brierley Hill had a restructure leaving them a DI spare, and we had a space.' He opened his hands expressively.

She understood. To the powers above it was a simple numbers game. Surplus here, a gap there. Perfect. It would have been if not for the part he'd played in the Symes investigation.

'I know you won't ask but my response is that the team has been chugging along.'

She nodded her understanding. There had been nothing major and he'd been keeping the team warm.

'Keep him around for as long as you need to. Ease in gently and stick to desk duties for the next week or two. You're not—'

'Are we done, sir?' she asked, standing.

His expression told her that there was more he wanted to say, but slowly he nodded that she could leave.

She got to the door before she heard his voice again.

'Stone, no one expects miracles. You've been through—'

'Thank you, sir, but I'll be fine,' she said, closing the door behind her.

She took a breath and readied herself for the journey ahead. It was three corridors and one flight of stairs. She gritted her teeth and went for it.

The calls came from all directions.

'Welcome back, marm.'

'Good to see you.'

She put down her head and surged forward, fighting her way past people who would never normally speak to her for fear of having their heads ripped off. She prayed that the novelty of her return would wear off quickly.

She arrived at the safety of the squad room and breathed a sigh of relief. She had sent a brief text to Bryant the night before saying:

Back tomorrow. No Fuss.

Unusually, the door to the CID room was closed. A rare occurrence on her watch. CID was already classed as a separation from the rest of the force and closed doors did nothing to dispel that fact.

She took another deep breath and realised she did that a lot these days.

She opened the door to silence, but four heads turned towards her.

Stacey's face instantly creased into a smile, as did Penn's. Bryant caught her gaze and nodded.

'Morning, boss,' Penn and Stacey sang together as the fourth occupant of the room who was seated at the spare desk stood and offered his hand.

'DI Burns. I was involved—'

'You're the idiot who refused to link the search for Symes with his hatred for me?' she said, ignoring his outstretched hand.

She'd been away for two months. She'd read everything.

His face hardened as his hand fell back to his side. 'I simply offered an alternative...'

'And how'd that work out for you?' she asked, walking past him.

From the pile of belongings on the spare desk it was clear that he'd vacated her office speedily.

'Carry on, folks,' she said, reaching the door to the Bowl. 'If you need me I'll be deleting twenty thousand emails.'

She closed the door behind her and leaned against it to get her breath. It felt like she'd entered a space that was now alien to her.

DI Ian Burns. Thirty-one years of age, unmarried, with a father and grandfather who had served before him. Ambitious, driven and hopeful that the capture of Symes was going to be the crowning glory on his application to DCI.

Her life had been a promotion opportunity. He'd shot and he'd missed.

She knew what had happened. His acute failure to connect the dots had resulted in him being sent to Siberia. Big promotions didn't come out of Halesowen, and DI Burns was now on his own.

Having read the files, there were some of his actions that she could understand and others she could not. But one thing she couldn't forgive was what he had used in defence of himself in his statement and the one fact that had kept him away from demotion. The fact that she had willingly given herself to the enemy. Somehow, he had managed to turn his own failings back on her.

She pulled her attention away from his bowed head and pushed away the violent thoughts that were running through her mind. She switched on her computer.

Take your time, Woody had said. Ease into it gently. Take back control when you're ready.

Right now she had no idea when that would be.

TWO

It took Kim around half an hour to empty her inbox of circulars, memos and updates.

After filing anything from Woody, Keats and her team, she had simply pressed 'delete all' and watched thousands of messages disappear with the touch of a button.

She was about to start ploughing through the ones she'd ring-fenced when she realised she hadn't heard one word exchanged in the squad room.

She peered over her computer screen and took a closer look. It was 8.57 on a Tuesday morning and you could hear a pin drop.

Penn finished writing a statement and pushed it across the line towards Stacey where their two facing desks met. He raised his eyebrows apologetically. She shrugged silently in response.

Kim continued to watch as Bryant handed a statement across the dividing aisle to add to Stacey's growing pile of paperwork.

'Rightyo, people,' Burns said, clapping his hands together as though his words alone wouldn't summon their attention in the deadly silence.

It was 9 a.m. precisely.

'Now we're up to date on the paperwork, we'll plan the day.'

Although she was in her own office, the glass panelling and gaps around the door meant she'd hear a newt fart if it was in the next room.

'Wood, can you take that boy's name off the board please?'

Kim instantly resented Stacey being referred to by her surname and the boy on the board being referred to by no name at all.

Why were there no photos, details, age, description, lines of enquiry? It was just a name, like it had been put there and forgotten about.

Who was Jamie Mills? she wanted to ask.

'Sir, is it worth just talking to his parents?' Stacey asked, picking up the kitchen roll.

'For what reason? The plods informed the family and we ruled it a suicide. Job done,' he said, picking up a piece of paper.

Kim saw the wavering determination on the constable's face. 'But I just think—'

'Take it down, Wood,' he said icily.

Kim saw the firm set of her jaw as she rubbed out his name.

She returned to her seat silently. Kim tried to focus on her emails but couldn't help listening to the events in the next room.

'Sticking with you, Wood. We've been referred a missing persons case that came in last night. Adult male. Probably nothing but take some details.'

Fob job, as Kim liked to call it. There was no real investigative interest. It was an appeasement task. Make it look like they cared. Take a statement and then no further action.

'Bryant, there's an assault that came in during the night. Take a quick look and see if there's anything there for us.'

'Will do,' Bryant answered without looking at him.

Burns didn't even notice.

'Penn, check the logs.'

Penn nodded his understanding but said nothing. This was clearly their daily routine.

It took Kim just a few seconds to realise the meaning of checking the logs. None of them ever needed to be reminded to do that job. They all logged on to the reporting system to see which jobs had been funnelled their way, but she was guessing that wasn't what Burns meant.

She knew that some DIs checked the logs of other LPUs to see if other local policing units had anything juicier on their patch. Something bigger, sexier that they could find a way to insert themselves into. At best it was nicking your mate's best toys and at worst it was ambulance chasing to get the next big case. After Burns's recent mess-up he was going to have to catch himself a whopper to ingratiate himself back into the good graces of the influential brass.

Personally, she'd always been happy to eat off her own plate instead of taking food from anyone else's, and the set of Penn's expression said he agreed with her.

'Right, chop, chop,' Burns said, loosening his tie.

Stacey stood.

'Oh, Wood, before you go, do you wanna put the—'

'I think I'm gonna make some coffee,' Bryant said, standing up.

The smile didn't quite make it to Kim's face, but trust good old Bryant.

She turned away from her team going about their business with only one question on her mind. A question that was going to need an answer.

Who the hell was Jamie Mills?

THREE

Bryant followed Stacey out the door with the kettle in his hand. DI Burns only drank herbal tea.

'Wait up, Stace,' he called. She paused and, for privacy, he nudged her into the small kitchen used by the dispatch team.

'What?' she asked, her eyes alight with rage.

'I saw you slip it in there,' he said, nodding down towards the notepad she was taking to the interview room.

'I'm requesting a meeting as soon as I'm done with this interview.'

'You know once you submit—' Bryant stopped speaking as one of the controllers entered the room to take something from the fridge. He waited until she was gone before continuing. 'Once you hand in your transfer request, it's done. You can't retract it without—'

'I don't want to retract it. I can't work with him any more.'

'Stace, just give it—'

'Bryant, we had this conversation three weeks ago. It's bad enough that we get lumbered with the gonk that almost got the boss killed but then he insists on treating me like a second- class citizen. You menfolk continue to do the policing and I'll make you all coffee to keep your strength up.'

Bryant could hear the bitterness in her voice, and she wasn't wrong.

For a man in his early thirties, Burns's attitude towards women in the police force was archaic. Both Bryant and Penn had tried ignoring Burns's instructions on the admin, which had made the man worse.

Bryant forced down the frustration that had been building for the last two months. Right now it seemed like his efforts had been for nothing.

Woody had privately given him the news of the guv's replacement on the day of the mock funeral. As if he hadn't been reeling enough from having to pretend to put her in the ground. Bryant had objected as strongly as he'd dared to a man who was his boss's boss, to be told there was only one other choice due to the shortage of DIs. Bryant hadn't needed any more explanation. If they didn't take Burns, they'd all be reassigned in the guv's absence to other CID teams, and a new team would be formed upon the guv's return.

He'd kept that news to himself and had been as professional and courteous to the man as he could manage. The hands that wanted to pummel him into the middle of next week had stayed in his pockets just so the team remained intact.

'Stace, just give it a bit more time. The boss is back.'

'Is she?' Stacey asked pointedly. 'Did you see her face? Does she even recognise us?'

He couldn't answer the question honestly. Yes, she was back at work physically, but he could only wonder when the rest of her would catch up.

'For me, Stace, just a bit longer, eh?' he pleaded.

She sighed heavily, trying to force the tension out of her jaw.

'One day, Bryant. I'll give it one more day and then I'm putting it in.'

He nodded and let her continue to the interview room.

One additional day wasn't a lot. It was a big ask for the guv to come back to them in that time. He just hoped he'd done enough.

FOUR

Stacey had regulated her breathing by the time she headed down the corridor towards interview room one. It was a conversation with Bryant she was sick of having.

Never once in almost seven years had she seriously considered transferring off the team, but right now she could think of little else.

It was fine for Bryant to keep urging her to wait but she didn't know how much longer her mental health could take it. She couldn't switch off at night, not from the investigating because she was doing precious little of that. It was her own anger. Her own anxiety, her own fear of the next day that kept her awake. She wanted to answer him back when he delegated all the admin and menial tasks to her. She was the lowest-ranking member of the team and now she felt it. At night her brain swarmed with all the things she wanted to say to DI Burns but couldn't because he was her superior officer. In his opening speech he'd told them all that he took insubordination seriously and no one wanted that on their record. Whether justified or not, it was a black mark for other DIs looking at your file in the future.

The only option she could see was to get away from the man as quickly as possible, she thought as she opened the door to what was undoubtedly going to turn into another report-taking mission.

The woman at the table was slim with well-cut chestnut hair that almost reached her shoulders. Stacey guessed her to be late thirties, early forties.

'Mrs Denton, DC Stacey Wood,' she said, offering her hand across the table.

'You're a detective?' the woman asked.

In name only, Stacey almost said but nodded instead as she flicked open her notebook.

'I understand you've reported your husband missing.'

'Yes, I called the police station last night. They told me if he hadn't come back by this morning to come in and file a report.'

Standard practice, Stacey thought, if they were talking fully functioning adult gone AWOL for a couple of hours. Children and vulnerable people were actioned immediately.

'Can you tell me what happened, Mrs Denton?'

'Beth, please,' she said, holding up a manicured hand. The only rings were her matching engagement ring and wedding band. 'Gabriel left for work yesterday morning, same time as usual, eight fifteen on the dot. I left shortly afterwards. I was busy at lunchtime; a meeting ran over so we didn't chat while—'

'Is that something you normally do?' Stacey asked. She and Devon rarely communicated throughout the working day, except for the occasional emoji-filled text message that required no response. There were no prescribed lunch breaks in either her work or Devon's job as an immigration officer.

Beth nodded. 'Yes, we usually check in with each other, either call or text but mainly call.' She glanced at Stacey's left hand. 'You and your husband don't do that?'

'Wife,' Stacey corrected.

'Oh, my, I'm sorry. I don't mean—'

'It's fine,' Stacey said, waving away the apology. The poor woman looked mortified. 'Please continue.'

'So we never spoke during the day. I was home by six and had dinner cooking and a glass of wine ready by half past. Around seven I started calling him, but his phone went straight to voicemail. I contacted his work to be told he hadn't been in, and they'd just assumed he'd been down with the flu.'

Stacey noticed that her words were coming faster.

'I rang the local hospitals, checked news reports and then drove his route to work to check he hadn't gone into a ditch somewhere.'

Stacey was sure that would have been noticed by someone, but she also understood the woman's need to do something.

'Friends?' Stacey asked.

'We don't really have many of those. We're quite self-sufficient,' she said, almost apologetically.

'Surely there's someone – old college friends, drinking buddies?' Stacey asked. She and Devon weren't hugely sociable with large groups of friends, but there were people they both had in their lives from along the way: high school, college, part-time jobs.

'Well, I suppose, if we went way back I could come up with a few names.'

'Have a think about that and let me know,' Stacey said, sliding a card across the table. 'Any colleagues he was particularly close to?' she asked. She had to consider that he'd just decided to take some time out, but who would he have told of his plans?

Beth shook her head.

'Family?' Stacey asked.

'His mother is in a care home in Hagley,' she said, tapping the side of her head. 'Dementia. He has one brother he hasn't spoken to in years.'

'May I ask why?' Stacey asked, making notes.

Beth shrugged. 'They argued not long after we got married but both are too stubborn to make the first move.'

'Were they close before?'

'Not really.'

'Can I get his contact details anyway?'

Beth nodded. 'I have an old address book somewhere. I'll dig it out.'

Stacey paused for a second, readying herself for the hardest question of all.

'Does Gabriel have any mental-health problems – depression, anxiety?'

Beth shook her head. 'No, nothing at all. He's always been level-headed and sensible.'

Stacey took a moment to glance over the details taken by the desk sergeant. She had an address, vehicle details and a good description. This information would be placed on the system, and she was guessing that would be as much as Burns would allow her to do with it.

'Can you send me through a photo?'

Beth opened her Mulberry bag and took one out.

The man in the photo was around six feet tall with fair hair and blue eyes. He smiled at the camera in front of a backdrop of stunning scenery.

'Taken two months ago on our last holiday in Croatia.'

Stacey slipped it inside her notebook. She really did have everything she needed.

'Mrs Denton... sorry, Beth, what do you think has happened to your husband?'

The tears filled her eyes and spilled over onto her cheeks. Her hands fussed with the handbag strap as she talked. 'I can only think he's been in some kind of accident. I just keep picturing him wandering around somewhere dazed and confused and alone. I just want him home.'

Stacey reached across and touched the woman's arm reassuringly. She couldn't imagine not knowing where Devon was so she felt the woman's worry.

'We'll find him, Beth,' she said, wondering if she'd just made a promise she wouldn't be able to keep.

FIVE

My eyes open, I think. I feel them opening but the view is the same. The darkness is as dense. I blink again. It takes effort: effort to blink.

The panic in my stomach is instant. I don't know where I am. The unfamiliarity that meets my senses hits me before anything else. My stomach is already coiled, and my heart is beating rapidly.

Everything about my body feels unfamiliar. The ground beneath me is hard. My wrists and ankles are handcuffed. There is some kind of cloth in my mouth. My brain is full of cobwebs, a maze of unreachable corners. I can't seem to think clearly. Where am I? How did I get here? What did I do? Why am I tied up?

I try to control my breathing as the fear rises up into my throat. I try to redirect the breath that's coming quickly out through my nose. It can't escape through my mouth. Calm down. Calm down. Get control. Think, I tell myself. Assess.

My entire body aches from head to toe. I'm filled with an exhaustion that I've never known. Every cell wants me to close my eyes, to succumb to the fatigue that seems to reach every part of my being. My bones feel like they have liquefied. My whole body is nothing but a bag of mush.

I have to focus. I have to try and understand where I am. I need to get my senses to work for me. I have to find a way out of here.

I try to lift my head to focus my hearing. A pain shoots from the back of my neck to the top of my head. My neck weakens and my head falls forward again. Why is there a pain there? Was I hit on the back of the head?

Nothing makes sense. My brain won't catch up and help me. I don't remember anything.

I feel the sudden urge to urinate. I try to tense my body to hold it in. I tell myself to wait, but the urine flows from me. Circles of shame heat my cheeks as the liquid soaks my crotch. My body isn't listening. It's as though the messages from my brain to the rest of my body aren't being sent. It feels like I'm throwing a letter into an open fire. There's no route, no channel, no track for the instruction to go. It won't do as I say. It wants to rest. It wants to sleep.

I try to yank my wrists apart. My hands barely move. The effort exhausts me. The struggle to think exhausts me.

I must stay awake.

I must work out where I am.

I must understand what happened.

A wave of fatigue washes over me.

I give in and close my eyes.

SIX

Penn was still scouring the reports when Stacey came back into the squad room, and he readied himself for the friction.

'Sorted?' Burns asked as Stacey took a seat.

'All a bit weird, sir. Perfectly normal, happily married man leaves the house and never returns.'

'You don't know if he's happily married,' Burns said. 'Probably had a row over the kids and he's gone to cool off with a friend.'

'No kids and apparently no friends,' Stacey said, shrugging.

'Don't get smart, Wood,' Burns said, raising an eyebrow.

'Her words not mine,' Stacey replied.

Burns began to shake his head. 'File the report and pass on the description.'

'Sir, I think it's worth a look,' Stacey protested.

Penn held his breath. It was normally at this point of pushing that Burns either snapped at Stacey or delegated the role to someone else. Both wound her up equally.

Burns closed his mouth, breathed through his nose a couple of times and then turned.

'Penn, get the details from Wood and go to his workplace. Ask a few questions and leave it at that.'

Penn saw the rage flash through his colleague's eyes.

'Sir, I'd love to but this dodgy stomach,' he said, patting his gut. 'Daren't be too far away from a bathroom right now. It's just exploding out of—'

'Okay, Penn, enough,' Burns said as Bryant turned away to hide a smile.

'All right, Wood, go get some details from his workplace and pass them to Penn, who can follow up from the safety of his desk.'

Stacey gathered up her belongings and was out of the office before he changed his mind.

Burns rubbed his hands together. 'Penn, you got...?'

'Just seen something on the logs. Female found dead in her living room in Walsall – called in just fifteen minutes ago.'

Burns grabbed his jacked despite the fact Walsall had its own CID teams and was nothing to do with their local policing unit.

'Get a car to meet me out front,' he said, tearing out the room.

Penn reached for the phone. Their acting DI liked to travel in style.

Once he'd made the request, he put down the phone and let out a long sigh. 'Is it just me or does everyone else feel the tension lift as soon as he leaves the room?' he asked.

Bryant shook his head. 'It's like that nervous energy, that desperation fills the whole bloody building.'

Penn glanced over at the Bowl as the boss stood up and headed their way.

'See you later,' she said, racing through the room.

Both he and Bryant watched her go.

Bryant caught his expression. 'Give her some time.'

Penn nodded. They all knew what she'd been through, and keeping her team happy was the least of her problems.

'Where do you think she's gone?'

Bryant shrugged and returned to his computer, unnerving Penn all the more. Most times his computer was for decorative purposes only.

Penn knew their team had a weird dynamic and that even on a good day the boss shared little of herself with him or Stacey, but she was as close to Bryant as she was to anyone, and if he knew nothing then she wasn't sharing anything with anyone. Weirdly, both he and Stacey drew comfort from the genuine friendship that existed between Bryant and the boss, and while that was good, all was well with the world. When it wasn't, it threw everything just slightly off-kilter.

Although they were colleagues not parents, it reminded Penn of when he was young. He'd never once seen his parents argue, but he'd always known when they had. The weight of the silence between the two of them had filled the house, leaving him and Jasper with a sense of unease that he felt right now.

The sound of Bryant's low chuckle broke the silence. 'Just got to the incident log for that job you sent Burns to in Walsall. The female found dead in her living room was eighty-seven years old and appeared to have died from natural causes.'

'Really?' Penn asked with mock surprise. 'I must have missed those details.'

Bryant chuckled again.

Either way it had got the insufferable man out of their hair for an hour or two.

'Good job, Penn,' Bryant said. 'Bloody good job.'

SEVEN

Fairfield was a village located in the district of Bromsgrove. It housed a church, a pub and a post office-cum-convenience store to cater to the immediate needs of the residents.

Kim stepped off the Kawasaki Ninja and removed her helmet.

The house she sought was a semi-detached new build with a small fence dividing a shared front lawn. Colourful daisy plants lined the border. There was no car on the drive, but the sound of a vacuum cleaner could be heard through the open windows.

She knocked the door twice before the vacuum noise stopped and she saw a figure approach through the frosted glass panel.

The door was opened by a plump woman in her mid-forties wearing jeans and a T-shirt. Her brown hair was tied back, and a silver cross around her neck was her only jewellery. She wiped at her glistening brow as Kim took out her warrant card for the first time in months.

'DI Stone,' she said. 'Halesowen CID.'

The woman frowned.

'I'm here to talk about Jamie.'

'Please come in.'

Kim stepped past her and waited to be directed.

'In there,' she said, pointing to a lounge on the left.

Kim stepped over the vacuum pipe and into a bright room that was plainly furnished but captured the sun from a large bay window. A beam of light cut across a crucifix above the fireplace.

'Please take a seat although I'm not sure why you're here.'

'It's just a follow-up, Mrs Mills,' Kim said, unsure herself why she had made the visit. All she knew was that a seemingly healthy nineteen-year-old lad had been found hanging from a tree, and his name had been rubbed from the board before anyone had bothered to find out why.

There was a surreal feeling at not having Bryant beside her, but it was unfair to involve him in something she wasn't supposed to be doing as it was. On her own, she was just asking questions. With Bryant by her side, she was investigating. In his absence she had to try and mind her own manners and think of what he might say to grieving parents.

'Mrs Mills, may I just say how sorry I am for your loss.'

'Thank you, Inspector,' she said, putting her hands in her lap.

There were no tears, only a look of confusion. 'I'm still not sure of the reason for your visit. The constable told us there was no one else involved and that Jamie took his own life.'

'You don't seem surprised?'

The woman took a deep breath. 'Neither myself nor my husband were surprised by the news.'

'Your husband?'

'Yes, he's returned to work today.'

A bit soon, Kim thought. Jamie's body had been discovered forty-eight hours ago, meaning his father had taken only one day off to mourn the death of his son.

'The devil makes work for idle hands, Inspector,' Mrs Mills said by way of explanation.

'Did Jamie suffer from mental-health problems?' Kim asked, feeling as though she could, given that his parents were not surprised by his actions.

She shook her head vehemently. 'Nothing so dramatic. He got a bit down sometimes, went into himself, but he wasn't suffering from any kind of mental illness.'

Kim detected mild offence in her tone. 'He wasn't taking any medication?'

'For what? There was nothing wrong with him. He had quiet times now and again.'

'You didn't consult a doctor?'

She shook her head. 'Never even gave it a thought. Far too much airtime being given to this disorder and that disorder. Every naughty child now suffers from ADHD, lazy kids are labelled as dyslexic and the quiet ones are offered drugs and potions from medical professionals.'

Kim was trying hard not to form a negative opinion of the woman sitting before her. Understanding mental health in children and young adults had progressed significantly in the last twenty years.

'They're not busy enough any more,' Mrs Mills continued, as though Kim had opened a can of her favourite subject to be incensed about. 'We used to go to school, come back, do our chores, do homework, watch a bit of telly and then off to bed. There was no time to indulge ourselves in depression, anxiety, or any other nonsense.'

Kim realised she was in the company of a person who ensured that stigma was still attached to mental health, especially for young people. She would have liked to debate the subject but that wasn't why she was here, although Jamie's reasons for not discussing any potential mental-health issues with his mother were becoming clearer.

'May I ask how old he was when the quiet moods began?'

'Not sure how it helps anything now but probably when he was early teens. He withdrew into himself, stayed in his room, stopped meeting friends. We assumed he was going through a phase. We tried to get him more involved with the church. We thought it would pass. We did everything we could. We sent him off to summer camp a couple of times and prayed for him every day, but he just seemed to move further away from us.'

Kim couldn't help feeling as though Mrs Mills was talking about a distant relative, not her own son.

'A couple of years ago he got into cycling. He became passionate about it. He did it alone, but he'd ride for miles, off into Wales, all over the place.'

Kim understood that, only with her it was on the Ninja. She'd been known to take off for hours on her own, but it was normally to escape something, in a way to escape her own head, as though she was riding through the fog towards clarity, that the answers would be at the end of the bike ride. Had Jamie been seeking answers? And if so why hadn't he sought any of those answers from his parents?

'Would it be possible to see his room?' Kim asked.

'Well you can but there's nothing left in there. It's my sewing room. I make cushions and curtains for the church raffle. Jamie moved out of the house when he was seventeen.'

'May I ask why?' Kim asked, feeling as though she was moving further and further away from learning anything about the young man.

'He went and stayed with friends as he didn't care much for the rules of the house.'

Kim waited.

'Learning or working. Those are the rules. College or a job, but he skipped so much school that he failed all his exams and couldn't get a job. After the accident, he—'

'Accident?'

Mrs Mills allowed her annoyance to show. 'Inspector, I don't have time to relate Jamie's entire life history. He's gone and that's the end of it.'

Were there some urgent cushions that needed her attention? Kim wondered, but even without Bryant she knew when she was outstaying her welcome.

'Please tell me about the accident and then I promise I'll leave you in peace,' Kim assured her.

'He was knocked off his bike, around eighteen months ago. He was badly hurt, in hospital for two weeks. Major injury to his right knee. It had to be fused back into place. He made a remarkable recovery but his bike-riding days were over. He went further into himself. We tried to shock him into action by giving him an ultimatum. Either stop moping around and get a job or move out. He chose to move out.'

'And when did you last see him?' Kim asked, breaking her own promise.

Mrs Mills stood. 'He visited around six months ago, Inspector, and now I really must ask you to leave.'

Kim stood and tried to shake the feeling of unease at the woman's detachment to the loss of her own son. She'd talked of him with no more emotion than that of a stranger.

Kim headed for the door and took a card from her back pocket. 'If there's anything you need, please call me.'

Mrs Mills looked at the card. 'Please keep it. There's nothing we need. We have each other and our faith. Jamie is in a much better place and at peace now. Please leave it that way, Inspector.'

The door closed behind her as soon as her feet rested on the path.

Kim took her helmet from the handlebars, wishing she'd been able to ask more questions. Why had Jamie preferred the option of moving out when pressed to find a job? What had been at the core of his bouts of depression? Had his religious

'Penn, get the details from Wood and go to his workplace. Ask a few questions and leave it at that.'

Penn saw the rage flash through his colleague's eyes.

'Sir, I'd love to but this dodgy stomach,' he said, patting his gut. 'Daren't be too far away from a bathroom right now. It's just exploding out of—'

'Okay, Penn, enough,' Burns said as Bryant turned away to hide a smile.

'All right, Wood, go get some details from his workplace and pass them to Penn, who can follow up from the safety of his desk.'

Stacey gathered up her belongings and was out of the office before he changed his mind.

Burns rubbed his hands together. 'Penn, you got...?'

'Just seen something on the logs. Female found dead in her living room in Walsall – called in just fifteen minutes ago.'

Burns grabbed his jacked despite the fact Walsall had its own CID teams and was nothing to do with their local policing unit.

'Get a car to meet me out front,' he said, tearing out the room.

Penn reached for the phone. Their acting DI liked to travel in style.

Once he'd made the request, he put down the phone and let out a long sigh. 'Is it just me or does everyone else feel the tension lift as soon as he leaves the room?' he asked.

Bryant shook his head. 'It's like that nervous energy, that desperation fills the whole bloody building.'

Penn glanced over at the Bowl as the boss stood up and headed their way.

'See you later,' she said, racing through the room.

Both he and Bryant watched her go.

Bryant caught his expression. 'Give her some time.'

SIX

Penn was still scouring the reports when Stacey came back into the squad room, and he readied himself for the friction.

'Sorted?' Burns asked as Stacey took a seat.

'All a bit weird, sir. Perfectly normal, happily married man leaves the house and never returns.'

'You don't know if he's happily married,' Burns said. 'Probably had a row over the kids and he's gone to cool off with a friend.'

'No kids and apparently no friends,' Stacey said, shrugging.

'Don't get smart, Wood,' Burns said, raising an eyebrow.

'Her words not mine,' Stacey replied.

Burns began to shake his head. 'File the report and pass on the description.'

'Sir, I think it's worth a look,' Stacey protested.

Penn held his breath. It was normally at this point of pushing that Burns either snapped at Stacey or delegated the role to someone else. Both wound her up equally.

Burns closed his mouth, breathed through his nose a couple of times and then turned.

SIX

Penn was still scouring the reports when Stacey came back into the squad room, and he readied himself for the friction.

'Sorted?' Burns asked as Stacey took a seat.

'All a bit weird, sir. Perfectly normal, happily married man leaves the house and never returns.'

'You don't know if he's happily married,' Burns said. 'Probably had a row over the kids and he's gone to cool off with a friend.'

'No kids and apparently no friends,' Stacey said, shrugging.

'Don't get smart, Wood,' Burns said, raising an eyebrow.

'Her words not mine,' Stacey replied.

Burns began to shake his head. 'File the report and pass on the description.'

'Sir, I think it's worth a look,' Stacey protested.

Penn held his breath. It was normally at this point of pushing that Burns either snapped at Stacey or delegated the role to someone else. Both wound her up equally.

Burns closed his mouth, breathed through his nose a couple of times and then turned.

'Penn, get the details from Wood and go to his workplace. Ask a few questions and leave it at that.'

Penn saw the rage flash through his colleague's eyes.

'Sir, I'd love to but this dodgy stomach,' he said, patting his gut. 'Daren't be too far away from a bathroom right now. It's just exploding out of—'

'Okay, Penn, enough,' Burns said as Bryant turned away to hide a smile.

'All right, Wood, go get some details from his workplace and pass them to Penn, who can follow up from the safety of his desk.'

Stacey gathered up her belongings and was out of the office before he changed his mind.

Burns rubbed his hands together. 'Penn, you got...?'

'Just seen something on the logs. Female found dead in her living room in Walsall – called in just fifteen minutes ago.'

Burns grabbed his jacked despite the fact Walsall had its own CID teams and was nothing to do with their local policing unit.

'Get a car to meet me out front,' he said, tearing out the room.

Penn reached for the phone. Their acting DI liked to travel in style.

Once he'd made the request, he put down the phone and let out a long sigh. 'Is it just me or does everyone else feel the tension lift as soon as he leaves the room?' he asked.

Bryant shook his head. 'It's like that nervous energy, that desperation fills the whole bloody building.'

Penn glanced over at the Bowl as the boss stood up and headed their way.

'See you later,' she said, racing through the room.

Both he and Bryant watched her go.

Bryant caught his expression. 'Give her some time.'

Penn nodded. They all knew what she'd been through, and keeping her team happy was the least of her problems.

'Where do you think she's gone?'

Bryant shrugged and returned to his computer, unnerving Penn all the more. Most times his computer was for decorative purposes only.

Penn knew their team had a weird dynamic and that even on a good day the boss shared little of herself with him or Stacey, but she was as close to Bryant as she was to anyone, and if he knew nothing then she wasn't sharing anything with anyone. Weirdly, both he and Stacey drew comfort from the genuine friendship that existed between Bryant and the boss, and while that was good, all was well with the world. When it wasn't, it threw everything just slightly off-kilter.

Although they were colleagues not parents, it reminded Penn of when he was young. He'd never once seen his parents argue, but he'd always known when they had. The weight of the silence between the two of them had filled the house, leaving him and Jasper with a sense of unease that he felt right now.

The sound of Bryant's low chuckle broke the silence. 'Just got to the incident log for that job you sent Burns to in Walsall. The female found dead in her living room was eighty-seven years old and appeared to have died from natural causes.'

'Really?' Penn asked with mock surprise. 'I must have missed those details.'

Bryant chuckled again.

Either way it had got the insufferable man out of their hair for an hour or two.

'Good job, Penn,' Bryant said. 'Bloody good job.'

SEVEN

Fairfield was a village located in the district of Bromsgrove. It housed a church, a pub and a post office-cum-convenience store to cater to the immediate needs of the residents.

Kim stepped off the Kawasaki Ninja and removed her helmet.

The house she sought was a semi-detached new build with a small fence dividing a shared front lawn. Colourful daisy plants lined the border. There was no car on the drive, but the sound of a vacuum cleaner could be heard through the open windows.

She knocked the door twice before the vacuum noise stopped and she saw a figure approach through the frosted glass panel.

The door was opened by a plump woman in her mid-forties wearing jeans and a T-shirt. Her brown hair was tied back, and a silver cross around her neck was her only jewellery. She wiped at her glistening brow as Kim took out her warrant card for the first time in months.

'DI Stone,' she said. 'Halesowen CID.'

The woman frowned.

'I'm here to talk about Jamie.'

'Please come in.'

Kim stepped past her and waited to be directed.

'In there,' she said, pointing to a lounge on the left.

Kim stepped over the vacuum pipe and into a bright room that was plainly furnished but captured the sun from a large bay window. A beam of light cut across a crucifix above the fireplace.

'Please take a seat although I'm not sure why you're here.'

'It's just a follow-up, Mrs Mills,' Kim said, unsure herself why she had made the visit. All she knew was that a seemingly healthy nineteen-year-old lad had been found hanging from a tree, and his name had been rubbed from the board before anyone had bothered to find out why.

There was a surreal feeling at not having Bryant beside her, but it was unfair to involve him in something she wasn't supposed to be doing as it was. On her own, she was just asking questions. With Bryant by her side, she was investigating. In his absence she had to try and mind her own manners and think of what he might say to grieving parents.

'Mrs Mills, may I just say how sorry I am for your loss.'

'Thank you, Inspector,' she said, putting her hands in her lap.

There were no tears, only a look of confusion. 'I'm still not sure of the reason for your visit. The constable told us there was no one else involved and that Jamie took his own life.'

'You don't seem surprised?'

The woman took a deep breath. 'Neither myself nor my husband were surprised by the news.'

'Your husband?'

'Yes, he's returned to work today.'

A bit soon, Kim thought. Jamie's body had been discovered forty-eight hours ago, meaning his father had taken only one day off to mourn the death of his son.

'The devil makes work for idle hands, Inspector,' Mrs Mills said by way of explanation.

'Did Jamie suffer from mental-health problems?' Kim asked, feeling as though she could, given that his parents were not surprised by his actions.

She shook her head vehemently. 'Nothing so dramatic. He got a bit down sometimes, went into himself, but he wasn't suffering from any kind of mental illness.'

Kim detected mild offence in her tone. 'He wasn't taking any medication?'

'For what? There was nothing wrong with him. He had quiet times now and again.'

'You didn't consult a doctor?'

She shook her head. 'Never even gave it a thought. Far too much airtime being given to this disorder and that disorder. Every naughty child now suffers from ADHD, lazy kids are labelled as dyslexic and the quiet ones are offered drugs and potions from medical professionals.'

Kim was trying hard not to form a negative opinion of the woman sitting before her. Understanding mental health in children and young adults had progressed significantly in the last twenty years.

'They're not busy enough any more,' Mrs Mills continued, as though Kim had opened a can of her favourite subject to be incensed about. 'We used to go to school, come back, do our chores, do homework, watch a bit of telly and then off to bed. There was no time to indulge ourselves in depression, anxiety, or any other nonsense.'

Kim realised she was in the company of a person who ensured that stigma was still attached to mental health, especially for young people. She would have liked to debate the subject but that wasn't why she was here, although Jamie's reasons for not discussing any potential mental-health issues with his mother were becoming clearer.

'May I ask how old he was when the quiet moods began?'

'Not sure how it helps anything now but probably when he was early teens. He withdrew into himself, stayed in his room, stopped meeting friends. We assumed he was going through a phase. We tried to get him more involved with the church. We thought it would pass. We did everything we could. We sent him off to summer camp a couple of times and prayed for him every day, but he just seemed to move further away from us.'

Kim couldn't help feeling as though Mrs Mills was talking about a distant relative, not her own son.

'A couple of years ago he got into cycling. He became passionate about it. He did it alone, but he'd ride for miles, off into Wales, all over the place.'

Kim understood that, only with her it was on the Ninja. She'd been known to take off for hours on her own, but it was normally to escape something, in a way to escape her own head, as though she was riding through the fog towards clarity, that the answers would be at the end of the bike ride. Had Jamie been seeking answers? And if so why hadn't he sought any of those answers from his parents?

'Would it be possible to see his room?' Kim asked.

'Well you can but there's nothing left in there. It's my sewing room. I make cushions and curtains for the church raffle. Jamie moved out of the house when he was seventeen.'

'May I ask why?' Kim asked, feeling as though she was moving further and further away from learning anything about the young man.

'He went and stayed with friends as he didn't care much for the rules of the house.'

Kim waited.

'Learning or working. Those are the rules. College or a job, but he skipped so much school that he failed all his exams and couldn't get a job. After the accident, he—'

'Accident?'

Mrs Mills allowed her annoyance to show. 'Inspector, I don't have time to relate Jamie's entire life history. He's gone and that's the end of it.'

Were there some urgent cushions that needed her attention? Kim wondered, but even without Bryant she knew when she was outstaying her welcome.

'Please tell me about the accident and then I promise I'll leave you in peace,' Kim assured her.

'He was knocked off his bike, around eighteen months ago. He was badly hurt, in hospital for two weeks. Major injury to his right knee. It had to be fused back into place. He made a remarkable recovery but his bike-riding days were over. He went further into himself. We tried to shock him into action by giving him an ultimatum. Either stop moping around and get a job or move out. He chose to move out.'

'And when did you last see him?' Kim asked, breaking her own promise.

Mrs Mills stood. 'He visited around six months ago, Inspector, and now I really must ask you to leave.'

Kim stood and tried to shake the feeling of unease at the woman's detachment to the loss of her own son. She'd talked of him with no more emotion than that of a stranger.

Kim headed for the door and took a card from her back pocket. 'If there's anything you need, please call me.'

Mrs Mills looked at the card. 'Please keep it. There's nothing we need. We have each other and our faith. Jamie is in a much better place and at peace now. Please leave it that way, Inspector.'

The door closed behind her as soon as her feet rested on the path.

Kim took her helmet from the handlebars, wishing she'd been able to ask more questions. Why had Jamie preferred the option of moving out when pressed to find a job? What had been at the core of his bouts of depression? Had his religious upbringing played any part in his decision to leave the family home?

The attitude of Burns reflected the attitude of the boy's mother: rub him out, make him invisible.

She'd just spent a good twenty minutes with the woman yet she felt as though she knew no more about a young man who had apparently chosen to end his own life.

EIGHT

The firm of accountants, Dunhill LLP, lay on the outskirts of Halesowen town centre and was an old Victorian house converted into offices. The car park was a mixture of reserved and open spaces. The space for 'G. Denton' was empty.

Stacey rang the bell, enjoying every second of being out the office. It had once been her safe place, but not any more.

The door buzzed and clicked, and Stacey entered.

The reception was a high semi-circle in front of an attractive woman in her early forties. Her black hair was impossibly shiny and her face made up perfectly. Stacey could only imagine the effort that went into getting ready for work.

Stacey held up her ID. 'Detective Constable Wood. Is there someone I can talk to about Gabriel Denton?'

'Is he okay?' the woman asked as alarm shaped her face.

'That's what we're trying to find out.'

'Everyone is in a budget meeting at the minute but I probably know Gabe as well as anyone.'

'Okay, and you are?'

'I'm Wendy Clarke, receptionist, secretary, office manager, take your pick.' She pressed a few buttons on the phone. 'Voicemail can take the heat for a few minutes.' She came around the desk and pointed to two sofas around a glass coffee table.

'I understand Mr Denton has worked here for many years,' Stacey said.

Wendy nodded. 'Twenty years. We have thirteen account executives and he has the highest customer retention rate of all of them.'

'And you've known him for...?'

'I've been here for almost ten years.'

'Any issues with colleagues?' Stacey asked.

Wendy smiled and shook her head. 'Everyone loves Gabe. I suppose a few think he's a bit boring, but accounting is hardly a white-knuckle ride. He's as straight shooting as they come; honest as the day is long, pleasant, professional and hard-working.'

That ruled out any work-related issues, Stacey thought. A part of her had wondered if he'd got himself into any financial trouble at work. She'd investigated her fair share of fraud and embezzlement cases over the years. People often chose to disappear before being found out. It wasn't something she could rule out completely. Perhaps he had done something he shouldn't have but it hadn't yet been discovered.

'Is he all right?' Wendy repeated, showing genuine concern.

Stacey ignored the question and continued. 'Do you know if Mr Denton suffers from any kind of mental-health problems?'

Wendy shook her head. 'I've never got that impression, and he certainly never mentioned it.'

'Any mood swings, outbursts?'

Wendy laughed out loud. 'No, that's absolutely not Gabe's style. He's a very calm man. He doesn't get ruffled – I've never once seen him lose his temper.'

'Did you find it strange when he didn't turn up for work yesterday?'

'Not really. All the accountants have the option of working

from home if they don't have client meetings. Gabe doesn't do it often, and I'm sure when he does he still wears his suit. Can you just tell me if he's been in an accident?'

'We really don't know, Ms Clarke. Mr Denton left the house yesterday morning and never returned home. He's missing and obviously Mrs Denton is very worried about him.'

'Of course,' Wendy said, her eyes widening. 'Have you checked the hospitals and—'

'All in hand,' Stacey said. 'But it is important for you to tell me if you've noticed anything strange or different in his behaviour recently.'

She thought for a moment and began to shake her head. 'We were only out back together on Friday and—'

'Out back?'

She nodded. 'We have a small courtyard area at the rear of the office. Just a couple of tables and chairs off the break room. Company policy not to eat at the desk, and we were often out there at the same time. We both enjoyed a later lunch, preferring to know the biggest part of the day was behind us and not in front.'

'So you spent a lot of time with him?'

'Well, if you call him with his phone and me with my Kindle spending time together, I suppose so.'

'Beth Denton tells me that they texted or spoke most days.'

Wendy nodded and straightened up the magazines on the glass table. 'Yes, I think they're very committed to each other.'

'Have you met Beth?'

'Just once. There was a big celebration party some years ago when one of the partners retired. It was a formal dinner with drinks afterwards. She looked a little uncomfortable during the meal and they didn't stay for drinks.'

Stacey could understand that. The first time she'd accompanied Devon on a work outing she'd felt completely out of it despite Devon's best efforts.

'She didn't come to any more company functions?' Stacey asked.

'And neither did he,' Wendy said.

'So you can think of nothing that might prompt him to up and leave?' Stacey asked.

'Obviously I can't be in people's minds, but there's definitely not been any indication here that there was anything wrong.'

'Okay, Ms Clarke, please take my card and contact me if you think of anything else or if Mr Denton gets in touch...'

'Oh, I don't think he'd get in touch with me.'

'I meant with anyone here,' Stacey clarified. 'Please pass my number around and ask anyone to contact me if there's anything they think might help.'

'Will do,' Wendy said, returning to her desk to open the door.

Stacey headed towards the town centre to cut through back to the station. Her stomach filled with dread, but if she was gone much longer, Burns would be blowing up her phone. She was sure there'd be some urgent admin task that needed doing by the time she got back.

She also knew that Burns had not one iota of interest in this case and would happily leave it to grow mould on the database. The only cases that piqued his interest were the ones that had a chance of reinstating his feet on the glittering career ladder.

She knew she had to let it go, but she desperately wanted to know why a happily married, trustworthy stable man had seemingly disappeared into thin air.

NINE

It was after one o'clock when Stacey walked back into the silent office, and Penn already knew how this was going to pan out.

Stacey's natural inquisitiveness meant she would want to follow this lead and see where it took her. His colleague took every case to heart and wanted every question answered. It was what made her a damn good investigator.

'Sir, I think there's something to look—'

'Park it, Wood. He'll be back by nightfall. They've had a row, he's kipped on a mate's couch and he'll turn up when he's hungry. It's a domestic and we're not investigating it.'

Penn could tell that she wanted to argue and he could see why. She wanted to investigate something, anything. Given half the chance, they'd all have investigated a suspected cake theft from the canteen. Right now, they were simply twiddling their thumbs waiting for the next big case to come in. Follow-ups to assaults and burglaries were being done by phone and email. Statement taking was being delegated to constables while they all stared at a computer and tried to look busy. Burns didn't want the team to get entrenched in a case that would mean the next biggie was passed to another team. He was constantly keeping them on ice until the career-making case landed on his desk. His colleague was desperate to feel that fire back in her belly. They all were. He could tell by the set expression on her face she wasn't done trying.

'Sir, I really think—'

'That's your problem, Wood – you think too much.'

Bryant's head shot up. 'Hey, just wait...'

'Calm down. I was only joking. She's not your sister, but if she can't take a joke, I'll spare her fragile feelings. Talking of fragile, does anyone know where Stone went?'

Penn shook his head as Bryant turned away to hide his rage. It was getting harder for the mild-mannered sergeant to control his emotions, but he was determined not to give Burns any reason to break up the team in the boss's absence.

'Maybe tomorrow she'll try working a full—'

'Anybody want anything from the canteen?' Bryant asked, standing.

Penn shook his head as his phone vibrated in his pocket.

He turned away from Burns to take a look. He hid his surprise that it was a text from the boss.

Meet me at Leasowes Park. Say nothing.

Penn slid his phone back in his pocket. Stacey was eyeing him suspiciously.

He held his stomach and groaned.

Burns looked his way.

'Sir, my stomach, it's getting worse. I think I'm gonna have to—'

'Go,' he said, waving towards the door. 'And if you're no better tomorrow, don't come in. If it's contagious, I don't want it.'

'Okay, got it. I'll let you know,' he said, reaching for his man bag.

He felt awful leaving Stacey on her own with the idiot, but right now he felt more alive than he had in months and there was a small fire burning in his belly.

TEN

Leasowes Park was situated on a 141-acre estate in Halesowen and comprised a house and gardens. The parkland was listed Grade 1 on English Heritage's register.

Outside of the golf course, the park was known for its simplicity and rural appearance. It wasn't the first time she'd visited in connection with her work and she was sure it wouldn't be the last.

Penn had texted her to say he was on the way, and she'd messaged back to tell him to park up at the warden's base and head for Devil's Armchair in the south. She was pretty sure he'd guess what she wanted to look at but not so much her reason for wanting him to meet her there.

She was surprised at the speed of his arrival even though they were only minutes away from the station. He must have hotfooted it out of there as soon as she texted him.

'Which one?' she asked, to save her reading through the statements.

'Sorry, boss, I'm not sure...'

'Which tree was Jamie Mills found hanging from?'

He shrugged looking along the row of oak trees. 'Sorry, boss, I...'

'How can you not know?' she asked, feeling her voice rise.

'We didn't investigate, boss. Burns attended alone, agreed the manner of death with Keats and dispatched uniforms to take the statements.'

'Is that how you investigate now? From your desk?'

'Boss, I swear, it's not by choice,' he said, holding up his hands. 'Every one of us is sick to death of the office. We've solved nothing cos we've investigated nothing. The locals have enjoyed your time off more than you have.'

By 'locals' Kim knew he was referring to the criminal community.

She pushed down her irritation. She wasn't being fair. She'd heard Stacey try and protest when Jamie's name had been rubbed from the board.

'So what do you think of the area?' Kim asked.

Penn shrugged. 'Nice enough, good view from up there. I once arranged to meet a girl at Devil's Armchair. I was fifteen and she never showed up.'

Kim just stared and waited. Oh yeah, they were rusty all right.

Penn coloured. 'Oh, you meant for suicide?'

'No because obviously I care more about your teenage love life. Of course suicide.'

Penn took a look around and began to nod. 'Yes, this could easily be a place he loved for some reason,' he said, looking back towards the viewpoint. 'People walk to the end of that path there, have a good look around and walk back into the park. They don't come down here. I think he was only found so quickly cos some guy was looking for his retriever's tennis ball.'

She'd already noted the absence of walking trails around this group of trees. Her own gut told her it was a secluded spot for suicide, if there even was such a thing.

'Here, hold this,' she said, thrusting her carrier bag at him. Time to get down to business. She took out her phone and accessed her emails. She clicked into a folder marked 'Jamie' and scrolled to the scanned statements. She read quickly.

'Third from the left,' she said, putting away her phone and moving to stand in front of the tree chosen by Jamie. Like the others around it, the branches were caught in that October transition stage of losing some of its leaves and clinging on to others.

'Reckon you can climb it. To that branch there?' she asked, pointing to a sturdy branch approximately three metres up.

Penn took a good look. 'Yeah, I think so, if I wanted to.'

Kim took the carrier bag from him. 'Let's assume you want to,' she said, nodding towards it. 'Go on.'

He read her expression to see if she was serious.

He got his answer and moved towards it. He reached up and used the remnants of broken-off branches to climb, before using his feet to dig into the bark and use those same stubs of branches as footholds. It took him a good seven minutes of careful planning and placement, going backwards and forwards again, before he reached the point she'd indicated.

'That it, boss?' he asked, with his legs dangling either side of the branch.

'Yep, you can come down now,' she said.

He rubbed the dead bark from his hands as he came to stand beside her.

She took the rope from the carrier bag.

'Okay, now do it like you're going to hang yourself.'

He raised an eyebrow as he doubled the rope and placed it loosely around his neck.

She reached into the bag again. 'Oh and put this on first.'

He took the knee brace from her and took a good look at it.

'Right knee,' she added.

He pulled the brace around his knee and pulled the Velcro strips tightly over the top of his trousers.

He approached the tree again, throwing out his right leg due to the sudden straightness of it.

As before he took a moment to plan his ascent. He raised his left leg first and then dragged his right leg up after it. He hit an immediate problem with there being not enough room on any of the stubs for both feet. He needed to place each foot higher than the other in a stepping-up motion.

He jumped down from the first stub and tried again but same problem. He tried for a third time by trying to jump and grab a branch to swing up, but to jump he needed to bend both knees.

He made his way back and stood beside her, scratching his head.

'Don't think I can do it with this brace on, boss. My leg won't bend.'

'Yes, Penn, my thoughts exactly,' she said, heading back towards her bike.

ELEVEN

It was after 3 p.m. when Kim pressed the buzzer on the doors to the morgue at Russells Hall Hospital.

Jimmy, Keats's assistant, buzzed her in and greeted her with a smile. 'Good to see you, Insp—'

'Where is he?' she asked, slamming her helmet on the work surface.

He pointed to the washroom where the pathologist usually prepared for the post-mortem procedure.

She stepped inside. The diminutive man was washing his hands at the metal sink.

'Keats, what the hell were you thinking?' she asked, placing her hands on her hips.

'Well, just now I was thinking about how tranquil my life has been for the last two months and I was trying to find the reason why.' He grabbed a towel and turned her way. 'And the reason has just come to me.'

'Funny, but have you seriously lost your mind?'

'Not according to my last check-up but with you back in the picture it may be imminent.'

'Jamie Mills did not take his own life, and how you could have agreed this with Burns is totally beyond me.'

He put down the towel and leaned against the counter. He folded his arms. 'Please continue to shout at me as though we don't have a long history of working together filled with mutual respect for each other's skills and abilities, masked by a charade of sarcastic humour.'

Kim paused. That was the closest Keats had ever come to admitting a grudging respect for her.

Her anger turned to frustration.

'He couldn't have done it, Keats. He couldn't even have climbed the bloody tree.'

'I'll take your revised tone as an apology, now follow me.'

He brushed past her and headed along the corridor to his office. He picked up a report and handed it to her.

'I've seen this,' she said. It was Keats's initial report citing suicide as the manner of death.

'Look at it again. All of it.'

She leafed through the parts she'd read, but there were an additional two documents. The first was the request to reclassify the manner of death, the second was an email.

'I sent that email to DCI Woodward not half an hour ago.'

She read it quickly. It was a request for a second opinion from a different investigating officer.

'Did you wait for my return to send this?'

'I can't comment on the coincidence of the timeliness of my request, Inspector, but I can say that my quiet suspicions were heightened when my initial examination discovered the fusion of the knee, at which point I had no choice but to stop the procedure pending reclassification.'

'Why wasn't any of this discussed at the scene?' she asked. Valuable time, not to mention forensic evidence, had been lost.

'If you've met Burns, I don't need to tell you that his motivations don't appear to be based solely on crime-solving, and certain incidents are sexier than others. In addition, some cases take more investigation than accepting what's right in front of you. Had he a seven-inch blade sticking out of him, I suspect we wouldn't be having this conversation.'

'Is that your way of saying he's both ambitious and lazy?' Kim asked with a smile tugging at her lips.

'Your hearing appears to have become impaired during your time away,' he responded, remaining the consummate professional.

'Well, he might show a bit more interest when Woody kicks his arse and throws it back at him.'

'You're not going to take it?' Keats asked.

Kim shook her head, trying not to show how exhausted she was. *Go slowly*, Woody, the doctor and the psychologist had told her. 'Burns needs to do his job – properly.'

He took the paperwork from her and then waved it about. 'I need a signature for the reclassification request. I could have authorisation by tomorrow if—'

'Pass it here,' she said, taking the paperwork back and moving towards the desk. She took a pen and signed the last page, then handed the form back to him. 'Woody can officially reassign the senior investigating officer tomorrow, but that'll get your authorisation.'

He nodded his agreement as she headed out of his office.

She was almost at the door when he spoke. 'Good to have you back, Inspector.'

She continued walking and didn't answer. She wasn't back yet. She wasn't even close.

TWELVE

Stacey stared out of the bus window with a feeling of hopelessness that had grown worse throughout the day.

From the moment Burns had been installed in their office, the three of them had been forced to fight back their emotions. Being lumbered with the person partly responsible for the boss's injuries was insensitive beyond belief on behalf of their superiors. Burns had refused to consider linking the search for Symes with his need for revenge on the boss. As a consequence, Symes had been able to watch the boss's movements from down the street. The top brass had seen a DI-shaped hole and filled it with a DI going spare, caring nothing for the repercussions. Added to that was the fact he was a complete and utter knob.

They'd all travelled their own individual journey of acceptance in the knowledge that Burns was a seat warmer until the boss returned. Penn and Bryant had tried to work around being given poorly matched tasks. They'd come to terms with the man being a glory hunter and his slapdash approach to investigating anything that didn't excite him. Stacey had also come to terms with all of these things but had been forced to swallow much more.

Her role had been revised to team administrator and general dogsbody. Every day she felt as though her brain was dying just a little bit more and her motivation was evaporating even quicker.

She'd tried to fight him, had tried to voice her own opinion over the months just as she had tried again today.

She had hated seeing Jamie's name rubbed off the board before they'd even spoken to a family member or friend, or made any attempt to understand his reasons for taking his own life. In her mind, he was still hanging from that tree because they'd made no attempt to cut him down. And maybe Burns was right about Gabriel Denton. Perhaps he would just reappear with a bunch of flowers and an apology, but that didn't quiet down the unease in her gut. She didn't need her intuition to check statements and make tea.

Like a prisoner, she had been counting down the days until the boss's return. When they'd been told a couple of months, she had taken the time frame as gospel and marked it on her calendar. That star that marked her return had become her beacon of hope and a target to aim for. Each day she'd got through was one day closer to the boss's return and normality.

But that day had come and gone and it had not been what she'd thought it would be.

Maybe it had been unrealistic to expect her to come crashing in like a superhero and save them all. Putting right all the wrongs that had occurred in her absence was going to be a tall order, but the woman Stacey had seen today wasn't even a shadow of the person she'd come to respect and admire above anyone else. It all but broke her heart to see this other person parading as her former boss. The passion, the drive, the determination, the sharp mind and dry wit appeared to have been left on the floor of the warehouse where Symes had beaten her nearly to death.

Just the thought of it brought the emotion to her throat. She couldn't even imagine what the boss had gone through during her physical and psychological recovery; but now, for her own sanity, Stacey knew she had to accept that this chapter of her life was over and it was time to move on.

THIRTEEN

Kim put the magazine down and reached for her coffee, aware that she was taking nothing in. There was a really interesting article on Great British V-Twins but her concentration wouldn't hold.

She reached for her coffee as Barney dropped his favourite ball at her feet.

During her convalescence, the two of them had spent many hours together out in the garden, although she'd tried to keep his routine similar by having Charlie come and get him every other day for his walk and shift of squirrel watching in Charlie's garden. Although only gone for the afternoon, she'd always been happy to see him return a few hours later. The time alone had been spent in the garage, which looked nothing like it used to.

Evening time she had taken to spending an hour or two sitting outside with a cup of coffee and throwing the ball for Barney.

She was pretty sure her neighbours weren't used to her using her outside space, and the positioning of the table meant she couldn't be seen. She'd hear the family to her left, the parents threatening their three boys that if they didn't behave, the 'police lady' from next door would take them away. She'd never met the mother, father or the children.

Kim wasn't sold on the merits of threatening kids with police officers, but from the sound of it, those boys needed threatening with something.

On the right-hand side of her, she'd heard hushed conversations between the married couple about pretty much everyone in the street. It was how she'd found out that Edna, her neighbour over the road, wasn't returning to her home a week before the 'For Sale' sign went up in the front garden. A subsequent whispered conversation had informed her that Edna's daughter Barbra had kicked out her lazy husband and was moving in with her mother.

The guilty part of her was relieved she didn't have to face Edna on a daily basis. Never would she be able to apologise for the damage that had been done to the elderly lady, all because a psychopath had wanted to hurt her and had chosen Edna's house as his base. Edna had been tied up, starved and terrified so that Symes could watch Kim as she came and went. She shook away the guilt. It did Edna no good.

'Come here, boy – bring your ball,' she called as the anxiety started turning her stomach. *Don't think about it*, she told herself over and over as Barney dropped his ball at her feet.

'Jesus Christ,' she said out loud as her phone sounded an activation. She had kept most of the safety measures installed by Leanne but had unregistered the system from the alarm receiving company. She didn't want strangers showing up at her door because she forgot to set her alarm. But still the activations had the power to make her jump out of her skin.

Her breathing normalised as she looked at the familiar face on the door-cam.

'What d'ya reckon, boy, shall we let him in this time?'

Barney picked up his ball and ran into the house.

There was her answer.

She reached the front door and paused. 'You got Jenny's lasagne?' she asked before opening the door.

'Chicken curry,' Bryant answered.

It came a good second.

'And?'

'An apple for the prince.'

She looked to Barney, whose tail had started swishing at the sound of Bryant's voice.

She turned the key and slid across the three bolts. Another habit she'd kept.

'It was the apple that clinched it,' she said, opening the door for him to enter.

The delicious aroma wafted out of the Tupperware tub he was carrying. She followed him to the kitchen while Barney began nuzzling the right-hand front pocket of his jeans.

'Easy there, tiger,' Bryant said, taking the apple from his pocket.

Barney immediately sat and Kim was grateful the dog had some manners.

Bryant gave him the apple and slid the curry halfway across the breakfast bar towards her. She pulled it closer.

'Thanks. You can go now.'

He sat on the bar stool and glanced over at the half-full coffee machine. 'No chance. It's taken me two months and a lot of Tupperware to gain entry. I'm not leaving now.'

A heavy silence fell between them. She guessed he was waiting for an apology. It wasn't coming. She hadn't wanted to talk to anyone and this was her home. Her only concession was to reach for his mug from the cupboard.

She filled it and pushed it towards him.

'New toaster?' he asked, nodding to the left of the kettle that the toaster no longer matched.

'Yeah, anonymous benefactor.'

'Wonder what she's doing now,' Bryant mused about her former protection officer.

Kim shrugged. She couldn't say she hadn't thought about it because she had. For a brief time, Leanne King had taken over both her home life and her work life, and a part of her wondered if they would ever meet again. In a perverse, masochistic kind of way, she missed the woman's presence.

'So, what you been up to on your nice long holiday?'

'This and that,' she said, picking up her mug and cradling it against her chest.

'In the garage?' he asked, his eyes brightening.

'Sometimes.'

'Bloody hell, you're talkative this evening,' he said, pushing himself off the bar stool. 'You know I've been dying to see how you're getting on with the Vincent.'

Bryant knew she'd been working on the restoration of the Vincent Black Shadow for months.

He approached the door that led to the garage. 'May I?'

She nodded. He was going to see it eventually.

He pushed the door open and switched on the light. 'Oh,' he said as he walked into the space.

She followed him in.

'Not really what I expected to see.'

He took a good look at all the parts she'd acquired for the Vincent that had been pushed into a pile in the corner of the space. The tools that were normally strewn over the workbench and floor were neatly stored on the wall board or in her Sealey tool chest.

He walked into the middle of the space, the spot between the treadmill and the weight bench.

'Not sure I like what you've done with the place.'

'Priorities, Bryant,' she answered, looking at the space that had once been her safe haven, her happy place, but which had been turned into a place of focus and steely determination; a place to better her achievements every day. Somewhere to push her body back to what it had been before.

She bristled at the look of disappointment she saw on his face. Not least because it mirrored the feelings inside. She was allowed to be pissed off at herself. He was not.

She headed out of the space, and Bryant followed her back to the kitchen. He took a sip of coffee and a deep breath.

'Listen, Kim, there are some things you should—'

He stopped speaking as her phone rang. It was a sound she'd got used to not hearing in her home.

She frowned at the caller ID. She'd said all she wanted to say to him earlier.

'Stone,' she answered.

There was a pause from Keats. 'Oh, my mistake. I meant to call Burns, but you two are close together on my contact list.'

Only if he had her listed as Bitch; otherwise the space between B and S alphabetically meant he had very few contacts.

'What've you got, Keats?' she asked, trying to stifle the natural curiosity that seemed to be waking up after a long sleep.

'Possibly another one. I'm not touching it until I have CID presence. But never mind, it's not your problem. I'll make the appropriate calls, and Burns can update you in the—'

'Where are you, Keats?' she asked, trying to count the buttons the devious, manipulative man had just pressed.

'Kingfisher Street, Norton. Why do you want to know?' Keats asked.

'You already know the answer to that. We'll be there in ten minutes.'

FOURTEEN

Penn closed the oven door on the muffins. 'Okay, twenty-five minutes,' he said, passing the timer to Jasper.

The oven had a built-in timer but Jasper preferred the portable one their mum had bought him when he'd first started cooking.

'Shall we roll out some dough and make a pizza while we wait?' Penn asked.

Jasper was already shaking his head before he'd finished the sentence.

'Okay, what do you want to do?' Penn asked.

Jasper started edging towards the door.

'You wanna go join Billy on the Xbox?'

Jasper nodded eagerly.

'Go on then,' Penn said, collecting up all the bowls and utensils.

Jasper trotted back and enfolded him in a bear hug.

'Thanks, Ozzy, love you.'

Penn shook his head with mock despair as Jasper headed up to his bedroom.

Last night he'd collected him from chess club, and

Thursday night it was a line dancing class he'd found himself online. Friday night he'd have his weekly sleepover at Billy's, which had somehow managed to stretch until Sunday morning.

He had checked that Billy's parents didn't mind the extra person in the house, but they had assured him they were relieved to see Billy spending time with a real person and not online. He felt the exact same way.

He began to fill the dishwasher, trying not to overthink the fact that Jasper couldn't seem to get out of the kitchen fast enough.

He'd felt as though he'd been close to begging his brother to do something with him that he had always loved to do. Jasper had given in and they'd made the muffins, but something had been niggling at him. There had been, at times, an expression on his brother's face that was familiar to him but he just couldn't place.

Suddenly the truth dawned on him. The expression had come from himself.

There was no question that raising Jasper had been a family affair. Their dad's overtime had provided the extra money needed for Jasper to attend a nursery for kids with Down's syndrome and other challenges. His mother had provided the loving and nurturing, and he'd provided the fun. Except some days he hadn't wanted to provide the fun. Some days he'd wanted to be out on his bike. Some days he'd wanted to go with his mates to meet girls at the park. And on those days, he could imagine the tolerant look of sacrifice he'd worn on his face.

He set the dishwasher to go and began preparing Jasper's lunchbox for the following day. Was this how it felt for a parent once their child sought the early stages of independence?

At no one's request had he moved his entire life around for Jasper's sake. The minute he'd known of his mother's terminal illness, he had given up his flat, moved back into the family home and transferred back to West Mids Police. He had never regretted that decision for a minute. He'd enjoyed spending the extra time with Jasper, and it had brought them even closer as brothers. He had always known that Jasper's long-term care and supervision would fall to him and he'd grown into that role. Except he hadn't expected Jasper to have a better social life than him, or more friends.

He smiled with pride. Jasper didn't let anything hold him back.

But, for himself, the future didn't look how he had once thought it would. Right now, he felt like the slowest guy in the race.

Jasper would always need him to some degree but more as a safety net than a full-on parent. And no one had ever warned him how hard making that adjustment was going to be. Penn knew it was time to let go.

But how the hell was he supposed to do that?

FIFTEEN

Kingfisher Street was approximately a quarter of a mile away from Norton Covert, a former sand and gravel pit naturally revegetated and now designated as a site of importance for nature conservation.

It was almost eight when Kim and Bryant showed their IDs and entered the ground-floor flat.

Keats was in the doorway to the living room holding out two pairs of blue plastic slippers.

'Dress-down Tuesday is it, Bryant?' he asked, appraising Kim's colleague's attire of rugby shirt and jeans.

'Shockingly I wasn't at work,' he answered.

'Then you're slacking,' he said, standing aside.

The stench from inside the lounge had already found her.

'Been a while?' she asked, stepping into the small space.

'At least twenty-four hours,' Keats called after her, meaning she was killed some time on Monday.

Mitch and one photographer blocked the view of the body. The lead forensic tech turned on hearing her voice. 'Good to see you back, Inspector.'

'She's not back, she's just nosey,' Keats clarified before she had chance to speak.

Kim remained silent as the pathologist ushered the photographer out of the way.

'Bloody hell,' she said as Bryant exclaimed behind her.

A figure dressed in jeans and a university sweatshirt sat in a single armchair, both hands resting on the arms of the chair. The scene was completely normal from the trainer-clad feet up to the chest area. Above that the head was covered with a bag made of thick clear plastic with the open edge of the bag taped closed with white masking tape.

The visibility was obscured by moisture stains left from the breathing once the bag had been applied, but Kim could see the victim appeared to be a female in her mid-twenties.

'Thoughts?' Keats asked.

Kim studied the scene for a moment before speaking. 'Initial opinion would be sex game gone wrong or suicide.'

Plastic bags were often used in extreme sex games where the brush with death was supposed to heighten the sexual pleasure.

It was also being used increasingly in the case of suicide, normally in conjunction with a cocktail of drugs.

'And yet...' Kim said, taking another walk around the body.

'Go on,' Keats urged.

'The tape is too evenly applied.'

The layers of tape were almost exactly on top of each other.

'It's too tidy,' she said, raising her right hand and circling her neck. 'The tape would have criss-crossed all over the place as she bent her neck to tape around herself.'

'Anything else?' Keats asked.

She looked closer. 'There are no scratch marks on the plastic. Even if you're taking your own life, there's a moment of panic when you're fighting for breath. Instinct would take over and you'd try and claw it away.'

'Agreed. Anything else?'

She turned to Mitch. 'Check her fingers for residue from the masking tape. If she touched it, there'll be a trace.'

'And here was me having never done this job before,' Mitch offered.

'Yeah, but were you gonna check her wrists too?' she asked.

Mitch looked down.

'Her wrists must have been secured somehow to stop her from clawing at the bag.'

'She got you there, Mitch,' Keats said, stifling a smile.

She turned to the pathologist. 'Did I pass?'

'You did indeed. You identified all of my reasons for being suspicious.'

'All of them?'

He nodded.

'Then you missed one,' she said as Bryant chuckled behind her.

He frowned.

'The tape used,' she explained. 'If you make the decision to end your life this way, you're going to make sure that the tape will withstand your efforts to rip it off. Masking tape is pretty east to tear. Duct tape would be a different story completely.'

Mitch chuckled. 'Sorry, Keats, but it looks like she got you too.'

Kim headed outside and began to remove her shoe coverings. Bryant followed suit.

'You want to harass me about two post-mortems now?' Keats asked from behind.

'That'll be Burns's call. Send everything along to him. I don't think you'll struggle to get his attention now.'

She could see the surprise on the pathologist's face.

'Yes, you did all the right things to pique my interest but you should know I'm not going to be manipulated into anything. I'll let you know when I'm back.'

She turned and headed towards Bryant's car.

'You really not going to take the case?' he asked, pulling off the car park.

'Yeah, I'm really not,' she said without further explanation.

Silence filled the car but she could feel the weight of his disappointment.

Go slowly, Woody had said. *Take your time. Jump in when you're comfortable. Let Burns take the strain.* And it was what she intended to do. The observations that had been made would help him kick-start the investigation. For her it was too soon.

'Thanks for the lift,' she said as Bryant pulled up outside her house.

'No problem,' he said, staring forward.

She got out of the car and waited for him to pull away.

The passenger window started to lower.

She leaned down. 'What?'

'I just want to say one thing. When you're ready to return to your team, you need to hope that it's still the team you left.'

The window slid back up and her colleague pulled away from the kerb.

She frowned. What the hell had he meant by that?

SIXTEEN

It was 7.05 a.m. when Kim entered the squad room. Her team was assembled and Burns stood at the head of the room.

She headed towards the Bowl.

'Thanks for taking the call-out last night, Stone,' Burns said as she drew level with him. 'But I can take it from here.'

She walked past him without saying a word. She wasn't sure why he was trying to have a pissing contest with someone who hadn't even taken their dick out. She had handed the case right to him.

She put down her helmet and smiled at the coffee that had already been placed on her desk. She'd been drinking the stuff since 4 a.m. when the nightmares had triumphed again. It didn't seem to matter how many miles her legs chewed up on the treadmill, the exhaustion wouldn't see her through the dreams that brought her out of sleep with a racing heart and sweat running down her back. Eventually she'd outrun them or they'd get bored and leave her alone.

She switched on her computer as Burns began to speak. She was disappointed to see that there were still no names on the board.

'Okay, people, it would appear that Keats made a mistake on the classification for the boy in the tree.'

Keats made a mistake.

The boy in the tree.

Kim tried to force down the irritation that was stabbing her insides.

When you fucked up, you admitted it.

'Apparently the murder was staged to look like a suicide so it was an easy mistake for him to make.'

From the expressions on the faces of her team, they were having as much trouble swallowing this blame shifting as she was.

'In addition, there was a second incident last night that may or may not be linked to the murder of tree boy.'

Kim felt the growl forming in her throat.

Tree boy.

Burns rubbed his hands together. 'So, it looks like we might finally have a case worth investigating. Detective Inspector Stone will be offering desk support on this one.'

Desk support.

'Bryant, I want you looking into the background of Jamie Whatsisname.'

Wrong.

'Penn, start doing door to door around his address.'

Wrong.

'Wood, start a log and go through all the statements to see what we missed.'

Wrong.

How the hell could the man not know how best to use the resources at his disposal after two months?

A movement from Stacey caught her eye. The constable leaned down and took a white envelope from her satchel. Her expression was anxious but determined.

Kim looked at the rest of her team. Penn looked confused but Bryant appeared sadly resigned.

What did Bryant know that Penn did not?

The answer came to her as Stacey began to speak.

'DI Burns, before we go any further, may I have a private...?'

'You can go now,' Kim said from the door.

Burns turned to look at her. 'Excuse me?'

'Thanks for keeping my seat warm, but I can take it from here.'

Stunned silence filled the room as she folded her arms and met his gaze.

'You're on desk duties,' he protested.

'And I'm sure we'll find some way to make that desk more mobile, but that's not your concern. Please just take your herbal teas and go. We can do this the hard way or the easy way, but either way I'm taking my team back.'

His eyes darkened. 'This is my investigation.'

'Okay, the hard way. Burns, not one person in this room has an ounce of respect for you. You don't know the team you've been tasked to manage and you treat them like shit. You were put here because the brass didn't know what else to do with you. You're lazy and ambitious to the point of incompetence.'

The rage flooding into his face did not slow her down. She'd given him the opportunity to go quietly.

'You can't investigate your way out of a paper bag without a map and a compass, which I can personally vouch for, and we have two victims who don't need to be viewed as opportunities for career advancement.'

'DCI Woodward will never allow you—'

'It was DCI Woodward who told me to step back in when I was ready and, guess what, I'm ready.'

Burns looked around at the team and, not liking what he saw, grabbed his jacket from the back of the chair.

He paused at the door. 'I'll be back, Stone.'

'Yeah, on your way, Arnie,' she said as he disappeared from view.

Her team broke into a round of applause.

She held up her hand and shook her head.

It stopped.

She focussed her attention on the detective constable. 'Anything in that envelope you'd like to share with me, Stace?'

'No, boss,' she said, ripping it in half and tossing it in the bin.

'Okay, now things seem to have been a bit lax around here in my absence.' She pointed to the spot where Stacey's desk butted up to Penn's. 'If there's no Tupperware box there tomorrow, I'll bake something myself.'

'Got it, boss,' Penn said.

'Oh, and, guys, do your own bloody filing,' she said, glancing at Stacey's desk.

Bryant wheeled over and took a pile as Penn reached across and did the same.

Before she did anything else, she had some explaining to do to Woody.

'I'll make the coffee, and you've all got five minutes to shake him off. After that it's back to work. Play time is over.'

SEVENTEEN

It took a little more than five minutes to give Woody the highlights and assure him she was fit to lead the investigation. What they did with Burns now was their problem, but at 7.34 a.m. her inbox pinged the arrival of confirmation that she was named senior investigating officer in the case of Jamie Mills and the unknown female.

Kim took her fresh coffee out to the squad room. The team had put her firefighting time to good use. Jamie's name was back on the board along with the term 'unknown female', which was something she wanted changed as soon as possible. Every victim had a name and every victim had lived a life, however briefly.

'Okay, let's get started. Stace, your gut was right about wanting to pursue Jamie's death so remember that. According to his mum, Jamie was a solitary guy prone to mood swings and introspection. We can't rule out mental-health problems; his moods deteriorated further after a serious bike-riding accident a couple of years ago. He wasn't living at home, so it's important to find out where he's been and who he's been with. Right now, we have absolutely no motive for the murder of either of our victims.'

Kim didn't yet want to elaborate on her feelings of unease surrounding Jamie's mother. She may have judged her too harshly, which she'd be finding out later today.

'Our second victim was staged to look as though she'd suffocated herself with a thick plastic bag and masking tape. Her body had been there for at least a day, so we're going to want a timeline from Keats on that before we talk to the neighbours. Penn, I'm pretty sure Keats will want to get both our victims done today because of the potential link, so it's a day trip to the morgue for you.'

'Cool.'

Stacey and Bryant both shook their heads. None of them would ever understand their colleague's fascination for the process of the post-mortem.

'One of you chase Mitch, chase Keats, chase Mitch again. I want a name for our second victim. Stace, get me everything you can on Jamie Mills.'

She paused. 'Everybody sorted?'

'Yeah, boss,' Stacey said with a wide smile.

'Absolutely, boss,' Penn added with a barely hidden smirk.

'Make that three,' Bryant said, raising an eyebrow at his colleagues.

'Don't get cocky, people. Those half shifts you've been doing are a distant memory and there's a lot of work to do so get cracking,' Kim said, wondering when the novelty of her return would wear off.

She pushed herself off the edge of the desk. She was at her door before she remembered. She turned. 'Stace.'

'Boss?'

'This missing man, what's your gut say, anything in it?'

Stacey nodded. 'It's a bit weird.'

'Okay, stay on it but obviously...'

'Absolutely, boss.'

The detective constable knew the murder investigation took priority.

'Look lively, Bryant,' she said, grabbing her coat.

It was just before 8 a.m. and a little early for a house call by anyone's standards, but this time she had no choice.

They were already behind the eight ball on this one.

EIGHTEEN

'What was in the envelope, Stace?' Penn asked once the boss and Bryant were out the door. Although she'd shared her intentions with Bryant, Penn knew nothing of her transfer request.

'It's not important,' she said, fighting back the emotion in her throat. The dark cloud above her head had been blown away, and the constant feeling of dread in her stomach was beginning to dissolve. For two months the anxiety had been with her from opening her eyes in the morning to the moment she fell asleep.

The boss walking out like that and giving Burns his marching orders had made her want to burst into tears. Whether it was through relief, pride, admiration, respect, she didn't know. But what she did know was that the boss had come through for her without even knowing it.

'Not all superheroes wear capes, Penn.'

'You know, that might be the most random thing you've ever said to me, but if you're talking about the boss, that was quite something, wasn't it?'

'I don't think Burns was expecting it,' she said, chuckling.

'Probably still crying his eyes out in Woody's office,' Penn agreed. 'But he did have it coming,' he said, catching her eye. 'If only for the way the knobhead treated you.'

Stacey was still struggling to believe the man was gone. She knew her colleagues had done everything they could to mitigate Burns's impact on her, and she appreciated it. She gave herself a mental shake. Time to crack on.

'So what did the boss text you for yesterday?' she asked.

'She wanted me to climb a tree,' Penn answered.

'And you say I come out with random shit.'

'With a knee brace on to disprove suicide.'

Stacey smiled to herself. It had taken the boss less than a couple of hours to act on something about which they'd all been concerned; but only the boss would have decided to carry out an experiment like that.

You didn't find a seemingly healthy nineteen-year-old boy hanging in a tree and not take the time to ask some questions. She was relieved to see his name back on the board. It should never have been wiped off, and they should have been investigating his death for the last few days.

Time to find out who Jamie Mills really was.

From the boss's chat with Jamie's mum, Stacey had the feeling that might not be so easy. If he was given to introspection and possibly bouts of depression, there was a chance he was a boy who had chosen to live his life quietly.

She put a search into Facebook as Penn ended his call to Keats to check timings. 'Oh,' she said out loud, immediately surprised at the results of her search.

She clicked and scrolled. 'Oh,' she said again.

'Gonna need more than that, Stace,' Penn said, reaching for his polka-dot bandana.

'I'm not sure how well his mother knew him but I may already have found the motive.'

NINETEEN

'That was quite the show in there,' Bryant said as they headed towards the village of Fairfield. 'If you'd have let me know ahead of time, I could have sold tickets.'

'Not one of my finer moments,' she said, aware of the lack of professionalism she'd demonstrated in front of her team.

'We'll agree to differ on that, but are you really ready to resume?'

'Bit late to ask me that now after needling me into it. You pretty much told me that my team was falling apart.'

'Hmm... I like the sound of "my" team, and I was just giving you the heads-up.'

'Was he really that bad?'

'Absolutely,' Bryant said without hesitation. 'And for Stacey it was a whole lot worse. I feel sorry for any women he works with in the future.'

Realistically, she had no idea if she was ready to head up a major investigation. It took full concentration and the ability to watch all the balls that were in the air. But she did know that given the fact Jamie's body had been found over seventy-two hours ago, they had some serious catching up to do.

'Next left,' she said as they passed the parish church. 'Behind the Toyota, the silver one,' she said, realising there were two other Toyotas in the street.

As she got out of the car, Kim had no idea of the emotional reaction of the parents to the news that their son had been murdered. In fact, Diana Mills's reaction to her son's death was still troubling her.

'One sec,' Kim said as her phone tinged receipt of a message.

She opened the link Stacey had sent and hid her surprise as the door opened before they'd even knocked.

Both Mr and Mrs Mills stood in the doorway, dressed in head-to-toe black.

Mrs Mills frowned. 'I'm sorry, Inspector, but I haven't thought of anything else and we're on our way out.'

She looked pointedly at Bryant.

'This is my colleague,' Kim explained. 'And if we could just take a few minutes of your time.'

She shook her head. 'I'm afraid not. We're just going to the funeral directors to make arrangements.'

'In which case we really do need a few minutes of your time.'

The woman looked as though she was going to stand her ground.

'We can talk right here, if you'd prefer.'

Mrs Mills looked around the street as a front door over the road opened.

'Diana,' her husband said.

'Oh, come in,' she said, stepping aside.

The man held out his hand. 'Stuart Mills.'

Bryant shook his hand. 'We're sorry for your loss.'

Stuart Mills was a bear of a man who towered over his wife.

'In here,' Diana said, pointing once again to the room Kim had been in yesterday.

Diana stood next to the fireplace, but Stuart pointed to a chair. 'Please sit.'

The three of them sat, but Diana stubbornly remained standing.

'Mr and Mrs Mills, I'm afraid we have some news about the investigation into your son's death.'

'What investigation?' Diana asked, looking from Kim to her husband in a 'why didn't I know about this?' kind of way.

'Any sudden death warrants investigation,' Bryant explained. 'Even if initial findings suggest suicide.'

'Initial?' Stuart asked, listening to every word.

'Yes, I'm sorry to have to add to your pain, but we don't believe that Jamie took his own life,' Kim confirmed.

'An accident?' Stuart asked with disbelief.

Kim shook her head. 'We believe someone else was involved.'

'M... Murder?' he asked.

'That's preposterous,' Diana exploded, finally moving forward and taking a seat. 'I told you yesterday that he had quiet times, that he was broody, unpredictable.'

'He may have been all of those things, but he didn't take his own life. Someone else was responsible for the death of your son.'

Disbelief contorted both of their faces, and Kim felt the situation was surreal. They'd had no problem believing it was suicide – normally a difficult and painful fact for family members to accept, but with these two it was the other way around.

'But you can't be sure?' she asked, looking to Bryant as though he would give her a different answer.

'We're as sure as we need to be to open a full-on murder investigation,' Bryant responded.

'A what?' Diana asked as abject horror shaped her mouth. 'Don't we have any say?'

Kim's mind went to the link she'd been sent by Stacey.

She no longer felt bad for the absence of empathy towards this woman. Whether the same applied to her husband she couldn't yet be sure.

'No, I'm sorry but you can't stop a murder investigation,' Kim said.

'But he's our son,' she said proprietarily.

'Why would you not want to know who killed your son and for his murderer to be brought to justice?' Kim asked as cordially as she could manage.

'The press, the papers, the news. I mean none of it is going to bring him back, is it?'

The news headlines over the weekend had not been sensational, and his death had made only the local news along the lines of 'man found hanging from a tree after taking own life'. There had been no follow-up, and the headline had pretty much disappeared unless you were specifically looking for it. Jamie hadn't even been identified by name.

A murder investigation was a whole different story, and the press would be banging the door down any minute now. Jamie's name and face would be all over the news, as well as any facts the press could uncover about him.

And therein lay the problem, Kim had realised.

Diana stood. 'Who is your superior? You've made a huge mistake.'

Kim had so hoped she was wrong, but every time Diana opened her mouth, she confirmed Kim's worst suspicions.

Diana looked to her husband.

'I think my wife is correct. I feel that we need to speak to your boss.'

Okay, so it was both of them. Poor Jamie.

'There's no mistake, I'm afraid. There is no physical way that Jamie could have climbed that tree, but you both knew that, didn't you?'

And neither one of them had mentioned it to the police.

They exchanged glances.

Mr Mills spoke first. 'Jamie could be very determined when he wanted to be.'

'Not determined enough to make a fused knee bend.' She paused. 'I'm afraid your trip to the funeral directors will have to be postponed. I don't have a date for when Jamie's body will be released to you, but a full post-mortem is being carried out today.'

'I didn't give permission for that.'

'You don't have to, Mrs Mills. It is a suspicious death so there's a legal process in place. We'll keep you informed of our progress, and please avoid contact with the press.'

She said this as a matter of routine, but she didn't think that was going to be a problem for these two.

Kim stood. 'We'll see ourselves out.'

She was at the door when Mrs Mills spoke.

'Why couldn't you just leave him be?' she asked quietly.

'Why would we do that, Mrs Mills?'

'He's at peace now. He's probably happier now he's gone.'

'Is that you or him?' Kim asked, meeting her gaze. There was fire in the woman's eyes which met the ice that was in hers.

'You chose not to accept your son's sexuality.'

'There was nothing wrong with—'

'I know there was nothing wrong with him,' Kim snapped. 'He was gay.'

'He was not gay,' Diana said, spitting the last word out of her mouth as though it was poison. 'He was confused. It was a phase. If he'd just tried harder when—'

'I think you should leave now,' Mr Mills said, standing beside his wife.

Kim looked at them both with contempt as she headed to the front door.

Sadness washed over her for Jamie. What chance had the poor kid had?

TWENTY

'Not quite the picture his mother painted, is it?' Bryant asked, scrolling through the Facebook profile of Jamie Mills.

Once past the numerous condolence messages posted on his wall, it turned into a colourful display of someone who was gay and proud of it. Jamie had over five hundred friends and thousands of photos. He was pictured amongst large groups of friends, at parties, at clubs, at Gay Pride events around the country. And in particular a young man whose hair changed colour and style almost as often as his clothing popped up in a lot of the photos.

'And there's our guy now,' Kim said as the familiar face appeared coming out of Tesco in Cradley Heath, already focussed on his phone.

His last Instagram post had been a selfie with a tray full of fresh fish stating how he couldn't wait to finish his long night shift at 9 a.m. He was easily recognisable by the shock of candy-pink hair they'd seen in a recent photo.

Kim and Bryant approached him as he reached a battered white Mini.

'River Harris?' she asked, showing her identification.

'Depends who's asking, darling,' he said.

She pushed her ID closer.

He rolled his eyes dramatically. 'Yeah, got three of those back home. You know, cos we all like a bit of role play.' He took it from her. 'Not as good as this though,' he said, squinting. 'That your real name?'

'Is River yours?' she asked, taking it back.

'I am destined for greatness, Inspector, and it won't find me with a name like John.'

She nodded her agreement.

'I'm assuming someone finally read my tweets then,' he said, folding his arms.

'Tweets?'

'Yeah, I know you say the account isn't monitored and I should call blah, blah, blah number, but I've been tweeting you guys day and night to say that Jamie didn't top himself. Never got a response or even a like, but obviously someone was listening.'

Did no one just come into the station any more? Was everything done on social media?

'We kinda came to that conclusion based on the evidence, but why are you so sure it wasn't suicide?'

'Err... Look here,' he said, moving his hands up and down his own body. 'Who'd want to die with me in their life?'

Kim had to admire his confidence.

'You two were good friends?'

'Besties,' he replied.

'Anything more?'

He twirled one of the three hoop earrings in his right lobe. 'Nah, tried it once. Couldn't stop laughing. Decided we were best as mates. He's proper gone, isn't he?'

Kim nodded.

He breathed in, blinked back tears and sighed. 'Well, you'd best find the bastard that did it.'

'We intend to. Was Jamie in a relationship?'

River scrunched up his face. 'Jamie didn't really do relationships. I mean, in our community, two and a half dates and you're booking the engagement party. Jamie always held himself back. He was the same when I first met him hanging around Spikeys.'

'Spikeys?'

'A club in Wolvo called the Green Nettle, stupid name. Went out for a smoke and saw him pacing around outside. I notice shit like that. You never know who's hanging around for a gay-bashing session. Popped outside for another later and he was still there, walking to and fro, down to the corner and back again with his hands in his pockets.'

'You approached him?' Kim asked.

'Yeah I asked him the golden question: Liza or Cher?'

'Sorry?'

'Gay icons, Inspector. You really should know these things. Anyway he answered "Cher" and I knew he was a keeper. I invited him inside, we danced, laughed, drank, hooked up our social-media accounts and we've been friends ever since.'

'And that was when?'

'Almost two years ago.'

'And Jamie never had a relationship in that time?' Kim asked.

River sighed dramatically. 'Let me light a smoke. If I'd known you were going to probe me this deeply, I'd have insisted on dinner first.'

Kim fought back the smile on her lips as he took a pack of smokes from his pocket.

She could see the look of longing on her colleague's face. Despite there being a good few years between him and his last smoke, the temptation was always there.

'It was complicated for Jamie. There was conflict in his acceptance of his sexuality.'

'His social media says otherwise,' Kim said, confused.

'Ah, Inspector, there's a difference between being gay and doing gay.'

'Not getting it,' she said.

'Okay, take me for example. I came out to my mom when I was thirteen. It took me weeks to build up the courage. I blurted it out, and her response was "tell me something I don't know, now put the kettle on". It was the most important cup of tea I've ever had.'

'Go on,' Kim urged.

'Over that cuppa my mum explained that life would be harder, that I would face bigots, homophobes, ignorance and stupidity. She told me that I had to rise above it and be true to myself and never to conform because of other people's opinions.'

Kim liked the sound of River's mum almost as much as she was warming to the lad himself.

'And Jamie's coming-out story?'

He rolled his eyes. 'Don't even. He tried to tell them in his early teens. They shut him down, told him he wasn't, called the whole thing a disgusting abomination, a crime against God and sent him off to all kinds of summer sporting camps where he got the shit kicked out of him numerous times.'

Kim tried not to let the anger show on her face.

'It's one thing admitting you find other men attractive and becoming part of that community. It's another thing acting on it.' Again, he swallowed back the tears. 'I like to think he was making progress before some fucking homophobe got their hands on him.'

'And that's what you think this is?'

'Don't you?' he asked, surprised.

Kim couldn't allow herself to think that there was nothing more to Jamie than his sexuality.

'Was Jamie having issues with anyone that you know of?'

River shook his head. 'He wasn't like that. Jamie didn't do conflict. We were on the train to Brum once and we got a bit of shit, couple of wankers calling us names. Jamie wanted to move along to the next carriage but I wouldn't go. I told the taller one that much as I loved to suck a dick, I couldn't get the whole of him in my mouth.'

Kim couldn't prevent the chuckle that escaped from her mouth. She liked people that were unapologetic.

'Jamie pulled me off the train before the lanky twat could catch me, but the whole thing completely ruined his night. One vodka and Coke and it was a distant memory for me.'

'Any new people hanging around your circle?'

River guffawed.

Kim rolled her eyes when she realised what she'd said.

'Okay, anyone strange hanging about?'

'Hard to tell in our community but no, nothing I'm aware of, and Jamie hadn't said anything about any weirdos or anything like that.'

'Okay, River, thanks for your time, and if you think of anything else, give me a call,' she said, handing him a card.

'Cool. Can I give you a shout if I'm getting my head kicked in as well?'

She smiled. 'How about you just keep yourself out of trouble.'

He raised his eyebrows suggestively. 'My mom always says if you can't be good be careful.'

Good advice, she thought as River busied himself putting the key in the door lock of the Mini. No central locking on that old girl.

'You wouldn't forget him in a hurry, would you?' Bryant said as they walked away.

'Hang on,' Kim said, turning back. She caught River as he was about to pull away.

'What now?' he asked, manually winding down the window. 'This bitch needs her beauty sleep.'

'You said something about Jamie doing better at something. What did you mean?'

'Oh, just that he was talking to some woman he knew from way back, somewhere up Rowley. Not sure where or who, but he'd chat with her every couple of weeks and he'd seem lighter afterwards.'

'Okay, thanks.'

She tapped the roof to signal he could go.

Who was this woman and what did she know about Jamie?

TWENTY-ONE

'Are you ready?' Keats asked as Penn pulled the face mask over his mouth.

Penn nodded. He'd foregone the smear of Vicks beneath his nostrils. Breathing it in beneath the face mask would have his eyes streaming in seconds.

'I have to say, Penn, that it is pleasurable to be sent an officer that appreciates the craft of what we do,' Keats said as he began his cursory examination prior to wielding his scalpel. Penn knew that the pathologist inspected every part of the body before he removed even one tool from the tray.

'And of course, the more we look, the more we find,' Keats said, taking a good look at Jamie's neck. He tipped the boy's head from side to side.

Penn was constantly amazed at Keats's bedside manner. Even while doing the most invasive acts on the body, there was a lightness to his touch, like a doctor who didn't want to cause any more pain.

He had learned to stay in the background and not get in Keats's way unless he spoke. That was normally permission to step forward.

'Look at the bruising of the rope around the neck.'

'Okay.'

'This didn't come from hanging.'

'Okay,' Penn said again, looking at the Adam's apple.

'Let me demonstrate,' Keats said, grabbing a tape measure from his desk.

Penn eyed him suspiciously.

'I'm not going to hurt you – now give me your neck.'

Climb a tree, get hung in the morgue. Oh yeah, things were definitely getting back to normal, he thought as he turned and felt Keats put the tape measure around his neck.

'When I say drop, just lower yourself quickly by crouching down.'

'Okay.'

'Drop.'

Penn did as he'd been told. He felt the tape measure tighten, but he also felt it shift.

'Ah, got it,' Penn said, straightening up and moving back to the body.

'The cause of death will either be due to strangulation or a broken neck. There is no doubt that our boy here was strangled but definitely before he was hoisted up onto the branch.'

There were two rings around his neck, Penn noted, pointing.

'The lower one was the one that killed him, and the upper one was from him resting in that position until he was cut down,' Keats said, waving him back to the periphery of the room.

Penn could only wonder at the physical strength of the person who had not only strangled Jamie Mills but also hoisted his dead-weight body up and into thin air.

He took out his notebook and scrawled.

One killer or two?

'While you've got that out, I'm going to estimate his time of death between the hours of 1 a.m. and 4 a.m. in the early hours of Sunday morning.'

Penn wrote that down while his mind did a quick calculation. Hours since death – approximately eighty-one. Hours between death and Burns's attendance – approximately six. Wasted hours – seventy-five. And that would have been more if the boss hadn't got involved.

Penn put his book back in his pocket and waited patiently while Keats moved around the boy's limbs, inspecting the feet and then the hands.

'Hmm...' Keats said, peering closely at the underside of the left wrist.

Penn knew better than to speak.

Keats moved to the right wrist and inspected the underside of that one. 'Hmm...' he repeated.

Penn said nothing.

'Approach,' Keats said.

He stood beside the man who was still holding Jamie's right wrist.

'See that faint white line there?'

Penn had to peer closely to see it, but sure enough there was a thin white line stretching across the wrist.

'Same on the other wrist,' Keats said.

'Suicide attempts?' Penn asked. Even though they knew his death wasn't suicide didn't mean he'd never tried in the past.

'Don't think so,' Keats said, frowning. 'Uncommon on both wrists and the line is too tidy. Pass me that razor.'

'Keats, I'm not doing any re-enactments with—'

'Calm down and pass me the razor.'

Penn looked around and located a Bic razor on the work surface. He placed it into Keats's hand as though he was a nurse assisting a doctor with major surgery.

The pathologist placed the boy's wrist back on the metal

tray. He began to gently and carefully shave the wiry dark hair that travelled down Jamie's arm. The process revealed pale skin beneath. Keats grabbed a magnifying glass and took a look. He handed the magnifier to Penn before taking his razor around to the other side of the tray. He repeated the process as Penn took a look. Sure enough, the faint white line was present on the top side of the wrist.

'Same on this side,' Keats said, putting the razor down.

Penn waited for Keats's explanation.

'Not attempted suicide marks at all. These are restraint scars, and they were made a long time ago.'

TWENTY-TWO

Stacey had received two emails within seconds of each other.

The first was from Beth Denton with signed permissions and passcodes into their bank accounts. The second was from Mitch with the personal details of their second victim.

Sarah Laing. Age 22.

A photo of her driving licence was attached.

Stacey zoomed in and did a double take, wondering if there had been some kind of mistake.

The girl in the driving-licence photo had long brown hair that draped over her shoulders. A thick, blunt fringe ran across the top of piercing blue eyes. She had a slightly hooked nose that gave her face interest and intrigue instead of natural beauty.

Stacey had already glanced at the preliminary photos Keats had taken of the body but she looked again to be sure. The young lady on the table had bleached-blonde hair, short and severely cut over her left ear. It hung fuller and longer on the top and over her right ear. Stacey counted seven hoop piercings down the length of her left ear and a single stud in the nose.

At first glance they looked like two completely different people, but the tell-tale signs were there: the shape of the jaw, the cheekbones, the full lips, the nose. It was definitely the same person but a very different attitude.

Stacey got up and moved around to Penn's desk where she could reach the wipe board easier. She breathed a sigh of relief as she wiped away the words 'unknown female' and replaced them with Sarah's actual details.

She was already intrigued with the difference between the two photos. The bank details of Gabe Denton were forgotten while she focussed on the main case.

'Okey-dokey, Sarah, let's find out a bit more about you,' she said, pulling the keyboard towards her.

She put the name into Instagram and came up blank. Nothing on Twitter, Facebook, Snapchat; and TikTok was a bust too.

She tried a general Google search and came up empty.

Stacey tapped her fingers on the desk. It wasn't that this hadn't happened to her before but not normally for someone in their early twenties.

She went back to Mitch's email. The only other attachment was a copy of a recent phone bill. She printed out the email and immediately sent a message to the provider requesting full details.

Perhaps the woman used another name. She typed in the phone number which came back as registered to Vodafone, which she already knew.

'What next?' she said, narrowing her eyes.

'Ah,' she said, focussing on the only thing she had left to try.

She took a screenshot of the photo from the driving licence and fed it into the face-recognition software.

Nothing.

She groaned out loud. Not something she wanted to do but she'd been left with no choice. She accessed the photos from Keats and took the headshot. For some inexplicable reason it felt intrusive. With the first photo Stacey knew the girl had been alive and so felt fine to use it, but the second photo, taken after death, felt like a violation.

'So sorry, Sarah,' she said as she dragged the photo into the box. She hit the search again and watched as the screen loaded the results.

'Oh my jolly good graciousness,' she said as she reached for the phone.

TWENTY-THREE

'We will get to leave this car in a minute,' Kim said as her phone rang again. They'd pulled up outside the office of Megan Shaw in Whiteheath. A red door with a nameplate was nestled at the edge of a carpet warehouse. It hadn't been too hard to find the woman Jamie had been seeing. Of the three psychologists listed in the Rowley area, only one listed sexual identity counselling.

The second they'd pulled up, Penn had called to update them on the post-mortem progress of Jamie Mills. The reason for those restraint marks on his wrists was something she intended to bring up with the counsellor, if she ever got in there.

'Go ahead, Stace,' she said, answering the call.

'Got a name, boss.'

Kim frowned. This was not news. She'd received the same email from Mitch and knew the girl's name was Sarah Laing.

'And?'

'Except that's not really the name she goes by. She calls herself Sarah Sizzle on the numerous dating websites she's subscribed to.' Stacey paused. 'Gay websites.'

Kim felt the world stand still for a moment. 'You're sure?'

'Oh yeah. I want to do more digging to see exactly what she was seeking, but she was on a fair few of them.'

Kim felt as though she was stepping into an area that was unfamiliar. She'd never downloaded a dating app in her life.

'Do these sites cater to all sexualities?' Kim asked.

'How am I supposed to know? I'm a happily married woman.'

'Stace.'

'They're a mixture. I need to go deeper.'

Bryant guffawed and, realising what she'd said, Stacey burst out laughing on the other end.

'Okay, enough, you two. Could Sarah and Jamie have been on the same site?'

'Definitely possible. Let me get back to it.'

'Quick as you can, Stace. We need to know if this is some kind of awful coincidence or if we're dealing with a rush of hate crimes.'

'On it, boss,' Stacey said before ending the call.

Kim didn't even want to consider the possibility.

'Come on, smutty boy, let's see what we can get without a court order,' she said, getting out of the car. She wasn't getting delayed again.

She pressed the buzzer beside the door and introduced them both into the speaker.

The door clicked. She pushed it open to reveal a carpeted staircase leading to the first floor.

There was no door on the upper level, and the stairs ended at an open-plan area that was part office and part lounge. At the far end of the space, she could see three doors: one marked 'toilet', the middle one was marked 'staff only' and the final one, key coded, had a 'no entry' sign.

The woman that stood to greet them was dressed in jeans, ankle boots and a V-neck sweater. Light brown hair curled beneath her chin. Her make-up was expertly applied and appeared minimal.

'Megan Shaw,' she said, holding out her hand.

Kim looked away as she surveyed her surroundings. The windows were on the rear of the property and looked out onto a trading estate behind, destroying the New York loft vibe she seemed to be aiming for.

'We'd like to talk to you about Jamie Mills,' Kim said.

Her face creased in concern. 'Is he okay?'

Kim shook her head as she took a seat. The reclassification of the incident had not yet hit the news and neither had Jamie's identity.

'I'm sorry to tell you that Jamie is dead.'

'Oh God, no,' Megan said as her hand went to her mouth. Her other hand landed on the back of the sofa to steady herself.

Bryant stepped forward, took her elbow and eased her down to a seating position.

'But why... I mean... who...?' she asked, shaking her head in disbelief.

A minute in and this woman had already demonstrated more emotion than his mother.

'Just take a minute,' Kim said. She caught Bryant's eye and nodded towards a bottle of water on the desk. He grabbed it and handed it to the counsellor before taking a seat.

She took a swig. 'Thank you.'

'Did you know Jamie well?' Kim asked to ease her into the questioning gently.

She nodded after taking another swig. 'I met Jamie when he was twelve years old. Initially I was seeing all three of them, as his parents didn't want me to talk to him alone.'

'Why not if they brought him to you for help?'

Megan took a breath. 'It was a certain kind of help they were seeking.'

'Go on,' Kim urged.

'They wanted me to help him but only in their way. There was a script they wanted me to follow.'

'Which was?'

Megan hesitated as her face hardened. 'They wanted me to convince him he wasn't gay.'

Kim took a moment to digest this. Maybe the woman had got it wrong.

'Are you sure they didn't just want you to help him explore—'

'No, officer. I was instructed to remove the very notion from his head,' she spat. 'It was made very clear to me what they expected me to do.'

'How were you supposed to do it?'

Megan shrugged. 'They seemed to think that prayer and denial were the only tools needed.'

'And did you try?'

Megan fixed her with a hard gaze. 'That's not what I do, and I'll try not to be offended that you actually asked me that question.'

Kim shrugged. She wasn't too bothered. She only wanted to know about Jamie.

'To be clear, I explained to Mr and Mrs Mills that my job is to help people come to terms with their sexuality, to under-stand it, to ensure they don't see it as a defect in their genetic make-up. To build them up, to embrace who they are. My work is about acceptance and exploration, about confidence to be who they are, so no I did not try and convince him he wasn't gay.'

Kim appreciated the woman's passion for her work but it was a question she'd had to ask. 'So what happened?'

'I managed to get a couple of one-on-one sessions with Jamie. He was conflicted. He was starting to feel attraction to other boys. When he told his parents, they called him every foul name they could come up with. They told him that such thoughts were not only ungodly but perverted, and they likened him to a paedophile.'

'What?' Kim exploded.

'I know it's hard to believe, but I feel they honestly thought it was some kind of disease for which they just needed to find the right treatment.'

Kim was struggling to believe that such people and attitudes still existed, but then she pictured Jamie's parents and it wasn't such a stretch. 'You say you only saw him a couple of times, seven years ago?'

She shook her head. 'He came back about a year ago.' She smiled. 'He knocked on my door, told me he'd got no money and asked if he could come in for a chat.'

'And you let him even though he couldn't afford you?'

'Of course,' Megan said, like it was a no-brainer. 'And do you always start off with such a jaded opinion of people?'

Kim nodded. 'Absolutely.'

Megan shook her head. 'Shame. Anyway, he asked if we could chat now and again and he'd pay me what he could. I told him that on Tuesdays, I normally spent an hour or so tidying up before going home and if he wanted to drop by then, he was more than welcome.'

Kim couldn't help but warm to the woman. The need to help the boy had far outweighed his ability to pay her. 'And your conversations?' she asked, readying herself with the threat of a court order.

'He was conflicted. I feel there was a lot he didn't want to tell me about the years since we'd last talked. He was all about moving forward. He wanted to explore his sexuality, but he couldn't rid himself of the guilt and self-loathing.'

Kim thought of River and his total acceptance of himself compared to Jamie.

'Unfortunately, Jamie's parents did him a great deal of damage during his adolescence,' Megan said, shuddering. 'He wouldn't speak about it, but God only knows what they put in his head during those years.'

'Why do you think they did anything?' Bryant asked.

'They brought a confused, frightened twelve-year-old boy to me and asked if I could "un-gay" him. I told them it couldn't be done. What makes you think they believed me?'

'But what more could they do?' Kim asked as the intercom sounded.

Megan regarded her for a second. 'Are you seriously asking me that question?'

Kim wasn't sure what she'd said wrong so nodded.

'Inspector, you have a lot to learn, and I don't have the time to teach you,' she said as the buzzer sounded again.

'What are you...?'

'I'm sorry but I have to end this now,' Megan said, standing.

'But...'

'Go start your education with Clifford – Cliff – over at The What Centre in Stourbridge,' she said, walking them towards the stairs. 'He'll tell you exactly what they might have done next, but get ready, Inspector, because you're not going to like what he has to say.'

TWENTY-FOUR

Stacey pushed her chair away from the desk and stretched her neck, feeling as though she'd had an education after trawling through a maze of dating websites.

She'd started off on Lex, which seemed to be a text-centred social app that modelled itself on old personal ads with a bit of erotica thrown in. At the other end of the spectrum, a site called Qutie seemed focussed on helping people, particularly LGBTQ people, build meaningful connections, including friendships as well as romantic relationships.

In between were apps like Thurst, HER, Feeld, Lesly, Open, Fem, OK Cupid. Stacey had been learning about them all. Not least that Sarah Sizzle was on every single one.

There were two things that struck her as odd. Sarah was on every site, indicating that she didn't seem to know if she wanted a quick fling with just one or even multiple partners, or if she wanted a deep and meaningful relationship with just one person. The second thing that struck her was that every profile she'd found had been set up in the last six months. Why everything all at once? Conversely, she couldn't find Jamie's footprint on any of them, making a link to some homophobe trawling the sites for people to kill an unlikely theory.

Even when she'd been single, Stacey had never really frequented the dating sites. Working as a police officer and watching too many episodes of *Catfish* had left her suspicious and jaded when it came to dating. Given the fact she was bisexual, she'd had no idea what to go looking for. She'd met Devon the old-fashioned way. She'd been in a pub with a couple of friends, and Devon had been in there with a bunch of colleagues from immigration celebrating someone's promotion. Yes, their eyes had met and Stacey had felt as though she'd been punched in the ribs. Breathing had ceased to be a natural bodily function that happened without her conscious instruction. Devon had found a way to be at the bar at the exact time Stacey had gone to buy a drink. Devon had apologised for bumping into her, and before she knew it, they were exchanging numbers. Numerous texts flowed between them where they discovered that their parents were both first-generation immigrants from Nigeria and their villages had been less than twenty miles apart.

Stacey had found the texting to be much easier than the meeting in person where she had found Devon to be as interesting and intelligent as she was beautiful. But Stacey had ended things after their first date, without explanation.

It had only been some months later when working on a slave-trafficking case that they'd met again, and a very wise man and a good friend had put her head on straight. Seeing the chemistry between them, Dawson had quickly identified her feelings of inadequacy and had told her she was a fool if she let Devon get away. She had followed his advice and the rest was history.

The memory was bittersweet as it combined her biggest gain in life with her worst loss. She glanced at the desk that had once been his and admitted that she still missed him.

'Okay, missy, enough of that,' she said to an empty room.

To distract her mind, she opened the bank statements for Gabriel Denton.

There were two accounts – one appeared to be a joint current account and the other a mortgage account. The mortgage account was straightforward. The money came in and the money went out. The couple had a standing order that was higher than their mortgage payment, which had been set when interest rates were higher. Because interest rates had fallen but the direct debit hadn't been adjusted, a small nest egg was starting to build of a couple of thousand pounds.

Stacey transferred her attention to the current account.

There was the regular payment to the mortgage account with all other utilities that went out at the beginning of the month.

She went through the debit-card payments and found a regular monthly spend at an Italian restaurant and a weekly variational cost to Just Eat.

Both healthy salaries went into the account except for one payment that was always transferred on the last day of each month manually. It was always the balance of the account minus £1,000.

Stacey reached for her phone and dialled Beth's number.

'Hello,' she answered, breathlessly.

'No news yet, Beth,' Stacey said, not to get her hopes up.

'Oh, okay,' she said and Stacey could hear the disappointment in her voice.

'It's just a question but I notice on the bank statements that there's a variable sum transferred into an unnamed account monthly.'

'Oh yes, we leave some emergency money in the current account and transfer the rest to our savings.'

'I don't have that account,' Stacey said.

'We never touch it. It's our pension top-up. We swore we would only use it in the most dire circumstances.'

'In the interests of thoroughness I'd like to check it.'

'Of course. It's the same bank and sort code.'

Stacey noted the account number and then opened up the log-in screen. Within seconds she was in.

'You'll see, I'm sure, that there have been no withdrawals for the last eight years, since our last IVF attempt.'

Stacey could see that the account held almost one hundred thousand pounds and indeed twenty-five thousand had been transferred just over eight years earlier.

Stacey felt a wave of sadness that clearly the treatment hadn't worked, as the couple were childless. She could only imagine the pain it had caused them both. Given that eight years had elapsed since their last attempt, she guessed they hadn't tried again.

But her heart sank even further when she saw something else.

'Anything big you were planning to purchase in the near future?'

'No nothing. Why do you ask?'

'Because ten thousand pounds was withdrawn from the account on Monday morning.'

'No, there must be some mistake. I've told you we never...' Her words trailed away as she put two and two together. 'But that's when he disappeared.'

Yes, it was.

'He must be in some kind of trouble. He must have been forced—'

'Beth, do you keep your passports together?'

'Yes, yes, of course. They're right there in the kitchen drawer next to the— Oh.'

'What?' Stacey asked, although she already suspected the answer.

'Gabe's isn't here. He must have moved it for something. Let me check around and give you a call back once I've found it.'

Stacey said goodbye and wondered how long it would be until she got that call.

TWENTY-FIVE

The What Centre was located on Coventry Street in Stourbridge, sandwiched between a chippy and a pub.

As far as Kim knew, it offered a counselling service for people aged nine to twenty-five accessed either by professional services or self-referral.

What she hadn't known before her Google search online was that they specialised in providing a range of support for young people who wanted to explore their gender identity and sexuality.

The green-fronted premises opened into a room with easy mauve furniture. Stairs descended out of the room but were blocked off by what looked like a kiddie gate. Posters and leaflets covered the walls. Opposite the entrance was a glass panel with a door to the left.

A man in his late twenties with hair tied back in a ponytail waved through the glass.

'Cliff?' Kim asked, approaching the office.

He nodded. 'I didn't do it,' he said, holding up his hands as they showed their IDs.

Oh, she hadn't heard that one in a while.

'Is there somewhere we can talk?' she asked.

'Anyone due in room one, Karen?' he asked the woman at the second desk.

She checked something on the computer. 'Nope, free until two.'

Cliff wrapped up what was left of his sandwich. She often forgot that many people observed proper lunch breaks. For police officers, it was a case of grabbing something on the go as they moved from one location to another.

By the time she thought about apologising for the intrusion, his sandwich had vanished and he was heading towards a key-coded door.

He keyed in the numbers and pushed the door open then held it for them to pass through.

'First left,' he said, disappearing from view around the corner.

Kim pushed open the door and the light automatically illuminated.

'Sorry,' Cliff said from behind. 'Our sessions are mainly one to one.'

In the small space were two green wing-backed chairs placed before an old fireplace.

She moved aside to allow him to enter, carrying a hardback chair which he placed beside one of the easy chairs.

'Thank you,' Kim said, taking the hard chair. Bryant sat beside her, and Cliff took the easy chair on the other side of the fireplace. The space was intimate for two but snug for three.

'So, how can I help you?' he asked, sitting back in the chair.

'Do you know a young man named Jamie Mills?'

He frowned and then began to shake his head. 'The name isn't familiar to me but I'd have to check our records to be sure.'

'Good friends with someone called River...'

'Oh, we know River very well, but he only ever comes in alone.'

'For what?' Kim asked out of interest. River didn't strike her as the type of person who needed help with accepting his sexuality.

'He treats it like a drop-in centre. Pops in for some of the group chats,' he said with a half-smile on his face. 'We don't actively encourage it, but he's not a bad example to have around.'

Yeah, Kim could see that. His confidence in his own skin was refreshing and a little enviable.

Kim was unsure why Megan had directed them to Cliff if he didn't know Jamie.

'Okay, well, thanks...'

'Hang on, you're here now. Maybe I can help. Tell me more about this boy.'

'He was nineteen years old and murdered a few days ago. His death was made to look like suicide.'

'Not the boy in the—'

'Yes,' Kim snapped, beginning to get annoyed at the reference.

'And it was definitely murder?'

Kim nodded. 'He'd been speaking to a counsellor, Megan Shaw.'

'I know Meg. So he had problems with his sexuality?'

'Originated from his parents. Deep-rooted by the looks of it.'

He nodded. 'Happens a lot.'

'Really?' she asked.

'Inspector, do you know what the DSM manual is?'

'Some kind of medical journal?' she tried. She'd definitely heard of it.

'It is the bible used for classifying mental illness.'

'Okay.'

'Care to guess when homosexuality was declassified as a mental illness?'

'Was it ever perceived to be one?' Bryant asked.

He nodded. 'And remained so until 1973.'

'When it was removed?' she asked.

'No. It was changed to sexual orientation disturbance, until 1980.'

'And then removed?' she asked.

'No, it was changed to ego-dystonic homosexuality.'

'I had no idea.'

'A new version of the manual is released this year, and for the first time there is no diagnostic category that can be applied to people on their sexual orientation. So, finally, we're not mentally ill. Woohoo for us.'

Kim took a second to digest this. How was this only being acknowledged now?

He continued. 'Richard Von Krafft-Ebing was a German-Austrian psychiatrist and one of the founders of scientific sexology. He became a proponent of the sickness model of homosexuality and believed that treatment came from the prevention of masturbating.'

'He thought he could change someone's sexuality?' she asked, aghast.

Cliff frowned. 'He along with many others both past and present.'

'What?'

'Have either of you never heard of conversion therapy?' he asked.

Kim shook her head, as did Bryant.

'You two really need more gay people in your lives.'

She considered mentioning Stacey, but she wasn't sure her colleague had heard of it either.

'Okay, you're going to learn some disturbing stuff,' he said, checking his watch. 'Conversion therapy in all its forms is designed to turn gay people straight. It is rejected by every mainstream mental-health organisation, but some practitioners continue to conduct it even though it can lead to depression, anxiety, drug use and suicide.

'America is pretty open about sharing its statistics and they estimate twenty thousand minors in the states without protections will be subjected to conversion therapy. Some right-wing religious groups promote the concept that an individual can change their sexual orientation either through prayer or other religious efforts. Research does not substantiate this claim and deems SOCE to be harmful.'

'SOCE?' Bryant asked.

'The full term is sexual orientation change efforts, widely known as conversion therapy.'

'Got it.'

'There's no proof it works but ample proof it causes significant medical and psychological harm. Confusion about sexual orientation is not unusual during adolescence and counselling can help, but therapy directed specifically at changing sexuality obviously provokes guilt and anxiety, because the belief that same-sex attraction is abnormal and in need of treatment is in opposition to those taken by mental-health organisations.'

'Surely a balanced view is offered by any counsellor?' Kim asked.

Cliff shook his head. 'Not in conversion therapy. The possibility that the person might achieve happiness and satisfying relationships is not presented, nor are alternative approaches to dealing with the effects of social stigmatisation.'

'But how can you treat something that isn't a disorder?' Kim asked.

'You catch on quick, Inspector. That's the whole point. Any intervention purporting to treat something that isn't a disorder is wholly unethical because it doesn't allow for the normal variants of human sexuality. People who have unsuccessfully attempted to change their sexual orientation experience considerable psychological distress.'

'Okay, back up,' Kim said, trying to take it all in. 'Where do these therapists come from?'

'Mainly they spring from far-right, faith-based organisations.'

'The church?'

'Not as a whole. We're talking extremists. Some groups have promoted the idea of sexuality as symptomatic of development defects or spiritual and moral failing. The inability to change is a personal and moral failure. How's that for a bit more self-hatred to add to the guilt pile?'

'You're gay because you didn't pray hard enough?' Kim asked.

Cliff nodded.

'And you say minors are at risk?'

'Absolutely, because it's often parents seeking intervention.'

Kim thought about Jamie and couldn't help but wonder what other methods his parents had tried.

'There's still forced SOCE in many countries, including the US, China, India, Japan. Recently, a Russian citizen was apprehended by the militia as a suspected lesbian, forced to undergo treatment such as sedative drugs and hypnosis. We're not just talking therapy. It goes a lot deeper than that. Methods include cognitive behavioural techniques, psychoanalytical techniques, medical approaches, religious and spiritual methods. There are —' He stopped speaking as a soft tap sounded on the door.

Karen's head appeared.

'Sorry, Cliff, but Bernie's here. She's in room two.'

Cliff pushed himself up from the chair. 'I'm sorry. I got carried away, but...'

'What would be the first step?' Kim asked, following suit and standing. 'Say a parent felt that her child was diseased. How would she take it up a notch to get her child cured?'

'Maybe have a chat with Exodus Plus. See if your boy was known to them.'

'And what's Exodus Plus now?' Kim asked.

She saw a flash of annoyance on Cliff's face as though she was asking him the first letter of the alphabet.

'Exodus Plus is an ex-gay movement, and now I really do have to go,' he said, leaving the room.

Kim forgave his impatience. He had someone waiting who needed his help.

She followed Bryant out to the car already googling Exodus Plus on her phone.

TWENTY-SIX

Although Penn had no problem attending post-mortems, he'd never been present at two in one day before.

When Keats had insisted on taking his lunch break between the two cases, Penn had taken the opportunity to get a breath of air in the cafeteria, turning down Keats's offer to join him in the office.

Because of what he was witnessing, he had little appetite for the beef pie or pork dinner so he'd settled on a cheese-and-pickle sandwich with crisps. There was little there to remind him of the sights on the metal table. He'd considered nipping back to the station but it wouldn't have been worth his time. Keats had made it clear he intended to resume at 2 p.m. on the dot.

For once he'd languished in peace and eaten his sandwich properly, with a warm coffee to wash it down instead of a bite here and a bite there in between urgent tasks. Who was he kidding? He wouldn't change his job for the world. In fact, after twenty minutes of peace and quiet, he'd texted Jasper.

Wanna do choc chip cookies tonight? he'd asked.

Got no choc chips, Jasper had replied.

Blueberry muffins?

No blueberries.

Shall I get some on my way home?

'*Ifulike*,' had been the response, and Penn had wondered when his brother had started abbreviating words and missing out spaces. Teenagers.

After lunch, he'd returned and watched silently as Keats had begun working through the process on Sarah Laing. In the very early days, Keats had explained the eight steps of post-mortem to him. He knew that the external examination was followed by the internal examination, which came before viewing the internal organs. Removal of the organs came next and was just before removal of the brain. The organs were then examined, weighed and measured before returning them to the body. The final act was to sew the victim back together.

Following Keats's guidelines, he guessed they were around number three. Keats was inspecting the internal organs but hadn't yet removed them. So far there had been no tell-tale grunts or beckoning actions for him to come closer.

When Keats had first wheeled the body into the room, Penn had texted Stacey for any update on Sarah Laing. She had texted him back with a link to one of her profiles on a dating site. He'd been unable to think of her as Sarah Sizzle, who appeared to be chasing after a good time. The pictures of the girl with a challenging expression and a wine glass were nothing to do with the girl lying on the table who was being disassembled by Keats.

Penn was starting to think of all the things he could be

doing back at the station when Keats spoke for the first time in over an hour.

'Aah, we have pockmarks.'

'We have what now?' Penn asked, putting away his phone.

'Shotgun-pellet-sized marks along the inside of the pelvic bone caused by the tearing of ligaments.'

'Meaning?' Penn prompted.

'Our girl here has given birth, and it wasn't very long ago.'

TWENTY-SEVEN

'So where's the baby?' Kim asked as they headed towards Kingswinford. She had left Stacey with the task of getting them an appointment with someone at the nearest branch of Exodus on the outskirts of Wolverhampton. In the meantime, they were heading towards the childhood home of Sarah Laing, a twenty-two-year-old woman that Kim didn't yet know. There had been little evidence of her personality in the small flat and no evidence whatsoever of a baby. Stacey had confirmed no mentions on any of the profiles.

'Maybe adopted?' Bryant said. 'Didn't fit with the lifestyle she wanted.'

'Seems she only chose that lifestyle a few months ago, when she started all these profiles on the dating sites. There's no mention of looking for men or of being bisexual so...'

'So how come she was pregnant in the first place?' Bryant asked.

'Exactly,' Kim said as the enigma of Sarah Laing continued to grow.

The house that Bryant pulled up at was a clean-looking semi-detached with a garage built on to the side.

One of Kim's burning questions was answered when the door of Sarah's parents' home was opened. The sound of a baby crying reached her immediately.

A man who appeared to be mid-forties was looking at her with a frazzled expression.

Kim introduced herself and Bryant.

'Mr Laing?'

He nodded, stepping aside to allow them entry.

A comfortably furnished living room appeared to have had a baby explosion. The carpet and furniture were covered in toys, blankets, cuddly toys, activity mats. Something squeaked underfoot as she stepped into the room.

A woman with blonde hair and a defeated expression sat on the single chair while holding the baby dressed in a pink Babygro on her lap. Her hand rhythmically rubbed the baby's back as it continued to cry. Kim guessed it was a little girl.

'Detectives,' Mr Laing said over her head, explaining the two strangers who had entered her home.

Mrs Laing nodded as Mr Laing cleared a space on the sofa for them to sit.

'We're very sorry for your loss,' Bryant said. An officer had been despatched to deliver the news first thing.

'Thank you,' Mrs Laing said as her eyes filled with tears. 'The officer said someone would be along to see us later, but I don't think we've processed it yet,' she said, swapping the baby to her other leg. She reached for a bottle and tried to put it in the baby's mouth. The little girl shut her mouth firmly and scrunched up her face before bawling again.

They really did have their hands full, and if Kim could have delayed her questions for a more suitable time, she would have done, but they needed to know about Sarah as soon as possible.

'Mrs Laing, I'm so sorry to have to ask you about Sarah at this time, but...'

'Please call me Elaine, and this is Pete. We're still new to this.'

'Been a while?' Bryant said, taking out his car keys.

'Not ever,' she answered, trying to bounce the baby into contentment. 'Sarah was adopted, eighteen months old. We skipped this part and went straight to fishing her out of the kitchen bin.'

Despite the gravity of the situation, Kim couldn't help the smile that lifted her lips as Bryant dangled the car keys in front of the baby.

Silence fell in the room and both grandparents looked at Bryant in awe. Even she was impressed.

'Shiny and jangly. Worked on Laura every time,' Bryant said, holding out his hands. 'May I?'

Elaine nodded and gratefully handed over the baby.

'I'm so sorry that we have to intrude but we're investigating your daughter's murder.'

The restrained tears broke free and washed over her cheeks. Her husband handed her a tissue.

She wiped at her face. 'It definitely wasn't suicide?' she asked. 'The officer didn't offer too much detail.'

'No. Sarah didn't take her own life. The scene was staged to look like suicide.'

Kim realised there was no relief in either scenario.

'But why?' asked Mr Laing as he came to sit beside his wife.

'We don't know that yet,' Kim said honestly. 'But could you tell us more about her?'

Elaine took a breath and composed herself. 'We'd been fostering children for a couple of years. Short-stay cases, mainly. Sarah came to us as an emergency case in the middle of the night after a raid on a drug den. She was found playing with needles beside her overdosed mother. There were no traceable family members so Sarah was brought to us. Her mum died two days later.

'We fell in love with Sarah straightaway. She was bright, intelligent, eager to learn and remarkably well-adjusted given her short life. The main barrier was physical contact. For years she wouldn't let us hug her or kiss her, and when she did it was on her terms. We knew that it was something she'd never had and just didn't understand.'

Tears began to escape again, and Mr Laing dabbed at his own eyes.

'Didn't matter. We already loved her like our own, and by the time she turned two it was official. She loved school, had every kind of doll there was, loved making tea parties. We both spent many hours eating invisible cake.'

A sad smile rested on her mouth as Elaine reached for her husband's hand.

'She gave all her physical love to the dolls. She cradled and cooed over them all day long.'

Mr Laing nodded at the memories.

Sensing the baby was getting bored with the keys, Bryant stood and began walking around the room, talking to her softly.

Elaine kept a watchful eye on his movements.

'Carry on,' Kim urged.

'She turned twelve and all hell let loose. We argued, she disobeyed every rule. At first, I thought it was typical adolescence, but then I saw a rage in her, a fierce anger that seemed to be consuming my daughter. She was a stranger to me, and it wasn't until she was fifteen that she told me the truth.'

Kim guessed what was coming.

'She told me she was gay. I was relieved. She'd finally shared what she'd been struggling to accept in herself. It broke my heart that she felt that way, but they were her demons and I knew we could work through it together.'

'And you accepted her?' Kim asked, thinking of how differently Jamie's mother had reacted to her son's sexuality.

Elaine frowned. 'Of course. She was still our daughter. We

loved her unconditionally. There is nothing she could have told me that would have made me love her any less. I thought we'd uncovered the demon, but I was wrong.

'Admitting to being gay wasn't the problem. She wasn't worried about telling us. The issue was that she didn't want to be. The very idea of it repulsed her. She didn't want to be different. She wanted a boyfriend, marriage, a family. I told her she could have anything she wanted with the right person.'

'What happened?' Kim asked, trying to imagine the conflict that had been raging in Sarah's mind.

'She didn't really speak to me about it again. It was almost like I'd given her the wrong response.'

Kim could see the irony in that situation. Elaine had been open and accepting yet it hadn't been right.

'It was like she'd expected me to take it away, somehow make it right. I felt awful because I couldn't solve what she perceived to be a terrible problem. I sought help from professionals to see if I'd done something wrong. I asked them if I'd made it worse. They assured me I'd done the right thing so I just waited to see what would happen.'

'Did she ever bring anyone home – friends, girlfriend?'

Elaine shook her head. 'No, and I didn't push her. I thought it'd be like your typical ten-year-old boy who hates girls and puts worms in their hair and then they reach a certain age and realise they weren't so bad after all. Truthfully, I didn't know what to do. I just hoped she'd eventually accept herself. I mean, how do you help someone not to be gay? It's who she is – was.'

Mr Laing squeezed her hand.

'The baby?' Kim asked.

Elaine sighed heavily. 'We don't know who the father is. Sarah left home when she was nineteen, and since then she grew more and more distant. The visits turned to phone calls and then the odd text message. I'd try to ring, I'd get no answer and then later I'd get a text saying "call you soon" or something like that.

'We lost contact completely for a few months before we saw her again six months ago. We hadn't even known she was pregnant. She brought Amy to us at just a few weeks old.'

Kim's brain was doing the calculation. It was six months ago that Sarah Sizzle appeared to have been born and the dating profiles initiated.

'She begged us to take care of Amy. She wouldn't tell us where she'd been or the circumstances around Amy. She would only say that right now she wasn't in the right place to take care of her child. She told us she was sorry and that she loved us. That was the last time we saw her. We offered to help her, have her move back home for a while to support her, but she refused.'

'She didn't return to see Amy?'

Elaine shook her head. 'I worked out how to send photos to her phone and I'd get heart emojis back, but she didn't come home again.'

There was little point asking her parents if they knew of any recent threat or conflict in her life, as they appeared to know even less about new Sarah than her team did.

Kim thanked them for their time and left a card in case they needed anything.

Bryant handed a sleepy Amy back to her grandmother.

If Sarah had been so keen to have a child, why hadn't she wanted this one?

TWENTY-EIGHT

Stacey opened up the footage sent to her from the bank.

The time clock showed that the staff member opened the doors at bang on 9.30 a.m. An elderly lady was first in the door using a walking frame.

Gabe Denton appeared right behind. He waited patiently while the woman progressed towards the open cashier's window, then waited patiently at the top of the line for his turn as more customers filed in behind him. Unlike others who started to look at their watches or shifted from foot to foot, Gabe just stood and waited. His body language was relaxed and open. He wasn't avoiding looking at the camera; nor did he appear to be in any hurry.

For some reason she'd expected him to be wearing a suit but he was dressed casually in jeans and a sweatshirt.

She continued watching as he waited his turn and then approached the counter. He rested his elbows on the ledge while answering questions from the teller. Her own mother had complained just last week about having to jump through hoops to get her own money and she hadn't been withdrawing anywhere near that amount.

A second staff member approached to do the double-check and still Gabe appeared relaxed as he answered the second round of questioning.

The second staff member disappeared with a set of keys and reappeared a minute later with the cash, which she handed to the teller.

The teller counted it and pushed it through the chute.

Gabe took the envelope and left the bank.

Stacey watched the footage again and began to shake her head. Either the man had no shame or he really felt as though he was doing nothing wrong.

The ringing of her phone startled her from her thoughts.

'Yeah, boss.'

'What do you know about Exodus?'

'It's the second book in the Bible,' Stacey answered.

'Exodus Plus as an organisation.'

'Never heard of it.'

'Get on it. It's an ex-gay movement, and I need an appointment with someone high up at the Wolverhampton branch.'

'On it, boss,' Stacey said, ending the call.

She closed the footage of Gabriel Denton and typed in a search of Exodus Plus in Wolverhampton.

'Oh, okay,' Stacey said aloud as Google gave her a brief description of the organisation.

Like the boss had said, Exodus was an ex-gay movement that encouraged people to refrain from entering or pursuing same-sex relationships, to eliminate homosexual desires and develop heterosexual desires and to enter straight marriages. The group was formed in America in the mid-seventies. At its height, the organisation had more than four hundred ministries around the world.

If it wasn't so despicable, Stacey would have laughed out loud at the fact that one of its founding members, and a leader within the ministry of Exodus, had left the group, divorced his wife and set up home together with another male member. Alan Chambers, the president of the organisation, closed it down in 2013 and then told anyone who would listen that conversion therapy didn't work. Despite his actions, many of its member ministries continued operating by either forming new networks or joining existing ones such as Exodus Global Alliance.

She clicked on any article with the Exodus name attached and was soon learning of cases of minors being forced to go to ex-gay camps against their will.

Stacey was growing more and more disturbed with each article she read. She had wrestled with her own sexuality in her teens and for the most part had battled alone. The confusion had been overwhelming when her first crush had been on a girl in the year above her. The object of her affections had moved house and therefore school, and once her fourteen-year-old heart had mended, she developed a crush on a boy that worked in the newsagents at the end of her road. It had taken another two years and many sleepless nights for her to understand that she was bisexual. A concept she'd had to explain to her mum when she plucked up the courage to tell her the truth. After her initial shock, Stacey's mum had finally spoken.

'Fifty-fifty not so bad,' she said, shrugging.

'Fifty-fifty what?' Stacey had asked.

'That I get grandchild,' she said before giving Stacey a big hug.

Stacey had opened her mouth to explain that same-sex couples were no longer forced to remain childless. One step at a time, she'd decided.

Stacey reflected on those years of confusion and loneliness. She had felt many things, a bag of adolescent emotions, but she'd never wanted to remove that part of herself or even pretend it didn't exist. She felt a deep sorrow for people who couldn't accept themselves the way they were.

She continued reading until she hit on one piece which

hinted that Exodus had links to a facility called the Judge Rotenburg Centre in Canton, Massachusetts.

'Bloody hell,' Stacey whispered as the link took her to an investigation of the facility which was founded in the early seventies to treat people with development disabilities, emotional disorders and autistic-like behaviours.

The centre openly used aversive therapy, ran contingent food programmes, used long-term restraints and solitary confinement, sensory deprivation and GED shocks as forms of 'treatment'.

Even though there had been six deaths since it was founded, the centre prided itself on being pioneers of behavioural treatment. There were numerous accounts of food being used or withheld as a reward and punishment for behaviour. Forced wearing of a helmet that restricted vision and hearing for extended periods of time. Patients being provoked into a behaviour so they could be punished. Humiliation techniques like being forced to eat like a dog or sleep in a kneeling position.

Stacey remembered watching a documentary on the treatment of prisoners at Guantanamo Bay. If the same conduct were applied there, it would spark world-wide outrage. And this was being done to kids.

Stacey shuddered, thanking God there were no such facilities in the UK. It was disturbing enough that a new branch of Exodus had made it across the pond.

She clicked into their website and punched in the number which was answered on the second ring.

'Exodus Plus, Lorraine speaking, how may I help you?'

The voice was perky, friendly and Stacey could almost hear the smile on the woman's face.

'Hi, I'm Detective Constable Stacey Wood from West Midlands Police. Just checking it's okay for my boss to meet with Charles Stamoran.'

'In connection with?'

The smile in the voice was gone.

'A current investigation.'

'I'm sorry, but Mr Stamoran is busy,' she said, ending the call.

Stacey stared at her own phone. 'What the hell was that about?'

TWENTY-NINE

'Go ahead, Stace,' Kim said, putting the phone on speaker.

'You're not getting in there, boss,' Stacey said. 'He's not free to speak and won't make an appointment until the end of the month.'

'Okay, Stace, we're just pulling up now. I'll get back to you,' Kim said, appraising the building. 'Hmm... don't want to speak to us, eh?'

'Have they already met you, guv?'

'Not funny,' she said, getting out of the car.

The office was the end building on a trading estate, which looked like it had been a small café at some point in its past. The sign above the door simply said Exodus with a plus sign; no explanation, no description and certainly no kerb appeal. The windows on both floors were blocked by venetian blinds that were closed. But for the two cars out front, a Jaguar and a Corsa, the place would have appeared empty and unused.

As she approached the door, she noted one single security camera. The door was locked but an intercom system was fixed to the wall. She pressed the call button.

'Exodus,' said the singsong voice.

'Detective Inspector Stone and Detective Sergeant Bryant. I believe my colleague called ahead.'

'Your colleague was informed that there was no one available and that hasn't changed in the three minutes since I ended the call.'

'It is regarding an active investigation,' Kim clarified in case she didn't understand.

'Doesn't make him any less busy.'

Kim wasn't warming to Lorraine. 'He can't spare us just a few minutes?'

'It's a no for the third time. Please step away from the front door.'

Kim took a step backwards.

Yes, she could wait for the man to leave the building. It was almost four, but she could be sitting here for hours. She considered making a few choice hand signs at the camera that was watching her, except, she realised, that it wasn't actually watching her.

She followed the trajectory of the lens.

Got it.

She stepped closer to the Jag.

'Hear that, Bryant?'

'Hear what, guv?'

'A noise from the boot.'

'Guv, I don't...'

'Yeah, your hearing isn't great. Call it in. Sounded like a child to me.'

Bryant took out his radio as she went and leaned against the Astra Estate.

Kim considered the differences in the two places she'd visited. The What Centre in Stourbridge was based just off the Stourbridge high street, open and welcoming. This place was locked and bolted out of sight on a trading estate.

'You do know this is gonna result in a formal complaint?' Bryant said, standing beside her.

She knew it. She also knew that right now she had a bit of leeway with Woody. Just a bit.

'Bloody hell,' Bryant said as they heard the siren in the distance. 'That was quick.'

Kim felt briefly guilty that officers had been temporarily diverted, but if she was right, it would take no more than a couple of minutes.

As the squad car came into view, Kim positioned herself so that the car had to park close to the Jag, especially for the viewing audience inside.

The siren stopped but the lights continued flashing as two officers got out of the car.

She flashed her ID. She wasn't as well known to the good officers of Wolverhampton.

'Something about the boot, marm?' asked the taller officer.

She nodded as they all approached the car. The smaller officer carried a crowbar.

Kim counted down. Five, four, three, two.

The door to Exodus magically opened.

A man wearing black trousers and a white shirt emerged followed by a slim woman in her early thirties with curly red hair.

'What the hell is going on here?' asked the man she assumed to be Charles Stamoran.

'Report of a—'

'Step away from my boot, officer,' Stamoran said, placing a protective hand on the metal.

'If you'd care to open it, sir.'

'For what reason?' he asked, looking around at all of them.

The red-headed Lorraine glowered in her direction.

'Sir, if you'd just open the boot.'

'Bloody hell,' he said, taking his keys from his pocket. A couple of beeps and the boot began to rise.

The space was empty except for a heavy jacket and a small toolbox.

'Happy now?'

The taller police officer looked to her.

She shrugged. 'Sorry, guys, my mistake. But thanks for your prompt attendance.'

The two officers headed back to the squad car. The shorter one was calling the result into the station.

'You did this deliberately,' Stamoran said accusingly.

'Hey, we all make mistakes, but now I've got you, we can either talk out here, in there or down at the station, but one way or another we are going to have a conversation.'

THIRTY

I don't know how long has passed since I last woke up but my muscles still don't seem to want to follow my commands. The fatigue is working its way into my bones.

A memory is forcing its way into my mind. I don't know if it was a dream.

This is not my first time of waking. There was a drink; food – a sandwich. My mind rebelled even when my body could not.

The memory is trying to come clearer. I woke and I was dry. My clothes had been changed. I had been washed. No, that must have been a dream. That couldn't have happened without my knowledge.

I squirmed around. There was no dampness on my clothes; there was no smell of fouling. How had I become that dependent, that pliable? How had I become no more of a challenge than a newborn baby?

I remember more. My hands, although still handcuffed, had been placed at the front of me. A piece of hard plastic rested against my fingers. I summoned my energy and felt all around it. It was a triangle. It was food. I put it back down. I would not eat their offerings. I would not help them keep me alive for whatever they had planned. I would not allow them to control me. It took more than a few seconds to realise that if I'd been given the chance to eat that could mean only one thing: the gag was out of my mouth. A fact that had so far escaped me.

'Help,' I called out.

In my mind it was a scream. In my mind it was a roar that could have brought walls tumbling down. In truth it was a whisper that barely travelled a foot away from me.

'Help,' I called again.

The effort of the task did not match the outcome. My head had swum with the exertion.

'No. No. No,' I cried, trying to fight the fatigue away. I needed to try again, to muster every ounce of strength and focus it into one almighty cry.

I had known what I needed to do even as the lids of my eyes fell and blackened my world.

That was earlier and now I've woken with a hunger so fierce I would consider eating my own left leg. I remember the sandwich. My heart pumps with excitement. It dies quickly. The gag is back in my mouth and the sandwich is gone.

Inexplicably I feel hot tears sting my eyes. I blink them back. Am I crying for a sandwich or am I crying because I now understand the game? I have no control. My captors have everything. They will decide when I eat, not me. And if I don't eat when they tell me to, the food will be taken away.

The grumbling in my stomach is louder than my cry for help.

When the fatigue comes again to claim me, I make no effort, this time, to fight it away.

THIRTY-ONE

Lorraine's glare had followed Kim around the building, only to soften every time she glanced at Charles Stamoran, who appeared not to notice the severe schoolgirl crush that the woman was doing little to hide. It was almost as though she'd taken it personally that the barricades had been breached. As though she hadn't kept him safe enough.

'Okay, Inspector, you have my attention. What was so important?'

The inside of the property was little warmer than the outside. Stamoran's office was for business and not for counselling. She wasn't sure where that took place.

'So, you un-gay people here?' she asked, looking around.

The bookshelves were filled with religious texts and faith-based guidance books. His own desk, although generous, held a laptop, a coaster, a phone and a framed photograph. Kim couldn't see the subjects in the photo from her black conference chair on the other side of the desk, and neither could Bryant.

'You already know of our purpose, Inspector, and as I can see you're not a supporter, I won't explain our work any further.'

'Oh no, please do. I'm very interested.'

She recrossed her legs. She was going to get comfortable for this.

'Okay, I'm not sure if you're aware that not everyone who is gay wants to be. For some, despite their attraction to the same sex, they cannot stand the thought of actual engagement. I don't feel that I need to spell it out,' he said as distaste pulled at his lips.

Oh boy, was he the right person for the job.

'We advocate abstention. Of not giving in to the temptation.'

'So to die lonely and unloved?'

Stamoran shook his head. 'I told you…'

'My apologies,' she said, holding up her hand. 'I'll stay quiet and save my judgemental comments until you're done.'

'We believe that it is possible to guide members into living a fulfilling life that doesn't overstep their boundaries and sensitivities.'

That sounded like a 'keep it in your pants' ideology to her.

'As an organisation, how do you feel that one of your founding members couldn't resist temptation? Does that not put a mighty big pin in your belief bubble?'

'Exodus International was dissolved. We're a part of—'

'Semantics, Mr Stamoran. You preach the exact same message. Please answer the question.'

'No method is one hundred per cent effective.'

'Just how effective is Exodus? What is your success rate?' Kim asked.

'We don't measure it in numbers. If we can just help one person lead the life they want then we consider ourselves triumphant.'

'Did you help Jamie Mills?'

His initial reaction was surprise. 'Who?'

His response seemed genuine, which gave her a good benchmark.

'Sarah Laing?'

His face tightened. 'Who?'

'Ah, you've lost me now, Mr Stamoran. Clearly you know Sarah but tried to intimate that you don't. Why would you do that?'

He coloured, having been caught in a lie. 'We don't discuss individual cases to protect the privacy of the—'

'Sarah's dead, Mr Stamoran. I'm not sure she's too fussed about that any more.'

'Dead?' he asked, although his body language remained the same, as though he wasn't as shocked as he was making out.

'Before you embarrass yourself, we know that Sarah struggled with accepting her sexuality. Counselling didn't help her; neither did the support of her parents. I'm guessing you were her last hope.'

'You make it sound as though our work is one step up from death,' he said and then seemed to realise what he'd said. 'I'm sorry, I mean, many of our members manage to lead reasonably happy lives if they follow our instructions.'

'Reasonably?' Kim asked. 'Is that the best they can hope for?'

He thought for a minute, before nodding towards the door that led back to the front office. 'Lorraine is addicted to pizza. It doesn't agree with her. She has some kind of food intolerance. She would eat it for every meal, but she has to be reasonably happy with a couple of slices once a month. None of us can—'

'Hang on,' Kim said. 'I'm talking to you about being free to love who you love and you're talking to me about food choices?'

'What I'm trying to explain is that some people don't want the consequences of their indulgence.'

'And I'm saying that sexual identity isn't like having a

bloody wheat problem,' Kim said, trying to keep her tone on the right side of being thrown out.

'It's about making a choice.'

'And did Sarah make a choice?'

'It's fair to say that Sarah tried her best.'

'In what way?'

'Sarah wasn't content to abstain and choose another way of life. I mean, she tried but it wasn't good enough for her. She wanted the urges, desires, thoughts removed. She did not want to be gay.'

'I understand that,' Kim said. 'So you had to explain that there was nothing more to be done and to recommend further counselling to help her accept herself, yes?'

He frowned. 'No. That goes against everything we believe in. Just because we couldn't help her didn't mean we just gave up on her. Sarah's sheer determination to change made her a suitable candidate for referral.'

'To where?'

'Change Clinic in Bridgnorth.'

'For what?'

'Specialised therapy.'

A pit formed in Kim's stomach.

'Can you spell it out for me, Mr Stamoran?'

'Absolutely. We sent her there to be cured.'

THIRTY-TWO

Unusually, Penn looked a little pale as he entered the squad room, Stacey noted.

Even though it was almost six and they'd been at work for eleven hours, neither of them would go home until the boss rang the bell.

'You okay?' she asked as he slumped down into his chair.

'Yeah, just two in one day is a bit much. I don't know how Keats does it,' he said, shaking his head.

A few blonde curls escaped from the power gel he used when leaving the office. Had it been earlier in the day, he'd have reached for one of the bandanas in the top drawer.

'Thought you didn't mind them?' Stacey said.

'I don't mind sprouts at Christmas but I wouldn't want a plate full of the little buggers.'

'Fair point,' Stacey conceded. 'But now you're back can I pick your brains?'

'Unfortunate choice of words given where I've been all day but go ahead.'

'If you wanted to leave your wife, how would you do it?'

'Well, seeing as I don't have...'

'Imagination, Penn. We're role-playing here.'

'Okay, why am I leaving?' he asked.

'Is that important?'

'Of course. If I'm angry cos she's cheated on me or broke my Bose headphones, I'm gonna pack a bag, shout a bit and storm out.'

'Over headphones?' Stacey queried.

'Role-playing, Stace.'

'Okay, what if you weren't angry?'

'Then I'd probably sit her down and explain the way I was feeling, the things that had led up to it and try to cause the least amount of heartache as possible.' He paused. 'Do we have kids?'

Stacey shook her head, again feeling the sadness for the failed IVF attempts and wondering how that had affected them both in the long term, especially Beth.

'Okay, so we don't need to explain it to the kids or wait for them to go to bed.'

'What time would you leave?'

'Probably teatime. If I knew what I was going to do, I wouldn't want to go through the pretence of acting as if everything was normal. That wouldn't be fair.'

'Then what?'

'I would probably have booked a hotel room for a few nights depending on my long-term plans. I mean, there's the house and possessions to sort out, but I wouldn't want to address that immediately. That would be insensitive, although I would make it clear that she doesn't get to keep the vase I was given by Aunt Edith.'

Stacey burst out laughing. It had been a bloody long day. Twelve hours ago, she'd been on the cusp of leaving this team behind forever, and now she was belly laughing cos Penn had invented a whole new reality.

She sobered. 'Would you take money out of the savings account?'

Penn shook his head. 'Not without telling her. I'd have to trust that she'd do the same, but no. I wouldn't touch money we'd built up together. Luckily, Lynne isn't much of a—'

'Penn, did you hear what you just said?' Stacey asked.

'The money belongs to both—'

'You called her Lynne. Your fantasy wife is called Lynne.'

He coloured. 'No, you misheard.'

'No, I didn't and you wanna get that seen to.'

He logged into his computer as his complexion returned to normal. Stacey still felt guilty for her own part in the ruination of what could have been a beautiful relationship. She had pretty much barged into their romantic evening during the last case, when she and the rest of the team had been in danger and advised that they weren't to be alone. She knew that wasn't the sole reason for the failure, but she still carried the guilt for being the straw that broke the camel's back.

She turned her attention back to the actions of Gabriel Denton. Everything about him screamed nice guy, and yet it was starting to seem that he wasn't quite the man people thought he was.

THIRTY-THREE

'Thanks for the lift, Bryant,' Kim said as they pulled up outside her house. She'd just sent the other two home, and she was equally ready herself to get this day done.

'You okay?' her colleague asked as she got out the car.

'I'm fine,' she lied. She wasn't prepared to admit just how much the day had taken out of her.

'See you in the morning,' he said, waving as he pulled away.

He knew she wasn't herself, and he also knew not to push her once he'd asked the question.

Kim couldn't help glancing down the road before she stepped inside her home. Soon, a new family would move in to Edna's house. They would make changes, inside and out, not knowing the horror and fear that had been experienced there. No matter what they changed, Kim would always picture Edna tied to that dining chair in the middle of the room, bathed in the stench of her own bodily functions, just minutes away from death.

My fault.
My fault.
My fault.

'Piss off,' she said to her thoughts as she unlocked her front door. They didn't help her but she couldn't stop them coming into her head. Regardless of the pep talk from Leanne about guilt being the most useless emotion the human mind could conjure, that vision of a helpless old lady would never leave her.

She turned on the light and there was Barney with his tail whooshing across the laminate floor in the hallway. The negative thoughts fell away.

'Hey there, boy,' she said, rubbing him on the head. 'Ah, bugger that,' she said, closing and locking the door. She lowered herself to the floor, and Barney walked all over her legs, whooshing his tail in her face before curling beside her left leg. She leaned over and fussed him roughly.

'I've bloody missed you,' she said, half stroking, half scratching him. She suspected he hadn't missed her nearly as much. She'd got used to spending a lot more of the daytime hours with him.

These first days were proving hard for a number of reasons. After two months away from her job, jumping straight back in to twelve-hour days probably wasn't what Woody had meant by taking it easy.

'Come on then, boy,' she said, giving him one last squeeze before getting up.

She opened the back door before brewing a pot of coffee. Minutes later Barney was back to the open door with a ball in his mouth.

'Give me a minute, eh?' she said as the doorbell sounded. She checked the camera but the person had stepped out of the frame.

Barney's ears had perked up and he headed for the door with the ball in his mouth.

She opened the door, stunned to see the figure that was standing halfway down the path.

'Ted?'

She hadn't seen the man in months, and although she had seen him at just about every stage of her life, none of those times had been at her home.

'Oh my goodness, it's you,' he said, approaching the door. 'How coincidental. My car has broken down and I'd like to use your phone.'

'Your car is parked perfectly fine right there and you have a mobile,' she said, opening the door for him to enter.

'Never could get a thing past you, could I?' he said, strolling past her. He bent down. 'Well, hello there, young man, I've heard a lot about you.'

Barney's tail responded to the warm, playful tone in Ted's voice.

'So, why are you here?' she asked, closing the door.

'I was just passing and wondered if you needed anyone to not talk to. I'm quite good at it.'

Kim laughed. Ted had been her counsellor from the age of six, appointed just days after she'd been found clinging to her dead twin, Mikey, who had succumbed to starvation after their mother had left them tied to a radiator. Ted was one of the few people who knew pretty much everything about her. And not one word had come from her mouth. At every stage of her life, she'd been sent to speak to Ted, deemed the best in the business. She'd never opened up to him but she had always felt better after an hour in his silent company. In her adult years, she had chosen to visit him by choice, often to seek guidance on a particular case, but never had he visited her at home.

'Coffee?'

'Yes please,' he said, patting Barney on the head.

Kim took down a mug and paused. 'How do you...?'

'Normally you pour the hot water into—'

'I don't think I've ever made you a drink,' she said, stunned at the realisation. No one in her life dated back further than this man and she'd never even made him a cuppa.

'White no sugar,' he said.

She made it and pushed it towards him.

'So how've you been?' he asked. 'Anything interesting been happening?'

Kim smiled. He knew exactly what had happened to her, and she could understand why he had happened along to her home. He had been a part of every traumatic time in her life.

'I got help,' she said, looking down at her feet.

'Ha. The only person who thinks you got help is the psychologist that was treating you. I'm prepared to wager that you paced yourself over the treatment and got gradually better over the allotted period. You played the poor sucker like a well-tuned violin.'

Ted definitely knew her as well as anyone. Her silence was his answer.

'So you've had no help through the whole Symes ordeal or in dealing with the loss of your mother?'

'I'm fine.'

'Ay, ay, ay, ay, ay,' he said, before shaking his head and taking a sip of his coffee.

Kim wasn't sure exactly what that meant, but it didn't sound good.

'Wanna sit outside?' she asked. Dusk wasn't far away, but the day had been mild for late October.

'Lead the way,' he said, grabbing his coffee.

Most evenings she struggled with the confines of the house. Her happy place had always been the garage, but it didn't have that role any more. Now it was to mend her body.

They both sat at her small bistro table, and Barney appeared with his ball.

Kim threw it. He ran off happily.

'I understand your mother passed away while you were in the coma,' he said, folding his hands and resting them on his stomach.

'Don't wanna talk about it.'

'The coma you were in following your brief demise at the hands of a madman who literally beat you to death. Not much to unpack there.'

'Don't wanna talk about that either.'

'Thank the Lord. I'm in my early seventies and I haven't got long enough left.'

Kim laughed.

'Did you know how long your mother had left?' he asked.

'You did hear what I said about not wanting to talk?' she asked, throwing the ball again for Barney.

'Yeah, report me.'

Ted was no longer working so he had her there.

'I just don't—'

'Look, my therapist powers don't work beyond my property boundary. I'm not trying to analyse you. I'm just trying to be a friend.'

Kim relaxed. 'Yeah, I knew how long and I'd already decided not to visit her, and before you start, I know your thoughts on that one.'

He took a sip of coffee. 'If we were back at the house and I had access to my superpowers, I'd have said it would have been cathartic to go see her regardless of how it would have ended. As your friend, I'd have advised against it.'

'How do you do that?'

'What?'

'Have two different opinions on the same thing.'

'Textbook says forgiveness is good. Textbook says forgiveness promotes healing and growth. Textbook never met Kim Stone.'

'Ah, I see.'

'In a normal situation, people would probably be ready to offer some level of forgiveness after thirty-plus years. Maybe the edges of their anger have been smoothed, maybe they want the negativity out of their lives. You're the opposite – you've fed it and cultivated the hatred over the years. Your anger is as fresh as the day Mikey died.'

'Using your superpowers there, Ted,' Kim said, teasing Barney with the ball.

'Not really. Just observation.'

'I thought you'd tell me I'd missed my chance.'

'You've only missed your chance for her to hear it, not your chance to do it.'

Exactly what Leanne King had said to her while she'd been deconstructing the toaster.

They sat in silence for a few minutes before Ted spoke again.

'So what about the other thing?'

'Nope. Not talking about that.'

'Okay. Not talking about it doesn't mean it didn't happen. But okay, I'll talk about it instead. There's a lot going on with this one. There's the actual incident itself as well as the aftermath.'

'Ted,' she warned. No one had ever been able to read her like Ted, and she wasn't sure she was ready to hear this.

'What you did was brave, selfless, stupid, foolhardy and the only thing you could do. You offered your own life to save those girls. During the attack you experienced so many different emotions: fear, rage, helplessness, vulnerability, inadequacy, which all left their mark and will have to be worked through over time. Your body was punished and beaten past its limits of endurance to the point it gave up. It closed down. You died.'

Kim could feel the tension seeping into her jaw. She didn't need to be reminded.

'All of that is bad enough to deal with. But it's not the thing. I'll come to the thing in a minute. You're also having to deal with the paradox. Everyone else sees the positives of what you did. You saved those girls and you were happy to give your life to do it. You were commended. You're a hero.'

'Ted,' she warned again.

'And you don't want it. You don't feel like a hero. You don't feel that you deserve the accolades because a true hero would be dead and you're still alive.'

'I'd do it again,' she said.

'I don't doubt it. We already have a lot to deal with which would take months if not years to unravel so I know you hoodwinked your therapist. Did you even mention the nightmares, the real ones?'

'How did you...?'

'How could you not? No matter how much you hide all this stuff away, it's still in there somewhere,' he said, tapping his temple. 'It's no less real because you ignore its presence. It's the way you've dealt with trauma your whole life. We both know there will come a day when your method no longer works, but you can't be told so I'll save my breath. As if that wasn't enough, there's still the thing.'

'What's the thing?' she asked, safe that he couldn't possibly know.

'You offered your life. You made a bargain, a deal and you survived. In making that deal, you said goodbye.' He paused. 'I had a colleague once who emigrated to New Zealand. Two days before he left there was a huge party, family, friends, acquaintances. There were presents, tears, farewells and good wishes. Two months later he came back. Few people were fussed. They'd said goodbye. That's what you did as you took your last few breaths. You said your farewells. You were ready to die, and then you came back, and nothing looks quite the same any more.'

Kim said nothing to be careful not to give herself away.

'It's like you've returned to a slightly different world, a parallel universe. You're displaced, a stranger in your own life.

You're detached, playing a part as opposed to living the life. Is that a fair assessment?'

'I have no idea what you're talking about,' Kim said as she reached for his mug to get a refill.

She prayed he didn't notice the tremble in her hand.

THIRTY-FOUR

'Morning, guys,' Kim said, stepping into the squad room.

She glanced at the Tupperware box, positioned between the two desks.

'Good call, Penn, and a lucky escape for you all.'

No one argued. She was pleased to see that Penn's time away from the office had been well spent. It was time to get things back to normal, or as close as she could manage. Her own downtime had been spent listening to her feelings being presented to her by someone who wasn't too wide of the mark. She'd managed to turn the conversation with Ted to small talk after making it clear she wasn't going to discuss Symes any further. He had finished his second coffee and left with the offer that even though now fully retired, his door was open to her at any time. It hadn't needed stating.

'Okay, catch-up from yesterday. We know there's a lot of folks out there trying to take the gay out of people. We also know that although Jamie never joined Exodus, Sarah did. We also know that Sarah handed over her child right before deciding to list herself on every dating website. Given her parents' assessment, it was a bold move, as Sarah was repelled by her own sexuality.'

'A rebellion?' Stacey asked.

'Go on,' Kim said.

'Well, what if all her life she'd dreamed of a family, a husband and children and then the reality didn't equal the fantasy? Maybe she met a guy, she liked him and he was like the picture in her head, they had sex and she fell pregnant. Perhaps she told the father and he wanted nothing to do with either of them.'

'Illusion shattered,' Kim said.

'Exactly. So she goes on with the pregnancy, has the baby and it's not what she thought. She's still running away from her true self and finally realises what she is and that she can't change it.'

'But why go so hard?' Bryant asked.

'How long you been off the smokes now?'

'Seven years, three months, two days and nine hours but who's counting.'

They all laughed.

'Okay, say someone told you that cigarettes were no longer harmful and wouldn't give you a bad cough. What would you do?'

'Smoke the bloody lot of them.'

'Exactly. It's like Sarah decided if she was gonna be gay, she was really gonna get out there and do it.'

'Makes sense,' Kim said. It was as though she'd finally accepted who she was and had vowed to make up for lost time.

'We also learned from Charles Stamoran at Exodus that there's a facility or a clinic called Change, located somewhere in Bridgnorth.'

'Change what?' Penn asked.

'Exactly. Mr Stamoran wouldn't say much about the place

except that Exodus Plus used it as a referral system for those people for whom abstention was not an option.'

'You think Sarah went there?' Stacey asked.

'Exodus referred her. Maybe they can help with the identity of the father.'

'What's the difference between Exodus and this Change Clinic?' Penn asked.

'Exodus focusses on abstention. Their theory is that you can live a wholesome, fulfilling life if you choose not to act upon your desires. The Change Clinic claim to be able to remove those desires completely.'

'You're saying this Change place actually professes to be able to change your sexuality.'

'So the website says,' Kim offered. She'd been checking their website the previous night in bed while sleep had eluded her.

'Ooh, hang on, maybe they have a special spell they cast on people. Perhaps they have wands and cloaks and pointy hats.'

'You been watching Harry Potter again, Stace?' Bryant asked.

'Or maybe it's a surgical procedure,' Penn offered. 'Perhaps they find the source of it in your little toe on the left foot and they chop it off.'

She and Bryant watched on in amusement as the two of them fed off each other.

'Or maybe an appendectomy isn't really that at all,' Stacey said.

Penn opened his eyes wide. 'Or maybe they exorcise it out of you.'

'I hate the bloody gym.'

'Not that kind. I mean full-on exorcism. The power of Christ compels you.'

'And the power of the boss compels you two to knock it off now.'

Both of them sobered.

'Stace, how's your other thing going?'

'Still missing, boss, except now we've got him withdrawing a large amount of money from their savings right before he disappeared.'

'Okay, I trust you to know when you've done all you can.'

Stacey nodded her understanding.

'Penn, I want you doing background on Change. Any scandals, any lawsuits, history, everything. And while you're in a digging mood, check out the past of Charles Stamoran and his loyal assistant and a quick check on the good doctor, Megan Shaw.'

'Will do, boss.'

'Bryant, do anything you can to help these two while I'm gone,' she said, checking her watch.

'Gone where?' he asked.

'Meeting with the boss,' she said, rolling her eyes. The instruction to attend his office at 7.15 a.m. had tinged to her phone just after 6 a.m. She was pretty sure it was just a welfare check and she didn't expect to be gone long.

She hoped not. She was eager to head over to this clinic in Bridgnorth.

She was interested to see if the organisation itself was any happier to talk to them than the people who recommended their service.

THIRTY-FIVE

Kim took a seat in front of Woody's desk and peered into the mug that was sitting right in front of her.

'What's that?' she asked.

'Coffee.'

She looked around. 'You expecting someone?'

'For you.'

Kim stared at it suspiciously. 'Sir, never once have you made me a cup of coffee,' she said, playing back the events of the previous day. Clearly she had done something either very well and she was in his good books or she'd done something really bad and she was about to get fired. Either way the drink was making her feel uncomfortable.

'Strictly speaking I didn't make it. It came out of the machine, but it is a welfare meeting after all.'

Kim sat back putting space between her and the offending cuppa. She didn't intend on being here long enough to drink it.

'Sir, I'm fine,' she offered.

'That doesn't quite satisfy the requirements of our welfare guidelines, Stone, so forgive me if I delve a little deeper.'

She glanced at her watch.

'Not subtle and not going to work,' he said, peering over the top of his glasses. 'Yesterday was your first full day back in the hot seat. Did you follow my advice and acclimatise yourself back into the role?' he asked, picking up a sheet of paper.

Kim thought about the 7 a.m. start, meeting with River, meeting with Megan, meeting at the What Centre in Stour-bridge, meeting at Exodus in Wolverhampton and uncovering a lead on a dodgy clinic in Bridgnorth before getting home around 8 p.m.

'I think so, sir. I tried to observe correct start and finish times with prescribed meal and rest breaks in between.'

From Woody's disbelieving expression she didn't know if he wanted to argue with her or straight out laugh in her face.

He did neither and returned his attention to the piece of paper.

'Did you at any point feel overly stressed or anxious?' he asked.

'Only with Bryant's inferior driving abilities.'

That landed like a lead balloon.

He waited.

'No, sir,' she confirmed, choosing to ignore the layer of tension that had lain in her stomach throughout the day and the fact she thought she saw Symes on at least three separate occasions. Her boss didn't need to know about that.

'Did you feel physically fatigued or mentally exhausted?'

So many answers but none that were going to get her a tick on the piece of paper he was holding.

'No, sir,' she said, hoping he couldn't read on her face the fact that she'd had to pause three times on her way up the stairs to get to bed.

'Did you at any time doubt your physical or psychological ability to execute your duties?'

'No, sir,' she answered, knowing that if she admitted the

pains that had been shooting through her hip, he'd confine her to the station.

'And do you understand the correct channels and help available should you need it?'

'Yes, sir,' she said, knowing she'd never use any of them because they would all lead her back to a stint in the office.

She held her breath, praying that Woody had bought her answers. She couldn't run this case from the other side of her desk.

He signed the piece of paper at the bottom and placed it to one side.

She was hoping she was now free to go, but she wasn't going to bet her house on it.

'So I hear your dismissal of Burns's services went well,' he said, sitting back in his chair.

She sighed. Of course that was going to come up.

'Tell me, was it as bad as he'd have me believe?' Woody asked.

'I'm not sure how prone to exaggeration he is, but I could have handled it better,' she said honestly. 'It wasn't my finest hour despite the fact that the man is a first-class idiot.'

Woody didn't agree or disagree but remained silent and allowed her to continue.

'It was his treatment of the team that boiled my blood, sir, especially Stacey. He'd relegated her to tea girl and filing clerk. But his incompetence and lethargy towards a dead body was almost criminal. I'm not sure what case he's waiting to run up and slap him in the face, but letting dead folks slip by because they're not sexy enough is inexcusable.'

Still Woody said nothing.

'I meant everything I said to him, but I should have said it privately. I accept that, and to be honest, that's all I've got,' she said, opening her hands.

'Thank you for your explanation,' he said, giving nothing away.

'I'm guessing he really went in on me when he came up here,' she said.

Woody nodded.

'Is it going any further?'

'Given your understanding of how you could have addressed it differently, no, but steer a wide berth. He's a man with not a lot left to lose.'

Kim caught the undertone of Woody's instruction, which sounded a little bit like a warning.

'Did he make threats?' she asked.

Woody shook his head. 'No, but it's safe to say you're no longer on his Christmas card list.'

'I'll live,' she said, rising from the chair.

Woody made no attempt to stop her, meaning their meeting was over. She thanked him for his time and headed out of the office, hoping that all interaction with Burns was now well and truly in her past.

THIRTY-SIX

Bryant took the route to Bridgnorth that Kim favoured when taking the Ninja out for a burn. A sudden longing washed over her. It had been too long since she'd felt that kind of freedom. Maybe once this case was over she'd set aside some time to just pick a road and see where it took her.

This one had already wound through Enville, past The Cat and up through Four Ashes and Six Ashes. They were now passing through Wootton. She was aware that Bryant hadn't yet spoken to her once, not even to ask about her meeting with Woody.

'You okay?' she asked.

'Yeah, sure. I was just thinking that was some heavy rain we had last night.'

'Pull over,' she said as they approached Stanmore. They were only a couple of miles away from the clinic.

He indicated and slowed, pulling into a parking lay-by.

'What's up?' he asked, turning the engine off.

'Early lunch,' she said.

'Guv, it's not even nine o'clock. And we never do lunch anyway.'

'And you never make small talk with me about the bloody weather. What's going on?'

'It's nothing. I don't wanna add—'

'It's lunchtime. I'm Kim not guv.'

'That only applies at your house,' he replied.

'Well, come on then, turn the car around if that'll help you get it out.'

'Look, it can wait.'

'Wait for what?'

'Just time. That's all.'

Kim saw the muscle jumping in his cheek.

'Aah, you're waiting for me to get my strength back, for things to be normal.'

He didn't reply.

'Not sure when that's gonna pan out for you so come on, out with it.'

'You shut me out,' he said.

Kim waved her hand for him to continue.

'I feel like a total arse for even bringing this up. You've got enough to think about.'

'Doesn't give you any less entitlement to how you feel. So go for it.'

'Okay, we're friends outside of work. I care about you. I wanted to help. I wanted to be there. I wanted you to be able to talk or be silent or to rant and rage at someone. I wanted to be able to do what friends do and support you through one of the worst times of your life. I was here for this and you wouldn't let me in.'

'Literally or figuratively?' she asked, thinking of the times she'd watched him drive away.

'Don't be smart, Kim. I know you struggle to understand, but it makes the people that care about you feel like shit. It's like you don't trust me with your pain.' He paused and shook his head. 'I dunno. I just thought we were more than that.'

Kim swallowed down the emotion in her throat.

This man had been her solid friend for years. She trusted him with her life, and he deserved to know the truth.

'You wanna know the last thing that went through my head before I died?'

He nodded.

'You. I hated the thought of the guilt you'd feel at not getting to me in time. I knew you'd never forgive yourself for that. It was my biggest single regret as I felt myself drifting away.'

'Jesus, Kim, I had no—'

'We are friends, Bryant, and you're absolutely right to be hurt by my actions. I don't share anything very easily, least of all my pain. It was a rough time and I couldn't face being around anyone, even people I trust, so you're right, and I apologise for not letting you help.'

Bryant frowned at her. 'You serious?'

She nodded. 'You deserved better. I'm sorry, and I'm not bloody saying it again.'

Bryant threw back his head and laughed. 'I ain't pushing it.'

'And we're not even out of the woods yet of me maybe needing some help. Your time may come, my friend. Now start the car and get us to Bridgnorth.'

'On it, guv,' he said, seamlessly reverting.

There were things that she had to say to him, but this was his moment, his chance to vent. His hurt was justified and the apology had been genuine.

She'd given him his opportunity, and she would wait patiently for hers.

THIRTY-SEVEN

The property in Bridgnorth was fifty metres or so from a double gate straight off the road.

There was no signage to indicate the name of the place. They had only found it because the satnav insisted it was on their right and they were about to enter open countryside.

The house sat in what looked like a couple of acres of well-maintained grounds. There was nothing fussy or ostentatious in the space. She spied a healthy-looking lawn, a border of trees and a couple of benches at the area where the tarmac road met the gravel that appeared to encircle the house.

As they drew closer, Kim could see a small parking area to the left of the house. There were no directional boards or information signs. It felt as though they were approaching someone's home.

Bryant parked with the other vehicles as a man came out of the side door dressed in kitchen whites. He lobbed a black bag into the bin as they got out of the car. He gave them a cursory glance before dismissing them and going back inside.

'Friendly guy,' Bryant remarked as they headed to the front entrance.

Kim would describe the property as an old Victorian villa which was set over three floors. It wouldn't have been a home for the super, super wealthy but it might have been a getaway retreat.

Only when they stepped inside did it become clear they had entered a facility and not a home.

The hallway had been transformed into a reception, and Kim immediately understood why it had been so easy to walk in the door. The reception desk was behind a sheet of glass with a grid of holes to speak through.

There were three gold velvet tub chairs around a smoked glass coffee table to her right. The walls were painted white but with a hint of something that took away the starkness of the colour. Wildlife prints covered one wall.

A solid oak door stood to the left, and Kim was willing to bet that one was locked.

This was as far as you went without permission.

A girl dressed in a black polo shirt and black trousers appeared carrying a mug of something hot. Her glossy blonde hair hung down to the middle of her arm.

She offered an open smile. 'Hello there. Welcome to Change. How can I help?'

She set the mug down, and Kim got a whiff of something lemony.

'May we speak with Mr or Mrs Gardner?'

'Do you have an appointment?' she asked pleasantly.

Kim shook her head.

'May I ask what it's about?'

'An active murder investigation,' Kim said, holding up her ID and preparing to do battle again.

'Ooh, serious stuff,' she said, widening her eyes. 'Let me check if they're free.'

The girl took a portable phone to the edge of the space and

turned away from them. The holes in the glass partition didn't afford them any opportunity to listen in.

She turned back.

'Yes, they're free. Well, budget meeting but who doesn't mind an excuse to postpone those?' she said, pulling a face. 'Please come through.'

A buzzer sounded on the door to the left.

'I'm Jessica, and I'll take you to their office.'

Kim followed her through the door along a brightly lit corridor, painted the same shade of white as reception but with summer prints on the wall.

'Just here,' she said, standing before another door marked 'Private'.

She tapped lightly before entering.

The door opened into one of the most impressive spaces Kim had ever seen.

The room was blessed with high ceilings and tall windows. An antique desk was placed before each window and Kim could see why. The view of the back garden area was stunning. Cherry trees and coloured laburnums intertwined with each other. Daisies and fuchsia plants fought each other at low level while *Salix* bushes and delicate acers popped up all over the place. Beyond the explosion of flowers was a view of the rolling countryside.

Kim brought her attention back inside the room. A round meeting table had three people sitting around it.

She knew she was looking at Celia and Victor Gardner and a young man, early twenties, also wearing the uniform of all black.

'Please come in, officer,' the woman said, standing and taking off her glasses.

Victor Gardner smiled in her direction, and Kim was struck by the handsomeness of the couple. She guessed them to be mid-forties.

'My husband, Victor, and my son, Eric,' she said, nodding towards the other person at the table.

She motioned to the files and papers on the desk. 'Post-audit accounts,' she said, rolling her eyes.

Jessica coughed from the doorway.

'My apologies. This is our other child, Jessica.'

'Who got introduced after the accounts,' Jessica said, raising an eyebrow.

'Firstborn are soooo sensitive,' Celia said, sending a humorous nod to her daughter, who chuckled.

Eric gathered up the papers. 'I'll carry on with the action points.'

'Good lad,' Victor offered, slapping him on the shoulder.

'Yeah, come on, good lad,' Jessica said good-naturedly, holding open the door for her brother.

Celia shook her head as she moved to an easy seating area against the far wall.

'I swear they couldn't be more different,' Victor said, taking a seat beside his wife. 'One's all for people and the other is all for numbers.'

'And they both work here full-time?' Kim asked.

'For now,' Celia answered. 'Jess has just finished her degree in hospitality, and Eric is nearing the end of his business studies degree. They're both cutting their teeth here, but I'm sure they'll want to go and do their own thing at some stage, which is only natural.'

For a moment Kim wondered if they'd come to the right place. Surely these respectable, reasonable people with grown-up intelligent children weren't really trying to change people's sexuality.

'You don't think they'll stay in the family business?' Bryant asked.

'I think not,' Celia said pleasantly.

'And what is the family business exactly?' Kim asked.

Celia gave her a half-smile. 'I think you already know that, officer.'

'Humour me. Spell it out.'

'We assist people who want to make changes to their sexuality.'

'You think that's possible?' Kim asked, unable to believe she was sitting here having a rational conversation about something she viewed as fundamentally wrong; but these people appeared perfectly normal and reasonable.

'I wholeheartedly believe it, Inspector. This facility has been operating for almost forty years and our results speak for themselves, as does our waiting list.'

These words were not offered defensively, more with a hint of weariness at having to explain herself.

'So how do you do it?' Kim asked simply.

'Our methods depend on the person. An individual is assessed before any treatment, and a full treatment plan is formulated between the patient and us.'

'You use the word patient as though they're suffering from some kind of disease,' Kim stated.

'In our mind they are,' Celia said easily. 'And in their own mind, they are too. Whatever your judgement of the service we offer, please remember that all our patients are here voluntarily. They want to change; they welcome the opportunity to be cured.'

'Cured?' Kim asked.

'Absolutely. It is a disease in the eyes of the person who no longer wants it. We help extract it.' Celia paused. 'I can tell by your micro expressions that you're horrified by what we do and you're looking for some sign of evil here. It doesn't exist. We don't torture animals and drink their blood. We don't sacrifice babies at any altar. We help people to change something about themselves they don't like. How is that any different to cosmetic surgery, Botox or assertiveness training?'

'Because it's inherent. It's a part of who they are.'

'When they were born?' Celia asked.

'I suppose so,' Kim said.

Victor crossed one leg over the other and looked on with amusement as though he enjoyed the passion with which his wife debated the subject.

'What about a child born with a bad heart, a cleft palate, even transgender cases, people who know they were born into the wrong body? Should they not be given every opportunity to live the right life for them or should they just shut up and play the hand they were dealt?'

Kim wondered how she had turned into the unreasonable one in this argument.

'I suppose it depends on the methods,' Kim countered.

'We use a whole range of processes which I'm happy to discuss in more detail once I know the reason for your visit.'

'We're investigating two murders. Both victims may or may not be linked to your treatment facility.'

'Please tell me their names.'

'Jamie Mills.'

Celia nodded and frowned at the same time. 'Jamie came to us a couple of years ago, brought in by his parents the first—'

'So not everyone is here of their own accord,' Kim noted. 'Jamie was a minor and would have had to be put in the facility by his mother.'

Celia sighed heavily. 'We do have occasional cases where the parents feel their child is at risk of suicide if they don't get help. In these cases we do a risk assessment, and in Jamie's case we found him to be suffering psychologically and deemed that it was in his best interest to have him stay for a while. I like to think we helped him see clearly.'

You sent him to the nearest gay bar and into the company of River Harris and probably the happiest days of his life, Kim thought. They had indeed helped him, just not in the way they intended.

'Are you saying Jamie has been murdered?'

'Yes, it was staged to look like suicide but it definitely wasn't.'

'Poor kid,' Victor said, shaking his head.

'But why?' Celia asked.

'Maybe because he was gay.'

'But he wasn't any more,' Celia protested.

'He actually really was,' Kim argued, thinking about his social-media page.

Victor shook his head. 'We should have kept him longer.'

Celia nodded her agreement.

Kim wanted to scream that it wouldn't have made any difference, but they wouldn't be convinced. They had built a lucrative business on their ideals.

'What sort of treatment did Jamie receive during his stay?'

'I'm sorry. I can't discuss that with you without his parents' written permission.'

Kim knew that was never gonna happen.

Celia continued. 'I'm sorry, I don't mean to be obstructive, but we could get into a lot of trouble.'

Having met Jamie's parents, she could imagine just how much trouble. They wouldn't want anything discussed about the son they wanted to bury and forget about as soon as possible.

'Can you elaborate on the types of treatment you offer?'

'I can certainly do that,' Celia said, allowing Kim the loophole.

'We offer substance-based methods, for example hormones, sexual stimulants, sexual depressants.' She paused.

Kim had no questions. She'd assumed that much, although she didn't see any of those options as a cure.

'We offer hypnosis and psychoanalysis and group therapy.'

'You try and talk it out of them?' Kim asked.

'We encourage them to look for alternative avenues of attraction, more conventional.'

'You recite over and over the benefits of being straight and then hypnotise them into believing they're not gay?' Bryant asked.

'We use many different methods alongside each other,' Victor replied.

'Okay, what else?' Kim asked.

'Aversion therapy and aversion reduction—'

'Back up. Back up. What's aversion therapy in this context? I get it for dogs. If they bark, a collar shocks them so they no longer bark. Horrific, but is that what we're talking here?'

'Very similar. We have sessions where a patient sits in a special chair. We show homosexual images and issue a small shock, not painful but not particularly pleasant. We show heterosexual images and the chair gives a short massage.'

'Association,' Kim said, feeling the distaste rising in the back of her throat. People were not dogs that needed training in who they could or couldn't love. 'Isn't that considered inhumane?' she asked.

'Without consent, of course, and yet it remains one of our most used techniques. It's no different to the foul-tasting nail polish to stop the habit of nail biting. It's a simple theory of associating any given stimulus with an unpleasant sensation. It's used in alcohol addiction.'

Kim ached to point out that nail biting and alcoholism were bad habits or addictions.

'But that's not sexual identity,' she argued. 'You're talking about unwanted behaviours.'

'It's unwanted if the patient wants to be straight.'

Kim knew there was no argument she could bring that they hadn't heard before. It was time to focus on getting any information she could to help her find a killer.

'Did you treat Sarah Laing?'

Celia visibly blanched. 'Sarah?'

'I'm going to take that as a yes.'

'She's dead too?'

Kim nodded. 'We suspect by the same person. Can you tell us about Sarah's treatment?'

Celia nodded. 'Yes, I can speak more openly about Sarah. She was an adult who signed herself in here. She paid for the treatment herself.' She shook her head as though trying to digest the information. 'I'm not sure I've ever seen a greater or more complex case of self-hatred due to sexuality. She begged us to help her.'

'What treatment did she take?'

'Everything. She was here for one week of intensive therapy. It was all she could afford.'

'Aversion therapy?'

'Daily.'

'And?'

'I didn't see her the day she left but all reports were positive.'

'You think she'd been cured of being gay within a week?' Kim asked with disbelief.

'In truth I thought she'd be back in a few months to continue the treatment.'

'Just so you know, it didn't work. Sarah had actually decided to embrace her sexuality and the lifestyle.'

Celia opened her hands. 'We can't control how much effort patients put into their own recovery.'

'So she didn't try hard enough and that's the only reason it failed?' Kim asked, trying not to let her exasperation show. This wasn't a new knee that stiffened up if you didn't go home and follow the physiotherapist's instructions. This was fighting your sexual identity.

'We're not monsters here, Inspector,' Celia said gently. 'I'm truly sorry about Jamie and Sarah, but we only help people that want to make a change.'

'I think we're going to have to agree to differ,' Kim said, standing up.

Celia followed suit looking genuinely saddened.

'I hate that you're leaving with a negative impression of us.' She paused. 'Would you like me to ask Jess to show you around the place so you can really understand what we do?'

Kim opened her mouth to refuse. Nothing was going to change her mind, but why not? Both her victims had spent time here.

'Okay, thanks, Celia. I think we'd like that very much.'

THIRTY-EIGHT

Stacey got out of the squad car at a multistorey National Car Park a stone's throw away from New Street station in Birmingham city centre.

The boss hadn't been out of the office for five minutes when she'd received the call that Gabriel Denton's car had been reported as abandoned: the five-hour ticket purchased on Monday had expired almost seventy hours ago. Three fixed penalty notices had been stuck on the driver's side window.

Damn it.

With over a million inhabitants in the city itself and thousands of visitors daily, he could stay in the middle of Birmingham city centre and she'd never find him.

This close to New Street station, with thirteen platforms and trains to pretty much every destination in the country, he had access to anywhere. He had his passport and a large amount of cash.

Stacey sighed heavily as she walked around the car. The tow-truck driver moved impatiently from one foot to the other, awaiting her authorisation to remove, but she wasn't taking any chances. There was no way the boss would allow her to eat into the forensics budget for what was looking increasingly like Gabe Denton had done a voluntary disappearing act.

Oh, Gabe, I really hoped you were one of the good guys, she thought as she took a look in the boot that had already been forced open. She scanned the space that held only an emergency triangle and a foot pump.

She felt around for any signs of wetness, blood, bodily fluids, but it was as dry as a bone.

She took out her phone and walked around the car once more, taking a few snaps to accompany her statement.

She bent and looked inside. The glove box contained a small map book, tissues and a comb. She reached across and opened the centre console. It was empty, except for one thing. A mobile phone.

Perhaps Beth would want it after she'd interrogated it.

She touched the home button and it sparked into life. There was no password, and she could see that only five per cent of battery life remained.

The messages on the screen told her that he had twenty-seven missed calls and eleven voicemail messages.

She didn't waste the battery life to look at or listen to them. They were all going to be from Beth. The last one had come in only an hour earlier. The woman was going out of her mind with worry, and right now Stacey had no good news to offer.

She was less interested in calls received than she was in calls made. Was there any indication of what he'd been planning to do? Had he called an airline? Booked tickets? Made reservations?

She scrolled to his call register as a battery warning message flashed on the screen. The five per cent had dropped to two.

She could see immediately that almost every outgoing call was to Beth, but just one entry got her attention.

He had made one call on Monday morning before he disappeared.

And it was to a name she already knew.

THIRTY-NINE

Kim followed Jess back into the reception area feeling as though she'd just been given a tour of Disneyland by a very perky cartoon character.

Jess's enthusiasm for the place had shone through as they'd walked from one therapy room to another and then one treatment room after the other. The pride in the achievements of her parents had radiated from her. Kim felt that if you cut the girl in half, the name of the clinic would be running right through her like a stick of rock.

Kim had been shown the kitchen and introduced to the qualified chef who had been no more pleasant than when they'd seen him throwing the rubbish out. They had passed other staff members dressed in the black uniform as they'd toured the dining room, the evening lounge and the quiet room. Everyone had nodded and smiled pleasantly. She'd even been allowed to view the therapy room that held the aversion chair. It was an innocuous looking piece of furniture and yet Kim had no wish to go anywhere near it. The drop-down screen made it look like a one-person cinema had she not known what had been shown on that screen and why.

'Thanks for taking the time to give us the tour,' Kim said.

'Happy to,' Jess said with a bright smile. 'I never get bored of showing people around.'

'You're very proud of what your parents have achieved here. It must have taken a great deal of work, which I'm sure wasn't without sacrifice,' Kim said. She'd seen the playful dynamics between the family earlier but wanted to probe deeper.

The smile remained on Jess's face but lost some of its sparkle. 'No different to any other family with working parents, Inspector. Of course things get missed or forgotten when you're building a business with two young children, but Eric and I have grown up in this environment and feel just as passionately about it as our parents. We understand why they didn't make it to every parents' evening or sports day. They were helping people.'

Kim could see that Jessica held no animosity towards her parents and was as dedicated to the cause as they were. 'And how deeply involved are they with the patients? Do they offer any treatment themselves?'

'Oh no,' Jess said, grabbing a bottle of water from her desk. 'My parents aren't hands-on with the patients. We have clinicians that follow the treatment plans laid out by my mother, and my dad is responsible for marketing and legal.' The bright smile was back. 'We all have our designated roles given our skill set and passion.'

Kim had the feeling of being given a one-sided view, offered the opinion only of the people that ran the place, not the patients who used it. She hadn't been afforded that pleasure as their maximum capacity of ten had been at the mandatory morning tai chi session. She needed a balanced view of what went on here, and she wasn't going to get that from any of the staff.

'Is there anything else I can help you with?' Jessica said, closing the door marked 'private' behind them.

'Actually, there is one thing,' Kim said. 'Is there any chance we could get a copy of Sarah Laing's admission form? It's for her mum, who's having a hard time believing that Sarah would have voluntarily signed herself in for such treatment. If she can see the black-and-white proof of it, she might be able to accept that this was what her daughter wanted.'

'Of course,' Jess said, reaching under the desk for a lever arch file.

She laid it on the desk and flicked to the appropriate page, then removed it and stepped to the photocopier.

Bryant looked at her questioningly, knowing that Mrs Laing needed no such proof. But the piece of paper Kim wanted wasn't the one that was in Jessica's hand. She glanced down quickly at the record that had been revealed beneath Sarah's sheet.

Stephanie Lakehurst, 22 Hope Street, Much Wenlock.

'Thank you,' Kim said, taking the piece of paper. 'You've been very helpful, but can I ask you just a couple more things before we go?'

'Of course,' Jess said.

'You said that this place is your mum's passion, her vocation, but if she's not hands-on with the patients, what exactly is it she feels passionately about?'

'Helping people to change into the person they want to be. She's driven by giving people the choice and opportunity to change something they hate about themselves. Her vocation is helping to take away someone's pain.'

'Do you really think any of this works?' Kim asked.

Jess smiled. 'Oh, I know it works, Inspector. We have the living proof of it just along the hall.'

'I'm sorry, I'm not sure what you mean.'

'My mother. She was sent here when she was sixteen years old.'

FORTY

'It's not what you think,' Wendy Clarke said from the other side of the reception desk. The colour was rising in her cheeks.

'You don't know what I think, but I do know that Gabriel called you right before he disappeared and you hadn't thought to mention it last time we spoke?' Stacey asked. She was trying not to make any judgement on the nature of their relationship.

It had taken less than twenty minutes for the squad car to get her from Birmingham city centre to the accountants' office in Halesowen, and Stacey had spent most of those minutes convincing herself that Gabriel wouldn't have done that to Beth.

'I didn't want to get him into any trouble,' Wendy said, looking down at her hands.

'With who?'

'Beth.'

'I thought you just said it wasn't like that,' Stacey said.

'One second,' Wendy said as a client entered the front door. Stacey stood to the side.

'Mr Greer is waiting for you, Mrs Hawkins.'

The woman nodded and continued through the reception.

Wendy waited until the customer was out of sight before speaking again. 'He called because he wasn't coming into work.'

'You said staff didn't have to call in,' Stacey reminded her.

'He wasn't calling on a professional level. He was calling me.'

'Why?' Stacey asked, thinking that so far it sounded exactly like what she'd been thinking since seeing the flush of guilt on Wendy's face.

'Because Monday was curry day. At lunchtime. It was a thing. I always brought in beef curry that I made on Sunday. We always shared it. It was a date but not that kind.'

'What kind?'

'Romantic. It was just a standing arrangement,' she said, colouring further. 'He wanted to let me know he wouldn't be in for our curry lunch.'

'And he didn't say anything else? Didn't tell you his plans for the day?'

Wendy shook her head vehemently. 'It was a short call. He was being polite. Obviously, I was disappointed.'

'Wendy, I have to ask,' Stacey said, realising this bush had been beaten around enough. 'Were you and Gabriel having an affair?'

'God no. Gabe would never... I mean... well... not really.'

'Okay, Wendy, you're gonna have to unpack that one for me. It's either a yes or a no.'

'Well it isn't actually. There was nothing physical between us. Gabe would never do that, but there was a connection, an emotional one.'

'Go on,' Stacey urged.

'Gabe had started to open up to me. He talked of regrets, decisions he'd made that he wished he hadn't.'

'Such as.'

'Not trying to mend things with his family. He felt guilty for not visiting his mother enough. He wished he was in contact with his brother. I think they were close growing up and one silly argument was the end of it.'

'What was the argument about?'

Wendy shrugged. 'He never said, but I think it wasn't long after he and Beth got married.'

Stacey mentally filed that away.

'Why would he confide all this in you?' Stacey asked. 'And not a friend?'

Wendy shook her head. 'You're not getting it, are you? He had no friends. The only time he was out of Beth's sight was when he was at work, and even then she would either call or text him at lunchtime.'

'And it was always Beth contacting Gabriel?' Stacey asked.

Wendy nodded. 'Pretty much.'

Pretty much but not always.

It wasn't up to her to judge the dynamics of the couple's relationship. Okay, in her view it might have been a bit secular and exclusive, but it clearly worked for them. What she did have to wonder was whether Wendy had an ulterior motive for mentioning it.

'Wendy, please be absolutely honest with me now. Just how deep was this emotional connection between you and Gabe?'

Wendy took a breath. 'We were starting to fall in love.'

FORTY-ONE

'Pretty sneaky, guv,' Bryant observed as they headed towards the address in Much Wenlock.

'Creative is the word I think you were after. Technically, I didn't really do anything wrong. I just happened to see the name on the next sheet of paper.' She shrugged without apology. 'I just want to hear from someone who's spent time at the facility.'

He frowned. 'It wasn't exactly what I thought it was going to be.'

'How so?' Kim asked, trying to pinpoint the source of her own unease since leaving the property.

'I dunno. I suppose I expected them to be more secretive about what they do. I thought we'd have to drag it out of them. Do you remember when we suspected that group on Hollytree of illegal dog fighting?' he asked.

'I sure do,' she growled. Although Bryant was going way back, it wasn't an arrest she'd ever forget. Fifteen bait dogs had been rescued from the two-bed flat.

'We had the proof right there, but not one of those idiots wanted to admit to it even though we told them we were charging them all with the same offence. They knew what they were doing was despicable but did it anyway. I expected something similar from the folks at the clinic.'

'They were pretty proud of what they do,' Kim agreed.

'Guv, I'm feeling a bit conflicted.'

'About what, whether that line belongs in an American soap opera?' she asked, turning to look at him.

He ignored her. 'It's like, we both know that what they try to do is impossible, right?'

'Agreed.'

'And yet, they seem so sure they can help people who are genuinely distressed and suffering. If they were helping anyone else with any other kind of inner conflict, we'd be applauding them.'

Kim wanted to argue the point but couldn't, even though her mind screamed that sexuality was different to any other facet of a person's identity.

'And what about that final revelation from Jessica about her mother?' she asked.

'Exactly. Apparently Celia is living proof that the process works, so we're either both wrong about the effectiveness of what goes on there or Celia is living a lie, which also seems unlikely. My head is all over the place, guv.'

Kim nodded her agreement as she sent a text to Penn asking that he start doing background on Celia and Victor Gardner.

'Maybe things will be clearer after speaking to this Stephanie Lakehurst,' Kim said as Bryant took a right just before a service station.

'The one with the caravan,' Bryant said, pulling in.

The house was a tidy semi-detached property with matching net curtain in every room.

'Okay, let's see what...' Her words trailed away as her phone sounded from her pocket. The dread filled her stomach as she saw the caller's name. 'Keats?'

'Whatever you're doing, stop it and head towards me now.'

'Where?'

'Harvington. The Willows. One mile on from The Dog.'

She knew where the pub was, and a mile away from it in any direction was semi-rural.

'Don't say it,' she said.

'Okay, but not saying it isn't gonna bring this poor fella back to life.'

Bryant had already pulled the car away from the home of Stephanie Lakehurst. Whether they were right outside her door or not, there was a body in the opposite direction.

'Forty minutes, Keats. We're on our way.'

FORTY-TWO

'Yo, comrade,' Penn said as Stacey came back into the squad room.

'I've only been gone two hours,' she said, removing her satchel.

'Your presence has been sorely missed. Felt much longer.'

'You don't do so well stuck in here on your own, eh?' she said, reaching for a muffin.

Penn didn't have the heart to tell her the constant supply was in danger of drying up and that he'd had to almost beg his younger brother to bake with him.

'What did you find out?' he asked, eager to have another voice in the room. These days he seemed to be spending way too much time in his own head.

'Found out that Gabe Denton was having an emotional affair at work and has most likely taken some time out to get his head straight.'

'What exactly is an emotional affair?' Penn asked, sitting back in his seat.

'Everything except the sex, I think. Either way I don't think his full attention was on his marriage. I've just got one call to make before shelving it,' she said. 'What you been up to?'

'Well, on my long list of people and places to research, I've got a bit of history on the Change Clinic.'

'Go on,' Stacey said, leaning forward.

'The organisation began in the fifties. You'll be surprised to know that there are many of its ilk around the world. A lot of them have links to religious bodies, and some are privately owned businesses.'

'This one?' Stacey asked.

'Is privately owned, and has been at that property since 1959. The whole thing was started by a baron who had three daughters and one son. There were rumours around town that Henry Balham, the baron's son was—'

'Baron Balham?'

'Focus, Stace. So allegedly the baron's son was gay despite having a string of girlfriends. He put on a great show because we were many years away from the legalisation of homosexuality.'

'In '67.'

'Correct. So the rumours say that Balham Junior was caught having sex with a man and was reported to the police. Allegedly, he told his father and then took his own life by jumping off the roof of the building.'

'Definitely suicide?' Stacey queried.

Penn shrugged. 'Either way he lost his life before the police could speak to him, so there's no full scandal or court case associated with the name. The alleged suicide happened in '57, and two years later the baron opened his doors to people who wanted to adopt a more savoury lifestyle. The details are sketchy as to what services were offered exactly. It was registered as a business in the mid-seventies. When the baron died in the early nineties, his three married daughters couldn't offload it quickly enough. They sold the house and business to the first person interested, which happened to be Victor Gardner and his wife Celia, who have now been added to my ever-growing list of people needing background checks. Victor Gardner's money came from a successful vitamin range launched by his grandfather.'

'And?'

'Well that's about it so far,' he defended.

'You've pretty much spent the last couple of hours reading gossip?'

Penn thought for a second. 'I suppose so, yeah. Although, I have got some financials.'

'Ooh, go on,' Stacey said.

'Rest of the nineties was a bit of a disaster. It's a good job Victor is minted because there was no profit in the business back then. The property needed a lot of work to bring it up to standard.

'Early in the noughties they started to turn a profit. A small one, barely enough to keep two small kids in nappies, but by the end of that decade they were making a healthy profit, which has increased year on year since.'

'Give me the numbers,' Stacey urged.

'The most recent set of audited accounts filed just last week detail a year-end profit of £1.2 million.'

Stacey's mouth fell open.

'Yeah, my thoughts exactly,' he said.

There was a lot of money to be had from turning people straight.

FORTY-THREE

It was almost one by the time Bryant pulled into the driveway of The Willows in Harvington.

The potholes had Kim jumping up from the seat.

'Sorry,' Bryant said every time he hit a particularly deep one. She was pleased it was only around thirty metres long. At the end of it was a single-storey barn conversion with a garage on the left-hand side. Kim had the strange sense that the property should have been breathtakingly stunning. But it wasn't. The overall sense was of neglect. Weeds peeped through the gravel driveway and all along the base of the property. Small squares of cardboard had blown around the drive from the overfull recycling bin. Four empty whisky bottles were visible on the top. To her knowledge, the bins were collected every fortnight, so unless they'd missed one, that was more than a nightcap being consumed in Scotch.

A plant pot outside the front door, holding some kind of fuchsia, was being swallowed by weeds, and as Kim approached, she saw that it was also a makeshift ashtray.

In front of the garage was a black Ford Kuga which she assumed to belong to the owner.

'Ah, shit, no,' she said, spying the kiddie seat in the back of the car. She thought of little Amy Laing. Another child without a parent.

As she turned, Kim noticed the fence leading off the garage and travelling the length of the property. She could see the return of the fence signalling the total of their outside space.

She took a few steps down and saw that the back fence separated the barn from a similarly renovated property no more than twenty metres away. The left fence separated the barn from a two-storey farmhouse that had probably once owned both barns.

The right side of the fence led back down to the road and a wooded area right opposite.

Even back at the front door she could hear the traffic thundering past on the main road.

Kim had the strangest feeling of this being the dream on paper but not reality.

She approached the front door between Keats's vehicle and Mitch's Transit, then took the protective slippers from the officer at the door, while Bryant introduced them both for the log.

The front door took her into a cramped space with a wooden bench and a coat rack. A row of wellies told her this was a type of boot room.

'Oh good God,' Kim said as the stench of blood reached her and directed her to the left into a small lounge that had been smothered with throws, cushions and rugs.

'Stop for lunch on the way, Inspector?' Keats asked, his voice tinged with irritation.

'Yeah, had a three course at the Beefeater on the way. Steak was a bit dry but hey ho. Now what have we got?'

Keats stepped aside to reveal a man dressed in jeans and a white shirt, drenched with blood.

'Meet Liam Sachs, thirty-two years old, husband and father.'

The man's left hand was hanging loose in his lap. A deep red gash cut across the wrist. The blood had run out and left lines over his jeans, down the front of the chair and onto the carpet. His right hand was resting on his right leg, and a kitchen knife had fallen to the floor.

His hair was a straw blonde colour, a little long around his handsome face. Lifeless blue eyes stared straight at her.

In front of him was a laptop in the open position. The whole thing was covered in blood.

'Okay, Keats, go,' Kim said, wondering as to the reason for the call. On first inspection this looked like a genuine suicide.

'Look closely at the wrist, Inspector,' he instructed.

She did so.

'It's deep,' she noted.

'Too deep, but not conclusive on its own.'

She looked again.

'No hesitation marks,' she noted.

Keats nodded. 'Never have I attended a suicide in this manner to find such a deep and decisive cut with no hesitation marks. One normally needs to build up to inflicting such a wound.'

'Rare but not impossible?' she asked.

'One more thing, and I'll forgive your tardiness if you get this one.'

She leaned down to take a closer look, careful not to touch anything. She took a look at his hand and then back at the wrist.

'Is that a small bruise?'

He nodded. 'Okay, you're forgiven. Yes, there's a chance that bruise came from having his wrist held in place, so for those three reasons I'm not prepared to classify the death as suicide, and I'm sure you agree with me.'

She nodded as a techie stood beside her and took a photo.

'How long?'

'Initial estimations are that he died in the early hours of the morning – around 1 a.m.'

Kim frowned. 'Where was...?'

'His wife returned from an overnight sales conference this morning and found him. She's in the kitchen.'

'And the child?' Kim asked.

'Is with his grandparents.'

Kim idly wondered why the child hadn't been left with his father, but she thanked the Lord he hadn't been in the house.

She headed back through the cramped boot room to a hallway with what she assumed were bedroom doors and a bathroom. Right at the other end was a barn-style kitchen complete with wooden cupboards and flagstones.

Liam's wife sat at a small round table with a police officer sitting to her left.

Kim introduced herself and Bryant.

'I'll put the kettle on,' the police officer said, taking the untouched cuppa from in front of the woman, who stared at the table.

'Mrs Sachs, we are so sorry for your loss.'

The woman nodded without raising her head.

At this point family members were often in a state of denial and were looking to her to tell them there'd been some kind of mistake. This woman had entered her home and the proof had been right in front of her. It was an image she would never forget.

'He was alone,' she said, gulping back the tears. 'He did this because he was alone. I wasn't here.'

'That's not true, Mrs Sachs.'

'Monica, please. I can't stand hearing his name,' she said, finally lifting her head. Her eyes were raw, and her skin looked bleached of colour.

'Monica, I'm sorry to have to intrude but can you tell us what happened?'

'You've been in there. Can't you work it out for yourself? My husband left us. He gave up and left us.'

'Gave up on what?'

'Everything. Himself, us, his life.' The tears came again, but she wiped them away angrily. 'I'm sorry. This probably isn't the correct response, but I'm bloody angry with him.'

Angry but not totally surprised, Kim realised.

'Can you tell us more about Liam and what led you to this point?' Kim asked, feeling she was going to learn more by just letting the woman speak.

'He's been depressed for a while. About eighteen months. Since he lost his job. Everything crashed around us. We bought this house when Liam was in retail management and I worked full-time as a teacher. This was the dream; we had it all – good jobs, a barn conversion in the countryside, our child. We were even talking about having another and then bang his job is gone a month after I'd reduced my hours to part-time. He had no warning. Just seven years' redundancy and a pat on the back.'

She took a breath.

'He tried so hard to get another job. He was scouring the job sites all day long. The bills started to mount up, so I went back to work full-time, which made him feel even more of a failure. I mean, he was getting interviews but just not nailing the job. His depression got worse, but I really had my fingers crossed this time.'

A fresh wave of tears spilled from her eyes.

'This time?' Kim asked, thinking that Liam Sachs did not fit their victim profile. Maybe she and Keats had acted too hastily. There was something else nagging at the back of her mind; something about the scene she'd just left that she should have registered.

'You said this time,' Kim prompted for her to continue as the constable set down three mugs of tea with a sugar bowl and spoon.

'He had a second interview this morning. It was a Zoom call for a position in Birmingham, good money but longer hours. He was really excited. He told me last night that he had a really good feeling that things were about to go our way. He was really chipper. I joked that I should go away more often. He just seemed so sure of this one.'

'May I ask where you were last night, Monica?'

'In Chester, new sales system training at the software company. I should still be there, but when I couldn't get Liam on the phone, I came straight back.

'His Zoom was at 9 a.m. so I waited until ten to be sure it was over. My hope was fading because I knew if it was good news he would have called me immediately. Even so, I was still too late. It must have gone badly and he did this to himself soon afterward. Unless...' A look of horrified panic contorted her features. 'What if I drove him to it? Maybe my phone call prompted him to do it because he just couldn't face giving me another disappointment.'

'I don't think that's the case at all,' Kim said, knowing that the Zoom meeting had never taken place. But there was more that she needed.

'Can you tell me what time you spoke last night?'

'Not sure, around elevenish. We Facetimed for about fifteen minutes. Liam was tired and wanted to get off to bed to be fresh for the interview.'

And yet he was still fully clothed at around 1 a.m., Kim thought.

Again, a little niggle came into her mind. She'd missed something. She knew it.

'Just one more thing for now and then we'll give you some peace.'

Monica nodded as exhaustion did battle with the grief.

'Why was your son not here with his father?'

'Liam wanted to focus solely on the interview. He wanted the night to himself to prepare. He suggested Joey go to my mom's. He knew that if Joey was here he'd spend the whole night playing with him. He didn't want to be distracted. He just wanted to be totally ready and have nothing go wrong.'

Kim nodded her understanding as the woman's eyes filled with fresh tears.

'How the hell am I going to tell a three-year-old boy that his daddy is gone, that he bailed when things got tough, that he didn't love us...?'

'It's not true, Monica,' Kim said, stopping her in her tracks.

'Of course it is. You saw what he did to himself.'

'I know you're angry, and it might be your anger that's holding you together right now, but I'm going to tell you something that's going to put that anger out of your head.'

Monica dabbed at her eyes with a look of disbelief.

'Monica, the Zoom call never happened. Your husband died in the early hours of the morning. Your phone call didn't prompt him to take his own life.'

She started to shake her head. 'That doesn't make any sense. I spoke to him last night. He was the best he's been in a long time. I would have known if he'd been planning to—'

'He wasn't planning to do anything,' Kim interrupted. 'I can't say too much, but we have reason to believe that Liam's death is connected to a current investigation and that Liam didn't take his own life.'

The colour that had been brought to her face by rage was quickly dissolved by shock.

'You think he was murdered?'

The hope in her voice brought emotion to the back of Kim's throat. What a thing to hope for but Kim understood it completely. He was dead and that was certain. Monica had managed to process that, but if it hadn't been by his own hand, she could let go of the rage, the disgust, the feeling of abandonment, the blame.

Kim nodded. 'He didn't leave you and your son, and we will find the person responsible.'

'B... But why?' she asked as Kim pushed her chair back.

'I can't tell you any more yet, but as soon as we have any developments, you'll be the first to know.'

Kim motioned for the constable to retake her place at the table.

She headed back to the lounge area wondering if they were barking up the wrong tree about the gay link. Maybe the fact that Jamie and Sarah were both gay was a coincidence. Perhaps there was some other link or the victims were more random than they'd thought.

The questions continued to circle around her head as she entered the room that still held the stench of blood.

Keats, Mitch and two assistants were removing Liam Sachs from the chair.

'Wait,' she said, standing in front of them.

She viewed the body from head to toe.

'Got it,' she said, turning and walking away.

She took a good deep gulp of fresh air as she removed the protective slippers.

'Okay, guv, what have you got and do I want to catch it?' Bryant asked as they walked to the car.

'Footwear, Bryant. It was 1 a.m. in the morning on a night that he wanted to get to bed early to prepare.'

'Yeah, I was there.'

'So why the hell was he wearing trainers?'

FORTY-FOUR

It was after two when Penn headed down to the cafeteria to snag them both some late lunch. Stacey had asked for whatever Betty's special was but she secretly hoped it was the cottage pie. Whatever the woman did with that mashed potato was either illegal or too high in calories to think about.

Stacey took the opportunity of a peaceful office to make a call. She was conscious of the pile of work Penn had on his desk, but she needed to finish up what she could do about Gabe Denton and then update his wife.

Craig Denton answered on the third ring.

'Hello,' his voice held a question at the unknown number.

Stacey introduced herself. 'Have you got a minute to talk?'

'I'm between trains right now but what's this about?'

Stacey could hear the background noise. Now was clearly not a good time, but his curiosity had won the day.

'I'm ringing about your brother Gabriel.'

'I know his name, officer. Is he okay?'

That was her first question answered. Gabe hadn't been in touch.

'Gabriel is missing. He left the house on Monday morning and hasn't been seen since.'

There was a moment of silence before he spoke.

'Finally seen sense, has he? Well good luck to him.'

Stacey put his animosity to the side for a minute to ensure that there'd been no contact.

'So he definitely hasn't been in touch with you?'

'I'm the last person he'd contact. If he can't go and visit his sick mother who's just eight miles up the road, he's hardly going to travel to Bristol.'

'Mr Denton, there's obviously bad blood between the two of you but—'

'Bad blood? Oh yeah, and I'm happy to tell you why. It's when you go through so much shit as kids, when you have no one so you rely on each other. We were best mates and brothers. Never did I see my life without him. But she soon put paid to that. Drove a wedge between us the day they were married. And it's because of her that he never visits our mother.'

Stacey had heard all this before, a family member blaming the spouse or girlfriend for everything. Even worse if the relationship had been a particularly close one, but Gabe was a grown man with a responsible job. If he wanted to visit his mother, he would. She was interested in what had caused the rift in the first place.

'I assume you're talking about Beth.'

'Of course – who else could convince him of something so foul?'

'Sorry?'

'She told him I came on to her on their wedding night, that when we had a dance, my hands were all over her. There were tears, words like violated that made me sick to my stomach. I'd never looked at her in that way. I may have had a few drinks, but I would never have disrespected my brother like that. There were things said in the heat of the moment that can't be unsaid. We never spoke again after that night.'

Stacey could hear the emotion in his voice. The pain was still there after all these years, and what made it worse was that it was probably just a misunderstanding.

'He never tried to call me once.'

'Did you try and call him?' Stacey shot back.

'No and I never will.'

'Even though you miss him?'

There was hesitation.

'Yeah, despite that. Look, my train is due any minute. He hasn't been in touch. This trip down memory lane hasn't been a pleasant one and I don't want to relive it all again.'

'Okay, Mr Denton, thank you...'

'I hope he's okay but do him a favour – if he's managed to get himself lost, let him stay that way.'

The phone went dead in her ear and Stacey knew that her last lead had dried up.

She couldn't help but be intrigued by what had taken place between Beth, Craig and Gabriel and the seriousness of the incident to warrant the two brothers not speaking for years. There must have been something to Beth's accusation if Gabe had believed her and cut his brother out of his life.

Whatever the story, the boss wasn't going to let her go any deeper because of a drunken fumble on the couple's wedding night. The work was piling up on Penn's desk, and she couldn't justify any more time away from the main case.

The only thing left to do was tell Beth Denton that they had no idea where her husband had gone and they didn't know if he was ever coming back.

FORTY-FIVE

'Where to, guv?' Bryant asked once they were back in the car.

'Hang on,' Kim said, tapping her fingers on the dashboard. She had the feeling that her work here was not yet done.

'Dare I ask what's going on in that twisted little mind of yours?' Bryant asked, switching off the engine. 'I mean, this may not even be related to our case. Liam appears to have been a happy married man.'

'Hmm...'

'What?'

'It's the shoes. I can buy everything else, but it's the bloody shoes. Who walks around their house at 1 a.m. with their trainers still on? Where was he going or where had he been?'

'To get a loaf of bread.'

'Spot any convenience stores close by as we were driving in? Looks like they're a one-car family, and that car was with Monica in Chester.'

'So what are you...?'

'Come on,' she said, getting out of the car.

Bryant followed as she strode out of the gate and turned left along the fence line.

'Can you search your phone and walk at the same time?'

'Search for what?'

'Never mind. Get Stace on the phone.'

She continued to walk the well-trodden path that ran along the east side of the Sachses' property.

'Yeah, Bryant,' Stacey answered on loudspeaker.

'Stace, there's a small wooded area in Harvington, about a mile away from The Dog and right off the main road,' Kim said, taking the phone from her colleague.

'Okay, boss,' Stacey answered.

'Find out if it has a name.'

'Okay, I'll have a—'

'Do it now,' Kim said. 'While we're on the phone,' she added, handing the phone back. 'Here's Bryant.'

She followed the path into the woods while she waited. Stacey was tapping away in the background.

'Bryant, can I ask exactly what it is you're doing?' Stacey asked.

'Following my new sniffer dog into the woods at the minute.'

Kim turned and offered him a filthy look before pushing a long thorny bramble out of her way.

She couldn't help but think about Monica's description of Liam's bubbly, excited mood the night before.

She continued along what appeared to be the only well-trodden footpath through the area. The route appeared to be popular with dog walkers, she thought, avoiding another pile of dog mess. Liam had wanted the house to himself and he'd been excited for the interview. Not nervous, not apprehensive, excited. And then there were the shoes, she thought as the path finally branched into two directions.

She instinctively turned right.

'Boss, I can't find any official name for the woods.'

Kim carried on walking. 'But?' she asked, hearing the hesitant tone in the constable's voice.

'It appears to have a nickname. It may once have been Harvington Woods cos now it's called Having It Woods and...'

Kim came to a stop and looked down at the ground.

'Oooh, boss, it's a local well-known spot for dogging.'

Kim looked away from the condom at her left foot.

'Yep, I was afraid you were gonna say that.'

FORTY-SIX

'Stace, I know you want to go see Beth so do it and get back as quick as you can to give me a hand,' Penn said, sensing her agitation.

'Thanks, buddy,' she said, grabbing her satchel and her coat.

The boss had just added Liam Sachs to the list of people he had to try and research.

So far, Penn was trying to get background on Charles Stamoran, his assistant Lorraine Abbott, Celia Gardner, Victor Gardner, scandal, lawsuits and now Liam Sachs as well.

There was no doubt he preferred to be busy, and it was all still quite a novelty after the last couple of months. It was just that all of the tasks were equally as important as each other.

He could certainly understand Stacey's wish to go and see Beth Denton in person. It was hard to step away from a case that hadn't reached any conclusion, and the least one could expect was an explanation in person. In truth, he was just as fascinated with the case as his colleague. What would possess a seemingly happily married man to withdraw a sizeable amount of money and just run out on his wife without any explanation? Experience told him there had to be a reason somewhere.

Maybe he wasn't as happily married as Beth Denton would have them believe. And if they were, then shame on Gabriel Denton. Some people just didn't know what they had.

His phone beeped receipt of a text message.

He breathed a sigh of relief. He'd texted Jasper an hour ago asking if he had a lift sorted for his dance class. Despite his best efforts, his brother had not been able to talk his best friend Billy into taking the line-dancing classes with him. Regardless, he'd gone alone and walked into a room full of strangers and come home buzzing. Since then one of his fellow line dancers had collected him and dropped him off each Thursday evening. Penn had stopped short of asking him for names and phone numbers. He was making progress in the whole 'letting go' process.

Not going tonight.

Penn quickly texted back.

Why not?

Don't feel well.

What's wrong. Have you checked your temperature?

Penn tapped his fingers as he waited for a response.

Calm down, Ozzy. Just feel a bit sick.

Penn was relieved but not totally appeased.

Have you eaten something bad?

Jelly babies.

A bag? Penn asked.

A box.

Penn chuckled at the row of sicky green emojis that followed his words. A frown accompanied his next thought or rather suspicion. Was he, the elder brother, the pity vote? Was Jasper putting it on so Penn wouldn't be on his own?

You sure that's all it is????

Penn pushed. Had someone said something unkind to him? Had he been singled out and bullied?

Huh?

Penn could imagine his face creased in confusion. Collateral damage of being a police officer was not taking anything at face value.

Never mind. OK, see ya later.

Cool beans. Later.

He smiled at the thought of an evening with his brother. Maybe he'd challenge Jasper to an Xbox championship complete with takeaway pizza.

He turned back to the mountain of work on his desk and hoped his colleague wasn't gone too long.

FORTY-SEVEN

It was almost four when they arrived back at the house in Much Wenlock, and Kim still had no idea how she was going to broach this line of questioning without revealing how she'd come by the confidential information.

'Just tell the truth,' Bryant said, reading her discomfort. 'It's been known to work now and again.'

'Novel concept but I'll give it a thought,' Kim said, getting out of the car.

She headed down the path and knocked on the door. The small Renault on the drive told her someone was home.

The door opened and Kim guessed they were looking at Stephanie Lakehurst. The girl was dressed in black leggings and an oversize jumper that fell off one shoulder. Her black hair was styled with an Elvis-type quiff. She had one single piercing in her nose.

'Stephanie?' Kim asked, holding up her ID.

Bryant did the same.

'May we come in?' Kim asked.

'Without a confirmation phone call to the nick, I don't think so.'

'Feel free.'

She frowned. 'Actually, I'll just give my cousin Sergeant Poole a shout at Halesowen.'

'Sergeant Poole works out of Dudley but nice try.' Kim already liked her style.

'Okay, not sure why you're here, but you're making the doorstep look untidy so you'd best come in.'

'Lovely house. Yours?' Kim asked, stepping into a clean, tidy hallway with animal pastel prints on the wall.

'Will be when the folks cark it,' she said, leading them into the lounge. A huge comfy-looking sofa curved and dominated the room around a big screen TV.

'Sorry, my attempt at humour and my way of saying I'm an only child.'

They all stood in the lounge.

'Before I ask you to sit, am I in any shit? You ain't getting comfy if I'm in trouble.'

'You done anything wrong?' Kim shot back.

'Hardly likely to admit it, am I?' she asked, taking a seat and indicating for them to do the same.

No sooner had Stephanie pulled up her legs than a Chihuahua appeared from nowhere, jumped up and nestled in the crook of Stephanie's arm.

'It's okay, Tyson,' she said, stroking the dog's head. 'I'll give you the signal if I need you to attack.'

'Tyson?' Bryant questioned.

'Why not?' Stephanie asked. 'Ain't no stereotyping going on in this house.'

Kim smiled as the dog seemed to look up at her owner in agreement. 'Stephanie, we understand you spent some time at a facility called Change in Bridgnorth.'

The girl's hand froze on the dog's head and her face turned to stone. 'How do you know that?'

'I accidentally saw your name while we were there on another matter.'

'I don't want to talk about it.'

Kim wasn't deterred. 'We're currently working an investigation where some of our victims seem to have a link to that place, and we need to establish whether we're looking at more than a coincidence.'

She shook her head. 'I'm sorry, but I can't talk about it,' she said.

'Why not?'

'I just can't.'

'We really need to speak to someone who spent time there and isn't dead,' Kim said, not unkindly but trying to drive the point home.

'I'm sorry, but I can't help you.'

'Did they help you?'

Stephanie offered no answer.

Kim sighed in frustration. 'Okay, what prompted you to go?'

Stephanie glanced up and to the left as though checking this was a question she could answer. 'Okay, my whole life I've been a tomboy, always liked wearing trousers, screamed the place down if Mum put me in a dress. I liked playing boys' games with boys' toys. Mum bought me a doll every Christmas hoping she'd find one I'd like. Her own brand of subliminal conversion therapy, I suppose,' she said with a smile.

'Did she find one?' Kim asked.

'Nah, they all met the same unfortunate end.'

Kim waited.

'Thrown over the fence for next door's dog. For my tenth birthday she bought me an Action Man with all the army gear. The dog didn't get that one. From that time, my mum let me be. She allowed me to make my own choices and never once passed judgement on the decisions or choices I made. Of course, that didn't pan out well for me when I went to high school.'

She paused and took a breath.

'Even before I knew myself that I was gay, I was taunted and called names. Every day for five long years. Any friends I made were scared away by the bullies. Not a time in my life I want to dwell on,' she said.

Kim nodded her understanding.

'All I could see was my entire future stretching out in front of me like my school years. I didn't want to be gay. I didn't want to be called names or singled out my whole life. I had no wish to be different.'

Kim's heart ached for the cruelty of kids and the long-lasting effects of bullies who probably hadn't given Stephanie a second thought once they'd left the premises for the last time.

'What did you do?'

'I conformed. I grew my hair long and changed the way I dressed. I got a job at a small roofing company and saved my money.'

'Did you already know about the Change Clinic?'

She nodded. 'I looked it up when I was sixteen. I did all the usual teenage things. I learned to drive, bought clothes, gave my parents board but always saved something for the fund. The time I waited was spent getting by, blending in, being part of the more widely accepted collective. By the time I was twenty-one, I had enough money for a month-long stay. I was sure that was long enough for them to fix me.'

'Is that really how you saw your sexuality – as a part of you that was broken?' Kim asked.

'Absolutely.'

'You didn't consider counselling to help you accept your identity?'

'Wouldn't have stopped the name calling, would it? Wouldn't have stopped the "lesbo" slurs shouted at my back. Wouldn't have stopped me feeling frightened that every day those calls would develop into something physical. Living with that kind of fear isn't living at all. I didn't want to stand out. I just wanted to be normal.'

'Did you read everything you could about conversion therapy?'

'Oh yeah. I researched it fully. I knew about the doubts as to its effectiveness, but I was gonna be the exception. I was going to do everything I was told, and I would be successful because I wanted it more than the people who had failed.'

'Did you understand the methods they might use?' Kim asked.

'Yep, I read about all the medical attempts, including hysterectomy, ovariectomy, clitoridectomy. For the boys castration, vasectomy, and one size fits all with the pubic nerve surgery and a lobotomy. I gotta be honest and say I didn't much fancy the clitorectomy. Didn't want no surgeon taking that away, but I was open for pretty much everything else.'

'Did you stay for the whole—'

'I'm sorry but that's all I can tell you.'

'Stephanie, we need more. People are dying.'

'And for that I am truly sorry, but I can't tell you any more.'

'Says who?'

'Says the non-disclosure agreement that I, other patients and every staff member signs before they're allowed past the reception desk.'

'You're forbidden legally to talk about the time you spent there?' Bryant asked.

Stephanie nodded. 'Not a thing.'

'You think they'd sue?' Kim asked.

'They have done.'

'Talk to us anyway,' Kim urged.

'They have good lawyers.'

'Ours are better.'

Stephanie appeared to consider her words.

Kim capitalised on the hesitation. 'We're not going to hang

you out to dry. We'll do everything we can to protect you, but we have two victims that spent time there, and we really need to know what goes on inside.'

Stephanie stood and Kim was convinced she was going to ask them to leave.

'Okay, but if you're gonna be here that long, I suppose I'd better find some manners and make you both a drink.'

FORTY-EIGHT

Stacey took a few deep breaths as she walked towards the home of Bethany and Gabriel Denton. There was no part of what she was going to say to Beth that was going to offer her comfort.

The woman must have seen her coming down the path as the door was opened before she had a chance to knock.

'Have you found him?' she asked, clasping her hands together.

Stacey shook her head as she stepped into Beth's home.

Beth pointed towards the lounge, and Stacey followed her instruction. The sound of a radio station came from the kitchen where Beth had obviously been keeping herself busy.

'Please sit,' Beth instructed.

'Thank you. We've had a couple of developments. None of which bring us any closer to finding Gabriel, but we have located his car.'

Beth sat forward as though this news was going to lead to something revelatory even though Stacey had tried to manage expectations before speaking.

'Where?'

'Not far from New Street station.'

'Birmingham?' she asked, scrunching up her nose. She shook her head. 'He hates crowded places. Someone must have taken his car, stolen it and dumped it.'

'The car was locked and didn't appear to have been tampered with.'

'Oh.'

Beth seemed to be forgetting the small matter of Gabriel withdrawing a large amount of money.

'I've spoken with Craig, and Gabriel hasn't been in touch with him.'

'Why would he if he's in hospital somewhere with amnesia?'

Oh dear, this was going to be harder than she'd thought. Maybe she could buy a little time until the penny dropped without her having to force it.

'He told me they haven't spoken since your wedding day.'

Beth closed her eyes for a second and shook her head. 'Oh, it was just awful. We had a dance towards the end of the night and his hands were all over me, running up and down my body. I tried to get away from him, but he kept pulling me closer and telling me I'd married the wrong brother.' She shuddered. 'The memory still makes me nauseous. I ran to the bathroom trying to hide my tears, but one of his cousins saw me in there trying to get myself together. I refused to tell Gabe at first; they were brothers. I knew how close they were. I didn't want to spoil that, but he just kept badgering me until I blurted it out. There was a huge argument and they haven't spoken since.'

'Did Gabriel ever talk about trying to patch things up?'

Beth shook her head. 'He would never have placed me in the position of having to spend time around him. Just the thought of it makes my skin crawl. I'm sorry you wasted your time, but Gabe would never contact Craig.'

Stacey nodded her agreement.

'So can you see on CCTV who drove the car? Maybe the direction in which they went?'

Stacey shook her head. 'No CCTV on this particular car park. His passport wasn't in the car, but his phone was.'

'That proves someone must have taken him. Gabe would never just leave his phone.'

The penny hadn't dropped and it was clear to Stacey that it wasn't going to.

'We think he did exactly that, Beth.'

'Wh... What?'

'Given that your husband withdrew a large sum of money on the morning he disappeared, parked his car close to a very busy train station and left his phone, it leads us to believe that Gabriel has decided to take some time out, away from his job, away from everything.'

'No. No. No. I don't believe it. He wouldn't let me worry in that way. He'd at least let me know he was safe. I think you're adding two and two and getting five. There could be any number of reasons for the money and the passport. He wouldn't just up and leave. You have to understand how close we are. We are everything to each other.'

Stacey took a breath. 'He may have decided to take some time to think things through, get his head straight.'

'About what?'

'Beth, there's no easy way to tell you this but it seems that Gabriel was developing feelings for someone else.'

Beth's mouth fell open and she stared for the longest minute.

'No chance. That's rubbish. Gabe would never cheat...'

'Nothing physical,' Stacey clarified. 'It's more of an emotional connection.'

Too late, Stacey realised that was probably the worst thing she could have said, but the truth wasn't hers to censor.

'No. I'm sorry but nothing of the sort was going on either

physically, emotionally or any other way. I would have known.'
She narrowed her eyes. 'Who told you this nonsense?'

'A colleague of Gabriel's has...'

'It's that Wendy Clarke, isn't it? The divorced woman who
couldn't stop making googly eyes at him at a Christmas party.
She's clearly a fantasist. You shouldn't believe anything she
says. It's wishful thinking on her behalf.'

'I'm afraid we do believe her, Beth. It all makes sense,'
Stacey said, fighting down the nagging doubt in her mind that
she was missing something. She still couldn't completely recon-
cile the picture of the polite, professional, hard-working Gabriel
with the man who had walked out on his wife without a word.
But the evidence said otherwise, and given that she had no clear
reason for her unease, the boss wouldn't let her spend another
second guessing her own findings.

She swallowed and continued. 'I think Gabriel needs some
time to clear his head and he'll be back soon,' Stacey said,
reaching across and squeezing Beth's hand.

She snatched it away. 'I suppose this means you're going to
scale down the search, stop actively looking for him because
you're convinced he's gone off to find himself.'

'There will still be observations, and the missing persons
record will remain open until he's found, but there's little more
we can do to actively investigate his—'

'Get out,' Beth said, standing.

'Please try to—'

'I mean it,' Beth said, pointing to the door. 'I trusted you and
you've completely let me down. Leave my house and don't ever
come back.'

Stacey gave her one last look before doing exactly as she'd
been asked.

FORTY-NINE

'If you're sitting comfortably, I'll begin,' Stephanie said, folding her legs beneath her again. Three mugs of coffee had been placed on the side table.

Her voice and tone were still the right side of cocky, but it was as though she'd now donned the attitude as a defence mechanism. Whatever it was she had to say, she was already in self-protection mode.

'The first day or two in there is okay. You talk with counsellors, you have group meetings where everyone discusses their reasons for wanting to change their sexuality. On day three they begin the therapy – aversion therapy.'

'We've seen the chair,' Kim said.

'No, you haven't,' Stephanie answered. 'If you've been given the guided tour, you'll have seen the show chair. That's child's play. I'm willing to bet you never made it to the third floor cos that's where the real fun happens. The show chair gives you a little buzz. You can feel it but it's nothing compared to the real one. There's no massaging on that one.'

And this was the exact reason Kim had wanted to speak to

an ex-patient. She wasn't going to get the truth from the guided tour.

'How does it work?'

'You're hooked up to a machine with electrodes all over your body, including your head. It's like a lie detector but extra. It measures your emotional responses. If you react in any way to the stimulus, you get a shock.'

'Can't you just get up?'

Stephanie shook her head and pointed to her wrists. 'You're tied in position. Obviously you're not told how bad it's going to be or how long you're going to be there, and once they lock the door and turn off the lights, it's just you and the big screen. Your sense of time and reality begin to blur. The screen never goes off. They start with pictures and videos of straight couples – having dinner, walking on the beach – and then straight into girl-on-girl action. You instantly get a good shock. Doesn't matter if you close your eyes, the sounds are still there. The videos get worse and more graphic, and the shocks get longer and more intense.'

'How long are you in the chair?'

'Depends on how long it takes your mind to give in.'

Kim thought about the scars on Jamie's wrists. She was guessing it had taken him a while.

'How long for you?'

'Twenty-seven hours.'

'Jesus Christ,' Bryant cursed.

'But how does your mind adjust?' Kim asked, trying to imagine the horror of what she was being told.

'Do you love or hate Marmite, Inspector?'

'Hate it.'

'After being shocked for hours on end, trust me – you're gonna want to give it a try.'

'Are you saying it worked?' Kim asked.

'I'm saying it does what it says on the tin. It's aversion therapy. It makes you want to avoid it. A week after I left, I saw two women on telly holding hands. I threw up.'

Bryant shook his head in despair.

'It's okay. I'm on the mend now. It was the worst time of my life, but I've been getting help to accept my sexuality.' She smiled. 'I've actually got a date tomorrow. First one ever.'

'Congratulations.'

'Thank you. Megan has been awesome.'

'Megan Shaw?'

'Yes, do you know her?'

'We've met. She works many of these cases it seems.'

'Because she can talk from experience. She faced her own identity demons and came out the other side. She understands exactly what we're going through.'

Kim hadn't realised but there was no good reason why she should.

'You said you got out before it got worse. What did you mean?'

'The chair is the tip of the iceberg. There are other, more forceful methods. The withholding or force-feeding of food, forced prayer, beatings, emotional and physical intimidation. I was forced to wear skirts and high heels. I was forced to wear make-up to feminise me – and worse.'

Kim wondered what was worse than the things she was already describing.

She waited.

'Corrective rape.'

'What?' Bryant asked with horror.

Stephanie nodded. 'It goes on. And it's happened there. I don't know any more details for sure, but it's definitely happened.'

Kim immediately thought of Sarah. Had she been raped? Was that why she had given the child to her parents to raise?

She made a mental note to ask for a DNA sample from the child. It was knowing who to match it to.

'I know you said you don't know any more details but can you point us in the direction of anyone else who would be willing to talk to us?'

Stephanie shook her head. 'Not likely. Not with those NDAs in place.'

'No one?' Kim pushed.

Stephanie sighed and looked to Bryant. 'She always this persistent?'

Bryant nodded. 'Oh yeah. She's not even warmed up yet.'

'Okay, there was a guy named John Dermot. We weren't supposed to know last names, but we once had a late-night chat and he let it slip. Don't know where he lives or if he'd even talk to you, but he was there at the same time as me.'

'Okay, Stephanie, thank you for talking to us about—'

'Aren't you going to ask me about the text?'

'Text?'

'I thought that was what had prompted you to get my details in the first place.'

'As I said, I saw your form by accident and we wanted to speak to someone with first-hand experience.' Kim sat back down. 'What's this about a text?'

Stephanie took her phone from her back pocket before answering. 'I made friends with someone in there. A man, Jerry, in his fifties. He's a kitchen hand, been there for years. He knew what went on there, but he was scared to say anything for fear of losing his job.' She opened up her phone. 'He sent me a text on Friday.'

Kim took the phone that was offered and read the exchange.

Jerry: Get ready shit's gonna hit the fan.

Stephanie: What shit???

Jerry: Got a letter out. Trustworthy guy. Put it in his bag.

Stephanie: Who???

Jerry: Gotta go speak soon.

Stephanie: It's been 2 days. Nothing yet.

Stephanie: What's going on?

Stephanie: Is everything ok?

The last message had been sent by Stephanie the day before. The last three messages had been delivered but not read.

'He stopped answering and I don't know why.'

Kim had no idea why either, but she did know she'd been shown around the kitchen earlier that day and there'd been absolutely no sign of a kitchen hand.

FIFTY

Stacey's shoulders were still carrying the weight of Beth's emotional outburst when she walked back into the squad room. She had argued with Burns to take the case on, so sure that such a loving and committed husband wouldn't just run out on his wife, and all evidence was pointing towards Burns having been right. That fact wasn't helping her mood one bit.

'Yay, the cavalry is here,' Penn said as she took a seat.

And that was exactly why she needed to blow it off. There was no more she could do, and another case needed her attention.

'Okay, where do you want me?'

'I'm waiting on the phone records, actual phone and computer from Liam Sachs so he's on hold for now. My first sweep for information on Charles Stamoran and Lorraine Abbott of Exodus has turned up very little and I'm now onto the Gardners and the clinic.'

'Okay, I'll take Exodus and you stick with the Gardners. Anything interesting so far?'

Penn sighed. 'Not a lot on the clinic and that's the problem. The website doesn't offer names of any staff members, or practitioners as they're called. I can't even find out what exactly a practitioner is qualified to do. The website mentions only that Celia was raised and schooled in the Black Country before attending university. The rest of the blurb is about her wanting to help people feel comfortable in their own skin.'

'Isn't that strange?' Stacey asked as a thought occurred to her.

'What?'

'Celia and Megan. They're a similar age, both gay, both brought up in the same area but with totally opposing views on how best to help folks feel better about themselves.'

'Yeah, but only one of them forces their patients to sign NDAs; actually that's both staff and patients so I can understand why there's not much out there on the internet to find, but—'

'You gotta wonder why they have to sign non-disclosure agreements though?' Stacey said. 'If the treatment they offer is all above board and they wholeheartedly believe in what they're doing, why is no one allowed to speak about it?'

'Good question,' Penn answered. 'Although I'm not sure where corrective rape falls in the list of approved treatment methods.'

Stacey felt her mouth fall open. 'No way that goes on there.'

Since the term conversion therapy had come up, Stacey had made it her business to find out more and educate herself. She now knew that Ecuador had more than two hundred treatment clinics that operated under the guise of drug addiction centres. She knew that although homosexuality had been legal since 1997, men and women were lifted from the streets and imprisoned in these treatment centres.

She'd read the story of a lesbian photographer who had gone undercover in one of these centres. She'd seen evidence of forced prayer, withholding food, force-feeding, emotional and physical abuse, beatings and corrective rape. Patients were only allowed to check out once they were believed to have been cured. In some South American countries, the network was vast and full of corruption. But that kind of thing couldn't happen here, she'd assured herself. These facilities were regulated, inspected.

'I can see the doubts on your face,' Penn said. 'But the source is credible and the boss is on her way back there now. Something about the third floor. She's got a name for us to look up.'

He pushed a Post-it note towards her, but Stacey's mind had gone into overdrive. 'If there's anything like that going on, people will have talked or tried to take action.'

Penn shook his head. 'No scandal, nothing.'

'Then you might be looking in the wrong place,' Stacey said. 'Go through their financials in more detail. If they've kept people quiet, it's going to have cost them a lot of money.'

FIFTY-ONE

'You're making a mistake, guv,' Bryant said as he headed back to Bridgnorth.

As honest as he was with her, he didn't normally phrase his doubts so clearly.

'You don't believe her?' she asked, wondering if he'd been in the same room. There was nothing in Stephanie's story, tone or demeanour that had caused her to doubt a single word.

'I absolutely do believe her, and that's the problem,' he said, pulling into a lay-by.

'Bryant, keep driving.'

'Just hear me out,' he said, switching off the engine. 'Did you even know the place existed?'

She shook her head. 'No, but I'd still prefer to be having this conversation with the car moving.'

'As police officers we had no knowledge of it.'

'Not our jurisdiction,' she defended.

'It's seventeen miles away from our station, a forty-minute drive. It's not the other side of the country. We've not heard any reports or rumours of wrongdoing. Not one. Penn worked for West Mercia and hadn't heard of it.'

'You're still sounding like you don't believe Stephanie.'

'Guv, work with me. I do believe her, which means we shouldn't underestimate how clever they are. I know you want to storm in there and demand access to the third floor, but we both know that with that attitude, you're not gonna get past Jessica's reception desk. But more than that, you give them warning that we're actually looking. It's private property. They let you in once for the guided tour. As far as they're concerned, we left happy. Why tip your hand and give them reason to hide anything?'

'Aargh,' she said, focussing all her frustration into that one cry. What she really wanted to do was go back there, punch someone in the face on behalf of Stephanie, Jamie, Sarah and anyone else that might have suffered at their hands. But another part of her knew when Bryant had a good point.

'Do you have to be quite so sensible at the points of an investigation when I really don't want you to be?'

'You can thank me later,' he said, starting the engine. 'Once we've got that search warrant signed and sealed, and we can go back and have a proper look.'

'Okay, head back to the—' She stopped speaking as her phone rang.

'Go ahead, Stace,' Kim said, answering the call.

'I've got a John Dermot, lives in a place called Stableford just six miles out of Bridgnorth.'

'Sounds good,' Kim said. 'Got anything else?'

'Not yet, but if you start heading towards, I'll do a bit more digging. I've sent the address to Bryant.'

'Good work, Stace,' Kim said, ending the call.

'Got it,' Bryant said keying in the postcode from the text message.

'Surely it's the same— Bloody hell,' she cursed as her phone rang again.

She was surprised. This caller didn't ring her direct very often.

'What's up, Mitch?' She had last seen him what felt like days ago at the crime scene of Liam Sachs.

'Our guy here might not be related to your case,' he said, telling her he was still at the house.

'Found something on the tech?' she asked.

'No. The computer and phone are already at Ridgepoint for fingerprinting and DNA. They'll be with your guys in the morning if you still want them.'

'Why wouldn't we?' Kim asked.

'Because once we'd removed the body and taken samples from the immediate area, we moved the seat he'd been sitting on.' He paused. 'We found a note. A suicide note.'

FIFTY-TWO

Kim took a few moments of the journey to read up on the village of Stableford. Classed as an affluent area, the properties were mainly detached with only four flats listed and no social housing provision at all. Statistics claimed that the population of just over three hundred was ninety-nine per cent white and that it was populated by an even mix of fully employed, self-employed and retired. In the last month, two crimes had been reported.

'It's a bloody hotbed,' Kim said as Bryant drove past the village hall.

'And here we are,' Bryant said, pulling onto a gravel driveway. A wooden gate had been propped open with some kind of ornamental rock.

They were guided through an arch of sycamore trees towards a stone country house, drowning under vines of wisteria and ivy. She guessed the house to be four to five bedrooms, but there were many outbuildings and what looked like a self-contained annexe behind the main house.

Accommodation also appeared to have been fashioned above a three-car garage.

'Hello there,' called a voice from the side of the house. The man heading towards them was early twenties with dark floppy hair that fell over a tanned and handsome face. He was wearing riding gear with a skull cap tucked under his left armpit and a riding crop in his left hand.

'John Dermot?' Kim asked.

'The third,' he said, nodding. 'Who's asking?'

She and Bryant produced their IDs as she introduced them both.

'Oh, thank God the parents are away. They'd just die of embarrassment having police turn up to the house. Mercifully you're not in a panda car or Mrs Fitzsimmons would have had a field day. She's the neighbour, and one of her cameras can just about reach to this spot here,' he said, moving two feet to the left. He held up and waved his middle finger. 'Just in case. Snotty bitch.'

'Err... Mr Dermot, may we take a minute of your time?'

'Of course. I don't think I've been a witness to anything illegal. Immoral probably, but that's another story.'

Kim stepped towards the house.

'Not that way, Inspector. I live over here.'

They followed him to the car port and up a set of wooden steps that led to the floor above.

He opened the door for them to enter. Kim caught a whiff of alcohol as she passed him in the doorway.

'Nice place,' Bryant said, stepping in behind her, and Kim had to agree.

The first room was a lounge-cum-TV-room with double-aspect windows showing views of open countryside to the rear. One entire wall was taken up with a huge television and entertainment centre including music system and at least two gaming consoles. Beyond this room she could see a light and airy kitchen with modern units and appliances.

'The bedroom and bathroom are just off the kitchen, but I'm guessing you don't want to see them.'

'Here is fine,' she said, taking the end seat on one of the oversize sofas. Bryant took the other end seat.

The man put his skull cap on a chair in the corner, and the clinking of glass told her he was fixing himself a drink.

He turned and the crystal tumbler was half full with a generous measure of golden-brown liquid. A glance behind him told her it was single malt whisky.

'So how may I help you, Inspector?' he asked, taking a seat opposite and snaking his free arm along the top of the sofa.

'Mr Dermot, we'd like to—'

'John, please.'

'Okay, John, we'd like to talk to you about a clinic called Change just down the road in Bridgnorth.'

He took a good drink. 'Okay,' he said, giving nothing away.

'We understand you spent time there.'

For the first time the hint of a frown shaped his features. 'How would you know that?'

'We understand that you signed an NDA, but would you be prepared to talk to us off the record?'

'Somewhat,' he answered cryptically.

Kim waited.

'If you ask me questions, I'll either answer or I won't, so go ahead.'

'What led you to the clinic?' Kim asked. She understood that John had been there at the same time as Stephanie, which had been last year. He was an adult. What had driven him to want to change his sexuality?

'My parents.'

'Can you elaborate?' Kim said.

'I've always known my parents' view on homosexuality. I'd never come out to them for fear of their reaction, but Mrs bloody Fitzsimmons had other ideas. She's the nosey bitch next door that caught me giving the gardener a blow job and told my parents. I should have resisted, but my goodness he was gorgeous and couldn't speak a word of English. He didn't need to. It wasn't his conversation skills I was—'

'So what happened?'

John continued after he'd poured another drink. 'Well obviously they wanted me cured, so they found this place who said they could rid me of the sickness and off I went.'

'But you were an adult. Your parents couldn't force you.'

He pulled a face. 'Not physically no, but there are other ways.'

Kim waited.

'I was told that if I didn't get help, I'd be cut off financially. Thrown out and disinherited. I'm a material guy. I love my life. I'm not very good at anything. I've never worked a day in my life and I don't intend to start now. I love being wealthy so they really left me no choice.'

'So you're cured?' Bryant asked doubtfully.

'Absolutely,' he said with a wide smile.

'Really?' Kim asked.

John laughed. 'Of course not, but I no longer shit on my own doorstep. I satisfy my desires miles away from this house, this village and the prying eyes and cameras of Mrs Fitzsimmons. Every month or so I bring back one of my girlfriends for a supposed nightcap and that keeps my parents off my back. It's a great plan with years of mileage left in it yet.'

Kim was trying to understand why she hadn't yet taken a dislike to this young man. He was rich, privileged, entitled and deceitful to his parents, and yet open and honest with them.

'Will you tell us about your time at the clinic?' she asked.

'Not really,' he said, shaking his head.

'Because of the NDA?' Bryant asked.

'Fuck the NDA. No, I deal with unpleasant things by pretending they never happened, officers. I put them in boxes and throw away the key. I am able to disassociate myself from past events and move on,' he said, taking a gulp of his drink.

The slight trembling of his hand said otherwise, but as someone who handled pain the same way, she couldn't really push him. But it meant she knew what to ask.

'Fair enough, but we're just trying to fully understand what goes on there.'

'It is a hell hole that has no place being in existence,' he said, taking another gulp.

'Could you share anything that you saw? Something that happened to someone else while you were there?' she asked.

He considered for a minute.

'Yeah, actually there was this one guy, jeez, he had a rough time of it. They threw everything at him. Cocky little shit at times. Reminded me of Jack Nicholson in that crazy film,' he said, clicking his fingers to remember.

'*One Flew Over the Cuckoo's Nest*,' Bryant supplied.

'That's the one. Yeah. We called him Jack, and they threw the works at him. They tailor your treatment plan to play on your worst fears, you see. Jack's fear was being disowned by his parents. They start off small and increase the pressure every couple of days. He had the shocks and stuff, but they didn't seem to bother him as much as the videos. Over and over again. Parents telling their kids they were disgusting, they were unclean, they were inferior, despicable. They showed Jack this one video of a guy who was kicked out of his home. He had nowhere to go so he ended up on the streets. He was on his own, no job, no money and beaten almost every night, while being called the most horrific names. Sometimes it was gay bashing and other times it was by other homeless guys. I think they got to Jack a bit because they just kept showing videos of this poor kid with nowhere to go, no friends or family, and he couldn't bear the thought of being alone.

'He was a spirited kid but he had his limits.' He smiled and raised his eyes upwards. 'I remember one time that Jack refused to belittle another guy in the group meeting. The lad had failed to hide his erection when the counsellor was talking about lewd acts. Everyone was supposed to kick him in the nuts, but Jack wouldn't do it so he got the hat.'

'Hat?' Kim asked.

'Yeah. It was big like a witch's hat but with a big D on it for Dunce. You had to wear it all day. Just the hat, no clothes, not even underwear. If you had the hat on it meant you got no food or water except a sip to take two tablets. And then you were supervised on the toilet.'

'For what reason?' Kim asked.

'So you couldn't use the toilet paper.'

Bryant got it first. 'The tablets were laxatives?'

John nodded. 'Jack had to walk round in that state all day.'

Kim swallowed back the emotion as John continued.

'They test you, you know. They tested Jack. They got one of the other patients to come on to him, give him the eye. Jack forgot himself and responded.'

'What happened to Jack?' Kim asked.

'They got him in the end, didn't they? In the film. He was lobotomised. They took his spirit. It was the same with Jack at the clinic. Made the poor kid cry his eyes out and beg for mercy.'

'Corrective rape has been mentioned,' Kim said, sensing where this was going.

John nodded. 'Corrective rape for the ladies and punishment for the boys if necessary.'

'Why would it be necessary?' Kim asked.

'To show Jack how foul and disgusting the act was. It wasn't sex. It wasn't consensual. It was rough and painful, brutal. That's what rape is. He curled into a ball and cried for his mum. They broke him in the end in the worst possible way. Jack was helpless, weakened, violated, broken.'

His voice croaked on the last word.

Bryant leaned forward. 'Did Jack know the name of…?'

'Never mind,' Kim said, standing.

'But if—'

'Enough, Bryant, we're done,' she said, taking a card from her pocket. 'Thank you for sharing Jack's story with us, and if you ever want to talk to someone about what happened to you, give me a call. I think we might know someone that can help.'

'I'm good,' he said with a smile. 'It's safely packed away in the boxes,' he said, tapping his temple.

'Just in case,' she insisted.

He took it and saw them to the door.

Bryant didn't speak until they were at the bottom of the steps. 'Guv, we could have got more. Maybe even a name.'

'Yes we could, Bryant, but at what cost?' she said, approaching the car. John wasn't ready to face his experience at the clinic the way Stephanie had.

That had been *his* story. They had been his fears. That was his tailored treatment plan they had forced him to recount. They were edging into territory that they didn't understand. They weren't professionals ready to deal with the aftermath of his pain because one thing was crystal clear.

There would come a time when John would realise that these things hadn't happened to someone else.

FIFTY-THREE

My eyes open and the rest of my senses take a little while to catch up.

The darkness is still dense. It's as though I haven't yet raised my lids. I blink twice to prove the fact to myself.

For the first time I can hear something in the distance. It's voices – or music. My mouth opens to cry out. I stop myself. Think first. Get the energy to make it count. Plan ahead.

The stiffness in my body is getting worse. My back has a line of pain stretching across the top of my buttocks. As I do the mental inspection of my limbs, I note that my arms have been brought to the front. Again. My mouth is uncovered. Again.

My heart leaps with excitement. That can only mean one thing.

The aroma of food breaks through the stale damp smell that has taken residence in my nostrils.

I feel in front of me, between my legs. There is a plate. I examine it like a blind person touching facial features. I want to know everything about it.

There is bread, a bun. I smell onions. There is a burger,

cheese, salad and fries. I know I must be dreaming until I manage to pick up the bun with both hands.

As it travels towards my mouth, I recall my stubbornness with the sandwich. The stand I tried to make about control. The lesson I learned. My mind would like to try and resist, but my body slaps the thought away.

I bite into the burger. It's real. Never have I tasted anything so wondrous in my life. I take another bite before I've swallowed the first. The cheese has melted onto the burger. It is like velvet in my mouth. I chew slowly and deliberately. Even the sensation of chewing is something to be treasured. How did I take such a thing for granted? I fight back the tears that threaten to spill out of my eyes. Two bites of a burger have brought every emotion swirling around my head to the fore. But mostly I am grateful. This is food and I am eating. Right now, it's enough.

After chewing the third bite, my jaw tires, but I want more. I bite off another mouthful and leave it sitting inside my mouth as I try to gather the strength to chew again.

I want more but I can't eat more. The fatigue is already starting to creep towards me.

I remember the music. It's low but I can still hear it. I want to shout, but I don't have the strength. I realise I made a choice. Eat or shout.

I swallow down the last bite of food before it moves to the back of my throat and chokes me.

My eyelids are drooping even though I want to stay awake.

I will rest for a short while and then use the strength from the food I've eaten to shout later.

Maybe then I'll finally see my captor so I can ask them: why do they want me and when are they going to let me go?

FIFTY-FOUR

'Okay, gang, it's been quite the day,' Kim said, sitting on the edge of the spare desk.

'If we can do a five-minute round robin before you go, starting with Bryant.'

'Guv, you were with me the whole—'

'Yeah, but they weren't and I'm parched,' she said, reaching for her coffee.

'Rightyo, we began the day at the torture chamber otherwise known as Change. All outward appearances offer no clue to what actually goes on. Obviously, we were given the tourist tour. We met the owners—'

'Bryant, it's called briefing for a reason – come on already,' she interrupted, tapping her watch.

'I'm being thorough. During our visit, the guv accidentally acquired the personal details of Stephanie Lakehurst, a previous patient at the clinic. We know that Jamie spent time there under his parents' instruction and that Sarah went there of her own accord. We learned that—'

'Okay, enough. I'll take it from here cos you brief as fast as you drive. We have a potential third victim who now appears to have left a note. Penn, it'll be here first thing tomorrow. Liam's wife has apparently confirmed that the writing is Liam's, but I still want you to look for any hint or clue this isn't genuine. Understandably, she's in shock. His phone and computer will be here too. We've spoken to John Dermot, who has confirmed Stephanie's account of treatment at the clinic. It truly is horrific and has no place being open at all.'

John's words about Jack's experience had been ringing in her ears all the way home. She just hoped that when the day came for John to open those boxes, he had the right support network around him. With everything they were learning, she needed everyone's full attention.

She turned to the constable. 'Stace, I'm gonna need you to shelve—'

'Already done, boss. I'll take over all the digging on Exodus, the Gardners and Liam Sachs while Penn deals with the tech.'

'Thanks, Stace. Any progress on tracking your guy down yet?'

Stacey shook her head.

Gabriel Denton was going to have to wait.

'Penn?'

'Financials are all in order for Change. They make good money, but they also shell a lot out.'

'Go on,' Kim said as the small hand on the wall clock grew ever closer to the seven.

'Every few months, at least twice, maybe three times annually they make a payment. It's always to different individuals and for different amounts but always high five figures. The highest is ninety-seven and the lowest is eighty-four. There's no explanation specifically in the accounts, and they appear to be included in the overheads.'

'That's some expensive lighting they've got there,' Bryant observed.

'What are your thoughts?' Kim asked.

Penn nodded towards Stacey. 'My learned colleague over there thinks they could be payoffs, settlements to unhappy customers.'

'Interesting,' Kim noted as Penn's phone buzzed.

He frowned as he glanced at the lit screen. 'Boss may I...?'

'Go ahead.'

He picked up the phone and read quickly.

'Oh shit, boss, I gotta... It's Jasper...'

'Go. Go. Go,' she said, aware of the toll such long hours took on family life.

He was out of the door in seconds.

'Drive safely,' she called after him.

'Actually, all go,' she said. 'There's nothing that can't wait until tomorrow.'

Stacey didn't need telling twice and was out of the office in under a minute.

'You ready?' Bryant asked.

She shook her head. 'Not yet. I'll get a car to drop me back once I'm done, and before you ask, yes I'm sure.'

Bryant grabbed his coat. 'In that case I'll go and offer my chauffeuring service to the female tornado what just whipped out of here.'

'Six forty-five,' she said as he headed out the door. A brief wave confirmed he'd heard.

She wanted to take one more good look at the application for the search warrant. She was giving the magistrate no reason to bounce it back to her.

Bryant had been right to exercise caution earlier. She wanted the element of surprise; but with or without the search warrant, tomorrow she was getting back inside that clinic.

FIFTY-FIVE

It was 7.20 p.m. when Kim got the call that the car would be with her in ten minutes.

She grabbed her jacket and headed downstairs to catch a bit of fresh air before the squad car arrived. She still hadn't shaken the meeting with John Dermot, and she seriously hoped that Megan Shaw had some time free in her schedule because Kim planned on sending every damaged soul they found her way.

She headed out of the building and zipped up her leather jacket. The temperature had taken a dive into the single figures.

She walked down to the wall that encircled the station so the squad car could just pull up on the road.

'What the...?' she exclaimed as a shadow rose up behind her.

Her heart leaped into her mouth as she swung her arm out and caught the figure in the stomach. Her heart was beating rapidly as a hand grabbed at her throat. She stumbled backwards but managed to stop herself from falling.

The smell of alcohol wafted towards her.

'Stone, I want a fucking word with you.'

She grabbed the hand at her throat by the wrist and turned it.

'Burns, what the hell do you think you're playing at?'

He swayed to the left and then the right and then almost fell against her. She moved out of the way and let him fall to the ground.

He groaned and then looked up, trying to focus on her face.

The man was blind drunk.

She stood over him and peered down at him, making no effort to hide the disgust on her face. 'You dare to try that on me after what happened, you stupid bastard!'

Suddenly, the anger infused her entire being. Rage tore through her whole body. How many more men were going to think they could put their hands on her and get away with it?

Her fists clenched, and every cell ached to punch the living shit out of him. It would be so easy to just let go. To let him have every ounce of frustration that had been festering inside her for the last two months.

'You think you're all that, Stone. You've got the respect of your superiors because you do everything right. You're a sancti-monious, arse-crawling bitch that tries to make everyone else look stupid.'

'I do my job, Burns. All of it. Not just the nice bits. Not just the bits that will get me noticed. Not just the soundbites or the press conferences. I bloody graft. I talk to people. I find out shit. I investigate. Looking stupid is something you've managed to achieve all on your own.'

'Everyone knows you're sucking the dick of—'

'Now you're reaching, Burns. You can say many things about me, but ain't nobody gonna believe that shit.'

'You threw me out the squad room,' he said, sounding like a five-year-old who hadn't been allowed a biscuit before bed.

'Grow the hell up and take a good look at yourself. I'm not the reason you're in Siberia with the brass. You messed up the

Symes case and you didn't even learn from that. You came to *my* team and carried on the way you always have, except people see you now for the lazy, arrogant shitbag you've always been, and no one wants you on their team.'

'It's all your fault. If you hadn't offered yourself to that psycho I'd have caught him and I'd be—'

'No you wouldn't cos you'd have still found some way to mess it up. You were moved here because there was nowhere else to put you. But do you wanna know the irony of this? You could have redeemed yourself by now. If you'd just listened to the one person you were determined to belittle and treat like shit, you'd now be working on the biggest case of your career. The case was right in front of you, and the person who was trying to tell you was too busy making your tea.'

He sobered, realising that she was speaking the truth. Stacey had tried to get him to investigate the death of Jamie Mills and he'd refused to listen.

'It's all your fault,' he repeated, demonstrating that neither drunk nor sober did he possess the ability to listen.

'Oh, sort yourself out, you useless sack of shit,' she said as the car pulled up at the entrance to the car park.

'I'm not done with you yet, Stone,' he called after her.

'Next time come see me before you go to the pub. At least that way you'll have a fighting chance,' she said before getting into the car.

FIFTY-SIX

Penn tried to keep his foot from pushing down on the accelerator pedal. The last thing he wanted was a speeding ticket and the delay of being pulled over.

The text had said that Jasper had burned himself on the oven. He'd tried to call but had eventually gone through to voicemail. He'd sent a short message saying he was on his way.

He tried to fight down the guilt. Had he caused this? Had he somehow willed this to happen to ensure Jasper's continued dependency on him? The feelings running through him were old friends: fear for his brother's safety and well-being, the state of alertness to be ready and available for anything Jasper needed. Except he hadn't felt this way in quite a while. He'd enjoyed the respite, the peace from the constant fight-or-flight state of being. He'd taken it for granted, he'd got used to it, he had relaxed, and now the old feelings were back. His stomach was in knots, his mind was racing with thoughts of something bad happening to his brother. He hadn't taken the time to enjoy the freedom of Jasper's increased independence and now he was right back in it.

They were not feelings he'd missed, he thought as he dumped the car in front of the house.

He rushed in and headed straight through to the kitchen.

He stopped dead.

Lynne was sitting at the kitchen table beside his brother, who had a bandaged hand.

Just for one second, his brother's injury was forgotten as his lungs forgot to breathe. He hadn't seen her for over two months and his heart suddenly felt every one of those moments.

He pulled himself together. His brother was injured.

'Lynne, what are you doing here?' he asked, moving towards Jasper, who was smiling apologetically.

'Second contact,' Jasper said.

Penn had forgotten. It was his own instruction that if he hurt himself in any way, he was to try next door or call Lynne, who he had known for years.

Penn nodded towards the wall that separated them from the neighbours.

'Bingo night,' Jasper said.

'I don't mind,' Lynne said. 'It's not like I was doing anything.'

Penn so wanted to read something into that, but their last meeting hadn't ended well when Stacey had turned up and disturbed their first real date.

'Does he need the hospital?' Penn asked.

Lynne stood. 'No, I don't think it's a hospital visit this time.'

Penn wanted her to sit back down. He wasn't ready for her to leave.

'Take a look while I put the kettle on.'

Ah, she was staying at least long enough to have a cuppa. He relaxed.

'Okay, buddy.'

He took Jasper's hand and began to gently unwrap the bandage.

'Where's it hurt, bud?' he asked.

Jasper pointed to the skin on Penn's hand that stretched between the thumb and the forefinger.

Lynne turned and leaned against the cooker with her arms folded.

Penn continued to unwrap the bandage until he reached the dressing that had been expertly applied.

'I'm gonna just take a quick look,' he said, touching around the area. 'I'll be as gentle as I can be.'

Jasper looked unconcerned.

Penn lifted the dressing gently to find a pale pink blemish no bigger than a few millimetres.

Jasper followed his gaze. His eyes widened. 'It's a miracle,' he said in wonder.

Penn looked to Lynne, who shrugged. 'He insisted on the bandage.'

'Jasper?' Penn asked, feeling the last drops of fear slip away.

'I'll live, Ozzy,' he said with great relief.

Penn was about to ask him what the hell was going on when he heard a car horn out the front.

Penn looked to his brother who smiled widely.

'Oobah.'

'You've ordered an Uber?'

Jasper stood and did a couple of dance moves before grabbing his jacket.

'See ya.'

And just like that he was gone.

Penn felt as though he'd been hit with a sledgehammer.

Lynne placed the two mugs on the table and sat.

'And just in case you were in any doubt, when I got here, the oven wasn't even on.'

Penn burst out laughing. He wasn't sure if it was the relief that Jasper was okay or because Lynne was sitting here in front of him or because his brother had turned into a scheming little urchin.

Lynne joined in, and any tension between them was broken.

Penn sobered. He cupped both hands around his mug. 'I owe you an apology. That night I should have told you what was going on when Stacey turned up.'

'What? That a psychopath had escaped from prison and was threatening the life of your boss and possibly her team; that you were all under instruction to not be alone and that Stacey trusted you enough to come here. Yep, that would all have been good to know before I got huffy and walked out.'

'It's a lot to—'

'We do the same job, Penn. I would have got it. I'd have understood. You should have trusted me.'

The words made him feel like shit.

He changed the subject. 'What did Jasper say when you got here?'

Lynne smiled and didn't fight the subject change.

'He told me he burned himself, which I knew was a lie. Even minor burns are worse than that. He insisted I wrap it up to protect it from infection, which I did while he just talked away about nothing, how he does.' She looked away.

'What was he saying?' Penn asked, dreading the answer.

'Just that you were lonely and that you'd been missing me. That you'd called out my name in your sleep.'

'I didn't do that,' he protested.

Lynne laughed. 'Oh, but you admit to missing me.'

'Oh yeah,' he said honestly

'We are pretty good friends, aren't we?' Lynne asked.

He felt the disappointment grab at his stomach. Friends.

She finished her drink and pushed her chair back. 'We should meet up a couple of times each month for a pint and a pizza. Let off some steam and trash the job how we've always done, yeah?'

He nodded and tried not to show his misery as she reached for her jacket.

Two months ago, he'd felt there was no chance for the two of them and now he knew it for certain. The moment had passed and he'd accepted it.

It wasn't until he'd walked in and seen her sitting with his brother that the full force of his feelings had almost knocked him sideways.

He'd missed her to the point of not wanting to ever be without her again.

She had come to tend to his brother, and he would always be grateful for the bond they shared. But she had set out her stall, as his mum used to say. She'd set the boundaries, and it was a thick white line of friendship that he had no choice but to respect.

He followed her to the door, fighting the panic rising inside him. Even though she'd suggested meeting up as friends and keeping in touch, he had the alarming feeling that she was about to walk out of his life forever.

She opened the door and turned. 'Now be sure to tell that scheming brother of yours...' She stopped speaking as Penn cupped her head and placed his lips on hers.

Electricity surged through him immediately, prompting his mouth to deepen the kiss, searching for a reply.

His answer came as her own lips responded.

It wasn't the kiss of a friend.

FIFTY-SEVEN

'You have to be kidding me,' Kim said to Barney as the door camera appeared on her phone screen. The door siren sounded at the same time. 'What the hell is she doing here?'

Only twenty minutes ago she'd been screaming at a drunken idiot on the ground and now she had to deal with this.

She pressed the speaker button on her phone. 'Piss off. I'm out.'

Tracy Frost shook her head and folded her arms.

Kim was smug in the knowledge that the door was locked and the insufferable woman could ring all she liked, but she wasn't getting in.

The siren sounded again.

'Frost, bugger off,' she called through the microphone. 'I'm out. I'm operating this remotely.'

'Where are you?' she heard through the speaker.

'AA meeting, now naff off.'

The siren sounded again.

'You're a liar – we both know you don't go out.'

'Frost, I will happily do the time for your murder,' she shouted and then hoped no one was passing by.

The journalist was undeterred. 'You've gotta open the door to do it.'

'Jesus,' she cursed, stomping towards the door. She unlocked it and threw it open. 'You do know this is completely unacceptable, don't you?'

'I brought Barney a cupcake,' she said, holding out a plastic dog toy.

'He doesn't like toys,' she answered as Barney sat and wagged his tail.

'Bloody traitor,' she said as Frost gave him the toy. He pranced off and took it to his chewing rug. The squeaking started immediately. Kim found herself hoping he broke it quickly. It wasn't a noise she relished the thought of through the night.

'You want one?' she asked, pointing to the coffee machine. Anyone knew the way to her percolator was through kindness to her dog.

'Err... yeah,' Frost said, as though it was a no-brainer.

Frost had hobbled behind her on the impossibly high heels she always wore to mask the limp she'd had all her life. She preferred people to think she couldn't walk in the shoes than for them to know she had one leg shorter than the other.

'Can we get something straight?' Kim asked as Frost took a seat on one of her bar stools.

'Yep.'

'When I let you kip here for one night because your life was in danger, it wasn't like giving you keys to the city.'

'The what?' Frost asked, tossing her long blonde hair over her shoulder.

'It wasn't an open invitation. You're a reporter, allegedly. I'm a police officer. We don't like each other, and I am never gonna welcome your presence at crime scenes.'

'Absolutely, but you do have the best coffee,' she said, taking a sip of the Colombian Gold.

Yeah, it was true.

'So what do you want?' Kim asked.

'A quote about the sudden surge of suicides that aren't suicides.'

'Liar. You know full well I won't talk to you about an active case out in the field so I'm not gonna do it here. Real reason?'

'Come to see my buddy here. He misses me.'

Kim laughed. 'You were here for one night. He's had pig's ears that have lasted him longer than that. I can assure you that the sense of loss is on your side only. He's hardly sitting at your side begging for attention. He's too busy disembowelling that cupcake.'

Although, for some reason, the dog had seemed to take to her. Kim had no clue why, and it was the only time she'd doubted his intelligence and judgement.

'Hey, I left you in peace for two months,' Frost offered as though she'd done some kind of favour.

'I wasn't at work so I should bloody well think so.'

'And don't we know it. Your replacement was a knob.'

Kim couldn't help the chuckle that broke free from her mouth. Finally, something they agreed on.

'You still haven't told me why you're really here,' Kim repeated.

Frost pulled a face. 'I suppose it's all about my little toe.'

'Your what?' Kim asked, pulling a face. Frost was many things but she didn't normally talk in riddles. Maybe she had, finally, lost her mind.

'I had a corn on it for years. Kept using those corn plasters on the little bugger, but it wouldn't go. Finally got it dug out. Didn't need the plasters any more, but my shoes never felt right without it. I'd really got used to having the little fecker around.'

Kim thought for a moment without speaking. 'You know, Tuesday night, Bryant came to see me. Last night Ted Morgan dropped by, so it looks like the good Lord decided to forego the third wise man and go straight for the donkey.'

Frost threw back her head and roared with laughter. 'Oh my goodness, corns and donkeys,' she spluttered. 'I wonder if we'll ever get to a point where we admit we don't mind each other anywhere near as much as we used to.'

'I hope not, now drink your coffee and piss off. I've got shit to do.'

'What, like catch up with friends and family? You've got no family and your only friend is busy extracting the squeak from a plastic cupcake so I'm pretty much the best you've got.'

'Shoot me now.'

'Are you still having the nightmares?' Frost asked, sobering.

'What nightmares?' Kim asked, feeling a chill steal over her body.

'Oh, come on, Stone. Who the hell do you think you're dealing with?'

Kim said nothing.

Frost continued. 'See, I had this incident a few years back when some crazy person kidnapped me and tried to kill me cos of some incident at school. He didn't beat the shit out of me and neither did I actually die, but I had horrific nightmares for months afterwards and even still get 'em now.'

Kim folded her arms. She hadn't known about Frost's nightmares. 'What's that got to—?'

'The thing is, we're not talking about bad dreams where you wake up with relief that it isn't real. The ones where you wait an hour, shake it off and get on with your day. Oh no, they're not like that at all. These beauties startle you awake in the middle of the night with screams and salty, messy tears and a heart that feels like it's going to beat right out of your chest. These monsters wake you with a fear that makes your limbs tremble. There's no throwing these off with a pot of coffee and a couple of smokes. The memory of it lives in your pores for the whole day. You relive it, think about it, analyse it. They're evil little bastards because they attack you at your most vulnerable time, the time when your brain should be resting, taking a break from the memories which plague you when you're awake.'

'Okay, I get—'

'Yeah, I'm not done yet,' Frost continued after taking a sip of coffee. 'The worst thing is that no one can help you. You can do all the practical safety stuff with cameras and alarms. You can surround yourself with people every minute of the day, but you've got to sleep again some time. It's like *Nightmare on Elm Street*. No amount of coffee, dog walking, working or cold water splashed on your face is going to keep sleep away indefinitely. Your body is going to demand it, and there's no protection you can take into your dreams, so you fear going to sleep and you can't really share this with anyone for two reasons.'

Kim said nothing, which Frost took as permission to continue.

'The first is because no words have yet been invented to describe the absolute terror that these beasts induce. No one will ever get that you're not talking about normal nightmares unless they've experienced them. People will think you're being overdramatic cos at the end of the day it's not real so get over it. The second is that people will always default to the "but at least you're alive" setting. You should be grateful to be here. They feel that because you got through the actual ordeal, everything else is okay. You're alive so deal with it. What people don't understand is that in some ways, the nightmares are worse than the trauma itself.'

She paused again and Kim made no effort to interrupt her or stop her from speaking.

'The incident happened only once. The nightmares keep coming. You don't know when and there's something else that's impossible to explain. You feel even more helpless in the dreams than you did at the time. How ironic is that?'

'Did you try therapy?' Kim asked, unaware that Frost had suffered like this after an incident where they had both almost lost their lives.

Frost shook her head. 'I'm not good with therapists. Everything they say reminds me of a cliché or a line from a movie. I tried it once and I found myself arguing with everything she had to say, and the second she asked me about my relationship with my mother, I was gone. I read somewhere that around five per cent of the population are immune to hypnotherapy. I think it's the same with therapists. They help an awful lot of people but I'm just not one of them.'

Kim laughed. She couldn't have put that any better herself.

'Okay, what did you do instead?' Kim asked. Damn it, the woman had piqued her interest.

'I wrote it down. Everything. I detailed what happened in the nightmare and the way it made me feel. I threw up all over the page. Total vomit. There was no rhyme or reason or structure, I just got a pen and paper and wrote everything down. Didn't care how long it took or how much I wrote. I didn't stop until I had nothing left to say.'

'Did it help?'

Frost shrugged. 'Something did, but it didn't happen overnight. I just found that I had less to write down and they weren't coming as often. That was a win for me,' she said, finishing her drink. 'Right, great chat and thanks for the coffee, but I gotta go.'

Kim didn't try and stop her, but she did have one question to ask. 'What about the other thing?'

'What other thing?' Frost asked, walking towards the door.

'You know, the whole somebody saving your life thing and feeling beholden to them for what they did.'

'Well in my case that person was you so I didn't feel anything of the sort, but their actions are on them. You don't owe that person your life, and neither are you obliged to feel or display eternal gratitude. You simply say thank you and move on.'

'Okay,' Kim said, opening the door. 'Thanks for the visit, but if you do it again, I'm filing a restraining order.'

'Yeah, whatever,' Frost said, giving her a backwards wave.

Kim locked the door and leaned against it.

What to do with the rest of her night? It was too early for Barney's walk and her body was too exhausted for a treadmill session, yet her mind needed to do something.

'Damn you, Frost,' she said as she headed for the kitchen drawer to take out a notepad and pen.

FIFTY-EIGHT

'Okey-dokey, let's get cracking,' Kim said, taking her usual place in the squad room. She'd said nothing to Bryant on the way in of her altercation last night with Burns and it was going to stay that way. She knew Bryant well enough to surmise that he'd go looking for Burns to give him an earful or at the very least insist she tell Woody. Neither option was acceptable to her because she just wanted to focus on solving this case. Burns was finished now, and she hoped she wouldn't be seeing him again.

'Stacey, you done with your missing accountant?' she asked.

Stacey nodded. 'His description is still being circulated, but there's nothing more I can do at the minute.'

'Full attention on this case then. I still want to know every-thing about Charles Stamoran and his guard dog Lorraine Abbott. I want to know about Celia Gardner and her sexual identity transformation. I want to know exactly what happened the night before last with Liam Sachs and...' She paused. 'Is anyone writing this down?'

'Got it so far, boss,' Penn said. 'And just to say that Megan Shaw seems to be as clean as a whistle. Only daughter of couple who divorced when she was eleven. All her schooling was done around Tividale. Took some kind of gap year before going to Dudley College and then Loughborough University. Returned to the Black Country and set up her own practice. Financials are all in order. Not a prolific user of social media and appears to have no current partner.' He opened his hands expressively.

'That it?'

He nodded.

She hadn't expected any kind of smoking gun, but for some reason she was surprised that the woman was unattached.

'Moving on, I don't expect the search warrant for the clinic through yet but it doesn't hurt to chase it. The very second it lands I want—'

'On it, boss,' Stacey said.

'Bryant and I will be focussing on Jerry Dwyer.'

'Address just set to Bryant,' Stacey said as his phone tinged.

'So soon?'

'There's a Jerry Dwyer listed as living in Quatford just three miles out of Bridgnorth, so I'm guessing that stands a chance. No one else listed at the same address on the electoral roll.'

'Thanks, Stace. It's one thing having the view of someone that's allegedly been mistreated, that's one experience, but speaking to someone who works there and has seen the treatment of many people is another matter.'

'Is he our killer though?' Bryant asked in his subtle way of hinting that they were getting a bit off track.

'We have three victims and two of them are linked to Change. We won't know about the third until we get access to their files.'

'Your gut?' Penn asked.

'Says that Liam Sachs was meeting someone he didn't want his wife to know about.'

'Which might have been either a woman or a man but, even so, that doesn't tie him to the clinic,' Bryant noted.

'Agreed, which is why we're going to shelve it until we get the search warrant for the records. In the meantime, after hearing Stephanie's story yesterday, I want to know what this Jerry guy has to say.'

'Even if it has nothing to do with the case?' Bryant asked.

She considered. 'Yep, absolutely.' As police officers they didn't have the luxury of ignoring one crime because they were investigating another. If rape and torture was happening under their noses, they couldn't ignore it because they were hunting for a murderer.

'If Jerry is to be believed, he felt strongly enough to slip an SOS letter into the bag of someone considered to be a good guy. What do we think?' she asked, turning to the rest of the team.

'I'd guess we're talking a visitor,' Stacey said.

'Could it be a delivery guy?' Penn asked. 'Jerry works in the kitchen.'

'Slipped into the bag of is quite specific,' Kim said. 'So I'm not sure that fits.'

'What about a visitor to one of the patients?' Stacey asked.

'They don't have them,' Kim said. 'No distractions while receiving treatment.'

'How about consultants like the therapists?' Bryant asked.

'Too risky. They're on board and most likely supportive of whatever goes on there.'

'So we're looking for a visitor who isn't there to see a patient, isn't involved in the actual business but is a good guy and can be trusted?' Penn asked.

'Maybe like a lawyer?' Stacey asked.

'Shit, wait one sec,' Penn said, turning to his computer. They all waited. He looked up from the keyboard. 'Or maybe an accountant?' Penn said, looking right at Stacey. 'Dunhill filed their last set of accounts.'

'Stace, ring your contact at Dunhill. The Gardners mentioned an audit when we were there yesterday.'

'You don't think Gabriel Denton was the—'

'Make the call and find out,' Kim said, not liking where this was going. Gabriel Denton hadn't been seen in almost four days.

'Hi, Wendy, it's DC Wood. Sorry to bother you so early but can you tell us where Gabriel was working last week?'

They all listened to the pause on speakerphone.

'I'd have to check the diary at work but I think Thursday and Friday he was at a clinic. I can't remember the name of it, but it's somewhere near Bridgnorth.'

Stacey thanked her and ended the call.

'Okay, Stace,' Kim said. 'Looks like we're not done with Gabriel Denton yet. You need to explain to Beth what's going on and have a bloody good look for that letter.'

FIFTY-NINE

'Seeing as the boss said to give Beth a little while longer, I'll take one of these to eat while I'm waiting,' Stacey said, swiping a cupcake from the Tupperware box.

Maybe she wouldn't notice, Penn thought, looking away.

'Err... what's this all about?' she asked, holding up the cupcake and inspecting it. 'This isn't one of Jasper's creations.'

He groaned. 'No, it's from the bakery. Jasper had a bit of a burning fiasco last night.'

'Is he okay?' Stacey asked, putting down the cake. 'Sorry, Penn, I forgot you had to rush off last night.'

'There's nothing wrong with him. It was all a ploy to get Lynne over. It worked, and that's all I'm gonna say about it right now,' he said, not knowing himself how to take the next step.

'Okay, spare me the salacious details. I only want to know if there's a chance of you two becoming a thing.'

He couldn't stop the smile tugging at his lips. 'Maybe.'

'Okay, I'm gonna let my imagination run wild, but I have two things to say before I go. First, it's about bloody time, and second, please let Jasper know that these shop-bought muffins don't even compare to his goodies.'

Penn waved his hand in acknowledgement as she walked out the door, leaving the half-eaten muffin on her desk. He worked hard to keep the smile off his face.

Last night had been surreal, but in the cold light of day, did Lynne feel the same way? Despite the fact they'd known each other for almost ten years, it felt like they'd rushed to the next stage. Was she regretting what had happened last night? Had it not been what she'd expected? Was she now filled with regret that they'd taken their relationship to the next level? Was she full of doubts and questions? The not knowing was almost painful.

He groaned as he took out his phone. Okay, what tone? How to ask a simple question and get a response that gave him the answer? He felt as though he might need some help navigating his way through the early stages of whatever this was. He hadn't had a serious relationship in years, and even then, he hadn't felt the way he did now.

He typed quickly. Did their tone of communication change because of last night?

Hope you weren't late for work.

At the last second, he added a smiley face. He read it back and face palmed himself. How the hell was he gonna get his answers in a reply to a text message that could have come from her neighbour?

The message was read immediately and a sickness started to rise in his stomach.

He took a breath and looked away. His phone vibrated.

Woulda been worth it.

Her text ended with a cheeky tongue-out emoji.

He laughed out loud as the natural rhythm of their relationship seemed to establish itself.

He sent a quick reply. Knowing she'd be about to start the working day too.

Weekend?

For sure.

She replied. Few words had passed between them, but it was enough.

He knew he had to push Lynne out of his mind or he'd never get a thing done.

Something else that was slowing him down was focussing on Celia Gardner. He was no closer to finding out anything about the woman. Her husband was an open book, and it had taken him less than an hour to chart Victor Gardner's entire existence from Hawthorn Primary in Oswestry to Wildcrest High School to Keele University to four jobs in sales and then to Change. Another twenty minutes and he could have found out what he'd had for his breakfast that morning. But no such luck with Celia. Even under her maiden name of Thatcher he could find no record of her education or work history prior to her marriage to Victor Gardner. Any general web search including that surname brought up millions of hits spread between the late prime minister and her headline-ridden children, which was slowing him down in digging into the backgrounds of other people.

He decided to work his tasks in chronological order. The boss had met Charles Stamoran and Lorraine Abbott first.

He entered Stamoran's details onto the system. There was no record. He wasn't known to them, and Penn knew that didn't mean he'd never done anything wrong. Only that he hadn't been caught.

He put in various searches for the Exodus leader. His social media was lacklustre at best. It was as though he'd opened accounts and then couldn't really be bothered to stay on top of them. Seemed a bit strange, Penn thought. Other than the odd retweet and share, he was pretty silent. Often when people had jobs such as his they shouted their opinions from the rooftops, defended their positions, justified their beliefs, even tried to convert the opinions of others. From this guy – nothing.

Penn clicked into his LinkedIn profile, the only platform that appeared to be up to date. Professional photos taken at various stages of his career sat beside lengthy profiles and listings of roles and responsibilities. Penn was intrigued enough to keep reading. He scrolled to the bottom of his employment history. The man had started working as a booker for a temping agency. Two years later he'd been promoted to recruitment consultant. Three years later he'd moved to a national chain of agencies in London. While there he'd risen through the ranks to become recruitment executive, area manager and then nothing for two years. Between 2017 and 2019 there was no record.

Penn had the realisation that it was a job to the man. His entire work history was listed and it had all been about recruitment, getting numbers. After two years out of work, the job could have been for anything. Recruiting people to go against their own sexuality or to go on a sightseeing trip. It was all the same to Charles Stamoran. It was all about the numbers. Penn didn't like the taste that information left in his mouth.

Content that he knew as much as he needed to know about Charles Stamoran, he turned his attention to Lorraine Abbott.

A search on the Police National Computer turned up a charge of ABH on her neighbour. He clicked into the narrative to find details of an ongoing feud between Lorraine and a Ms Roberts for at least three years. Various calls had been made by both parties but far more from Ms Roberts. Apparently, an argument over a shared border had erupted into violence and

Ms Roberts had suffered a broken nose and cheekbone, a black eye, a bruised stomach and a cut to her arm. Lorraine Abbott had sustained no injury. All a bit much for the sake of some overgrown pansies.

Ms Roberts had stated that it wasn't about the pansies. She'd made it clear that Lorraine Abbott had beaten her up because she was gay.

Penn reached for the phone. This was something the boss needed to know.

SIXTY

'Bloody hell,' Kim said when Penn finished reeling off the list of injuries. 'And that was over daffodils?'

'Pansies,' Penn corrected. 'But the neighbour claimed it was a hate crime and that Lorraine had been verbally abusing her for years before the assault. The jury agreed.'

'We'll be paying the lovely lady a visit later. Good work, Penn,' she said, ending the call as they pulled off the main road.

Quatford was a small village in Shrewsbury, just south of Bridgnorth. It was listed in the Doomsday Book and once had a bridge that was a key crossing of the River Severn. A bridge north of Quatford was built some years later, giving the market town its name.

Bryant pulled into a narrow street just behind The Danery pub. A row of seven small cottages lay just half a metre back from the road.

'Going back to the pub,' Bryant said, turning around in a small drive. There was nowhere to park that wouldn't block the road.

'Bloody hell, Bryant, it's not even nine.'

'To park,' he said, as though it needed explanation.

She waited until they were out of the car and heading towards Jerry Dwyer's house before speaking. 'What do you think of the news on Lorraine Abbott?' she asked.

'Other than the woman is an absolute charmer,' Bryant answered. 'I thought she was hostile to us because we're police but no, it looks like she's just a nasty piece of work.'

'To beat someone to a pulp because they're gay. That's a special kind of rage,' Kim observed as she came to a stop outside the middle cottage in the row.

Bryant knocked hard.

Kim allowed herself the brief hope that Jerry was going to answer the door and tell them he'd just been off sick for a day or two.

They waited. No answer.

Bryant knocked again, harder.

Nothing.

She leaned down and opened the letter box.

'Bloody hell,' she said, stepping away. She covered her nose and pointed. 'Bryant, have a sniff at that.'

He did so. 'Absolutely foul,' he said, wrinkling up his nose. 'Something is festering in there.'

'Okay, let's do it.'

He didn't need telling what she meant. Over the years they'd perfected the art of breaking down doors by synchronising their weight against the upper and lower part of the door at the same time.

'Jesus Christ,' Kim cried out in pain as the wood of the frame splintered. For an old door it put up quite a fight, and Kim just about saved herself and Bryant from collapsing into a heap on the floor. She made a mental note that her body wasn't quite up to exerting that level of force.

'Uggghhhh,' she said, moving closer to the source of the smell.

She covered her nose and stepped into the kitchen.

'I swear, guv, I've attended post-mortems that don't smell this bad.'

Kim nodded her agreement as she looked around the kitchen. No surface had been left uncluttered with dirty plates full of half-eaten meals. Stale, mouldy bread was everywhere, bowls holding sour milk, fish that was dried and shrivelled. The stench of rancid meat came from the swing bin in the corner.

'I'm thinking he didn't have time to clean before he took off somewhere,' Bryant said.

'Or was taken,' Kim added.

'I'll take a look up there,' Bryant said, climbing the stairs two at a time.

Kim went through to the living room, which was surprisingly tidy compared to the kitchen. There were no dirty plates or mouldy food, and although the furniture looked dated, it was well taken care of.

There was no bathroom downstairs to check so Kim headed straight outside. The garden was small and boxy, around ten metres long. The space was formed of gravel and slabs with no flowers or shrubbery of any kind. The space was encircled by a six-foot fence on top of double gravel boards, offering an eight-feet-high privacy screen all around. There was no shed or storage box and Kim could see why. The gate at the rear was double bolted.

'Nothing upstairs, guv,' Bryant said, joining her. 'Two bedrooms. Double has a fitted wardrobe and smaller one is a storage room.'

'Hmmm...' Kim said.

'Oh, I hate when you do that,' Bryant said as she headed back into the house.

She went to the front door and touched where the bolt keeps had been ripped from the door frame when they'd forced the door open.

'Hmmm...' she said again, entering the kitchen.

She moved around the space, touching things as she went, then headed up the stairs and came to a stop on the landing. She put her finger to her mouth as Bryant frowned.

'Well, he's obviously not here,' she said clearly. 'Which gives us a bit of a problem.'

'What's that, guv?' Bryant asked, following her gaze up to the attic door.

'We can call the locksmith but we can't hang about and wait for him. We'll have to pull the front door to and hope no one notices that you can get straight into the property.'

She flicked her fingers towards the stairs.

'Best we can do then, guv,' he said, walking heavily down the stairs.

She kept quiet as Bryant made a noise of trying to secure the front door.

And then silence as he stood at the bottom of the stairs.

Five. Four. Three. Two.

The attic door slid open and a set of stairs fell down.

A pair of feet emerged.

Kim waited until the man was halfway down the ladder.

'Good morning, Mr Dwyer. I'm DI Stone. This is DS Bryant, and we're both very pleased to meet you.'

SIXTY-ONE

Kim didn't need a full appraisal to see that this average blonde man looked awful, and he didn't smell a whole lot better. Aside from his creased clothes and armpit stains, his eyes were haunted, wary, darting around her as though she was hiding the object of his fear.

Kim had guessed that he was hiding somewhere in the property when she'd seen the back gate double bolted. She knew the front door had been bolted, so if he'd left the house, how on earth had he bolted both exit points? A quick mooch around the kitchen had confirmed that the kettle wasn't stone cold. He hadn't long made himself a morning cuppa.

'I'm sorry about the mess,' he said as she followed him down the stairs.

Kim got it. He'd been leaving the attic long enough only to do the bare minimum. He'd quickly dropped off his empties, grabbed some more food and then hot-footed it back to his perceived place of safety. He hadn't showered in days because he was so frightened to be out in plain sight.

Her only question was why.

'I won't embarrass you by asking if you'd like a drink,' he

said, passing by the kitchen and leading them to the neater lounge.

'Mr Dwyer, do you think your actions might be a little extreme?' Kim asked as she took a seat. She could hear Bryant in the hallway making arrangements to have the man's door fixed.

'Not at all. I've been terrified. Ever since I wrote that letter. I regretted it as soon as the man left the building. I knew they'd find out it was me and they'd come looking so they could shut me up. Even if they'd forced their way in, they wouldn't have found me up there. They don't want anything negative getting out, and I think they're capable of anything to shut folks up.'

'What prompted you to write the letter?' she asked. 'You've worked there for some time and you're clearly terrified.'

He shrugged. 'Just all seemed to be getting worse.' He shook his head. 'I'll be honest. At first I didn't take much notice. I'd signed the secrecy form and it was a job. I'd been out of work for almost a year and I would have taken anything. No matter, the wife left me two months after I started, so it was all for nothing except to earn enough so that I could keep the house.'

'Sorry to hear—'

'Never mind all that,' he said, waving away her words.

'Okay, Mr Dwyer, do you mind telling us what you've witnessed at the clinic?'

'Terrible, awful treatment of people. Locked in their rooms. Taken to the third floor, which is restricted access. Patients are force-fed. I once had to cook enough for a small army. I thought there was a party. It was all taken to one room. Others are starved. One girl wasn't allowed food for five days. Some are humiliated. One guy, in his early twenties, was forced to lick the urinals until he either puked or cried. He cried.'

Kim felt the rage start to build in her stomach. Convicts who had murdered innocent people weren't treated this way.

'Are all the staff aware of what's going on?' she asked,

hoping that there was someone, anyone, trying to put a stop to it.

He nodded. 'They're called practitioners. I don't know what qualifications they have or what they're practitioners of exactly, but there's eight of them and they all follow instructions.'

'No one questions this abuse?'

'They all sleep just fine at night because the patients are there voluntarily. No one is forced to stay.'

He looked to her and then at Bryant. 'Why aren't you writing this down in a statement?' he asked.

'We're not quite at the point of—'

'But that's why you're here, isn't it? That accountant gave you the letter and they've all been arrested?'

Kim stole a glance at her colleague before answering.

'I'm afraid not, Mr Dwyer. We're here because Stephanie told us about your text messages. We're hoping to search the premises later today, but I'm afraid we have even more bad news. The accountant to whom you passed the letter hasn't been seen since Monday morning.'

The colour that had reached his face prematurely drained again as though she had turned on a tap.

'I'm in danger, aren't I? They definitely know what I've done. If they've got him, they're going to come here. They're going to kill me. I know they are, and now you've broken down my door. I'm a sitting duck.'

'The locksmith and carpenter are already on their way,' she assured him. 'We won't leave until you're totally secure, but just to be safe, is there anywhere else you can stay, just for a day or two?'

'I have a nephew who lives in the Cotswolds,' he said. 'But I can't get there without exposing myself.'

Kim ignored the poor choice of words. She got the point.

'We'll get you there safely,' she said. 'You just need to pack a few things.'

He looked to the front door.

'We're not going to leave you alone, Jerry. Go pack,' Kim said.

He got to the door and turned. 'You are going to get them for all the hurt they've caused, aren't you? Victor and Celia, I mean?'

'It depends how much they know,' she said honestly. 'They weren't in the room for every terrible act that took place.'

'I understand that, but make no mistake, Inspector: every instruction comes from them.'

SIXTY-TWO

Stacey took a deep breath before knocking on the door. Without a doubt, Beth wasn't going to be pleased to see her and she'd be lucky to get inside. The fact she wasn't yet able to offer the woman a full explanation wasn't going to help her case one bit. A search warrant was unlikely given that the link was only a suspicion.

Stacey knocked again. There was a chance that Beth wasn't going to let her in at all.

She was about to knock a third time when Beth opened the door.

The surprise on her face turned to dismay.

'Have you come back to sully my husband's name even further, officer?'

In addition to the anger that Stacey had been expecting there was a tinge of something else: hurt. It was as though she'd let the woman down somehow by not understanding the depth of the relationship she shared with her husband. That she had trusted Stacey to understand that Gabe would never do that to her, and right now Stacey had to concede that she might be right.

'Beth, there's been a development,' Stacey said, hoping the admission would gain her entry.

The surprise was back on her face. 'There has?'

'I can't say much more, but may I come in for a minute?'

Beth nodded and stood aside. 'I'm in the kitchen,' she said, closing the door. Stacey followed her to the back of the house.

'What's happened?' Beth asked, taking a seat at a round dining table and indicating for Stacey to do the same.

She seemed to have caught the woman clearing away breakfast dishes. The faint smell of sausages and toast lingered in the air. Stacey applauded the woman's determination to eat well and stay strong. When Devon was away she lived on Coco Pops and Pot Noodles.

'I don't want to alarm you but there may be a clue to Gabe's disappearance in his work papers,' Stacey said to open the conversation.

Beth frowned. 'Excuse me?'

'I really wish I could tell you more, but at this stage I can't. I need to ask you if I can look through Gabe's briefcase.'

'After what you implied when—'

'I'm sorry, Beth,' Stacey said, trying to appease her. 'Maybe we did jump to conclusions too soon. Access to his briefcase would certainly help us establish where to go from here.'

'So you haven't stopped looking for him?'

Stacey shook her head.

'What do you need?' she asked, seemingly satisfied with the answer.

'Whatever he used to take with him regularly to meet with clients.'

'One minute,' Beth said, leaving the room.

Stacey could taste the humble pie in her mouth, and she'd happily eat some more if it got her what she wanted.

'Here it is,' Beth said, placing the briefcase on the coffee table.

It was a combination lock.

'My birthday, his birthday. Nineteen twelve and eleven eleven,' she offered.

Stacey turned the dials and the case sprang open. She felt a brief flash of guilt, wondering if a man's briefcase was like a woman's handbag. Was she overstepping some kind of personal boundary?

Beth peered over too.

In the lid of the case were various pockets and compartments. A quick look told her the letter wasn't in there. In the body of the case were two sets of bound accounts ledgers with the name **CHANGE** in bold capital letters on the front. She took both sets out and inspected the bottom of the case. Nothing. She held them by the metal spine in each hand and turned them both upside down. A single sheet of paper fell from the one on the left.

'Is that what you're after?' Beth asked as Stacey reached for the folded sheet.

The note was handwritten and began with the words:

Please help

Stacey nodded as her heart thudded in her chest.

'What does it—'

'I'm sorry, Beth. I can't share it with you,' she said, refolding the letter and putting it in her satchel. 'Thank you for allowing me to do this, and I promise that as soon as I can give you an update, I will.'

Beth looked as though she wanted to press further but chose not to.

Stacey headed for the door and closed it behind her.

She got back into the squad car and let out a breath. Yesterday she'd told the woman her husband had likely left her because he'd developed feelings for another woman. Eventually she might have to tell her that her husband was now missing and presumed dead.

SIXTY-THREE

'Read it out again,' Kim said, putting the phone on speaker so Bryant could hear. They had left Jerry Dwyer's house fifty minutes ago after the door had been secured and the man himself put into a squad car to be taken to Stow-on-the-Wold.

Stacey coughed and started again.

'"Please help. Both staff and patients are sworn to secrecy. This is not the professional clinic it seems to be. Patients are being starved, beaten, humiliated and raped. Please let the authorities know so they can investigate properly. They need to access the third floor. Please help before someone else dies."'

'Jesus,' Bryant said, pulling into a spot in front of Megan Shaw's premises. 'It was like a letter to nowhere. Just sat in Gabe's briefcase. A cry for bloody help.'

And a poor, desperately frightened man had been hiding in his attic since sending the letter.

'Okay, both you and Penn feel free to make a nuisance of yourselves until that search warrant comes through.'

'On it, boss.'

Kim ended the call as Bryant switched off the engine.

'Guv, how come we don't know about this place? I mean, why does no one know about this place?'

She shrugged as she got out the car. 'I have no idea, but I'm hoping this particular lady can help us out a bit.'

'But aren't they on totally opposing sides?' he asked.

'Of the same industry,' Kim said. 'I'm willing to bet your house that she knows more about Celia Gardner than she's letting on.'

She pressed the buzzer, and Megan answered immediately.

'DI Stone and DS Bryant. Do you have a moment?' Kim asked.

'What if I had a client, Inspector?'

'Do you?'

'No.'

'Then, may we—' She stopped speaking as the door clicked open.

As she ascended the stairs, Kim was met with the aroma of freshly brewed coffee and warm pastry.

Megan was carrying a mug and plate to the room at the back.

'Please excuse me. Most days I can't face food first thing and take a mid-morning snack instead.' She disappeared and then her head came back into view. 'Can I get you a coffee while I'm in here?'

'No thanks,' said Bryant.

'Yes please,' said Kim. 'Unless you have an appointment,' she added.

'I'm fine until twelve, Inspector, so if you're not done by then, you can take your coffee with you and I won't even charge you for the mug.'

Kim took a seat on the fabric sofa. Not too soft and not too hard; just comfortable. Bryant sat in the single chair and threw her an accusatory glance. He always expected her to refuse refreshments, and she normally did, but it smelled like damn good coffee.

'Milk or sugar?' Megan shouted.

'Neither,' Kim called back.

Megan appeared with a single mug and placed it before her. 'So, how can I help?'

'Why not just send us to Change in the first place?' Kim asked. 'You knew that was where Jamie had been treated after you refused to carry out his parents' wishes. You're treating another of their ex-patients named Stephanie Lakehurst. Why did you not just direct us to the clinic in the first place?'

'Two reasons,' Megan said, making no attempt to hide her subterfuge. 'The first is that you probably wouldn't have believed me if I'd told you the truth right off the bat. Whatever you now know is because of your own investigation and not because someone told you. Second is that you needed the education.'

'You sent me to school?' Kim asked incredulously.

Megan nodded. 'You knew absolutely nothing about conversion therapy or the reasons behind someone making the choice to try it. Now you understand why that awful place exists at all.'

Kim had to concede both points. She probably wouldn't have believed or understood had she not spoken to Cliff and then visited Exodus. And she certainly knew more now than she had the last time they'd spoken. She still didn't appreciate being given the runaround, but she knew why the woman had sent her on the journey.

'Now I'm suitably educated, what do you know about Celia Gardner?' Kim asked.

'More than I'd like to. Why do you ask?'

'There are a lot of accusations being made against the clinic she owns. Not least from Stephanie Lakehurst.'

'But why would you think I know Celia Gardner?' Megan asked, crossing her legs.

'Your paths must have crossed,' Kim insisted.

'They have indeed, but I'm not sure what you want to know.'

'Did you know Celia in your youth?'

'Why would you ask that?' Megan said, frowning.

'You're a similar age, both from the Black Country. You never met her?' Kim asked.

'You do know that the Black Country is 138 miles square?'

Kim shrugged and waited for an answer.

Megan continued. 'Oh, wait, you think that us gay kids wore magnets so we could find each other in a crowd?'

The questions had been asked with humour but Kim got the point. She moved on. 'Okay, there's a polish to her that doesn't feel real,' Kim said honestly. 'I feel as though I could wipe hard at the shiny silver exterior and find something not so palatable beneath.'

'I think that's a fair assumption. My understanding is that she's determined, ruthless and will always get what she wants.'

'She was sent to the old version of the clinic in her late teens, we understand.'

Megan shrugged. 'I've heard that rumour but it's not as if we speak. She has her little empire. She has the life she's constructed for herself with her perfect straight marriage and perfect children.'

'You sound bitter?' Kim noted.

'I deal with the aftermath of what she's created.'

'But it was there before she was,' Kim countered.

'It was the brainchild of an ignorant, bigoted man drowning in grief. It should have died with him.'

'Agreed,' Kim said. 'We're hearing horror stories. Can you confirm?'

'On the record, no.'

'Off the record, even though we're not reporters?' Kim said, taking a sip of her drink. She'd called the quality right.

'Even so, I'll answer direct questions if you ask them, but I'm not giving you a narrative.'

Kim wondered at her evasiveness but decided to put that aside for the moment.

'Have you treated anyone other than Stephanie after they've spent time at the clinic?'

'Poor word choice for the facility but we'll go with it. The answer is yes.'

'Are you prepared to give us a name?'

'No.'

'Has anyone ever spoken to you about electric shock treatment?'

'Yes.'

'Starvation?'

'Yes.'

'Humiliation?'

'Yes.'

'Violence?'

'Yes.'

'Corrective rape?'

'Yes.'

Bryant sat forward and Kim could see the muscle jumping in his cheek.

'Why haven't you reported it?' her colleague asked.

Megan was ready for the question.

'Because you guys insist on a complainant. And no one is going to speak up.'

'Why not?'

'Because they'll be slapped with legal action before the sentence is out of their mouth, and you guys won't do a thing about it.'

Bryant shook his head. 'I'm sorry but I have to disagree. Any serious complaint would be investigated.'

'Third November 2017, Sergeant. Go check it out. See if a complaint was acted on.'

Bryant made a note.

'You remember that date for a reason?' Kim asked, taking another sip of her coffee.

'I do, indeed, Inspector. There was a young man, twenty-two years old. He came to me after a month-long stay at the clinic. Electrodes were placed on his penis daily while being shown pornographic material. If his body responded to the stimulus, he was zapped.'

'He couldn't leave?' Bryant asked, crossing his legs.

'This is wrapped up as treatment. It's a rod of steel in a furry glove. It's for your own good, you're a freak, you're repulsive, you're disgusting, hour after hour, day after day. Trust me, you're going to try and conform.'

'How did he leave?' Kim asked.

'His body stopped responding to the stimulus and he was deemed to have been cured. He was filled with self-loathing and hatred of his own body. He couldn't look at himself in the mirror, and even talking about his own sexuality induced a panic attack.'

'What happened?' Kim asked, finishing her drink.

'I actively encouraged him to make a report, despite the NDA he'd signed. He spoke to a police officer anonymously, but the officer refused to take any action. Trying to tell your story and not being heard is worse than just keeping it to yourself. After that he was too frightened to raise it again, but he did put a negative comment on the clinic's website. Two days later he received a legal letter suing him for defamation. The letter also stated he would be sued for legal costs likely to run into tens of thousands.'

'A scare letter?' Kim asked.

She'd heard of them before. A letter that hints at everything that can go wrong and the repercussions. It was designed to scare people into backing off completely and keeping their mouths shut.

'Yes, and it worked,' Megan continued. 'He deleted the comment. He was terrified. He had no way to pay legal bills and thought they would take his mother's house.'

Kim felt the rage growing inside her at the injustice. Always David and Goliath.

'He was too frightened to continue our sessions. He wouldn't talk to me in case it got back to them.'

Kim tried to imagine that level of terror. To be too paralysed by fear to share what had been done to you. 'What happened to him?' she asked, fearing the worst but needing to know anyway.

'He died of a heroin overdose a year later.'

Kim said nothing while she swallowed down the emotion in her throat. Such pain, such suffering, such a waste.

'And that's why I no longer encourage anyone I treat from the clinic to speak out. I've seen what they can do, the tactics and underhand tricks to silence people. My job is to try and mend them as best as I can. Of course I'd like the place shut down. I'd like to meet with every person they've got there to try and help them accept themselves and heal, but it's not gonna happen because people who try and speak out lose their lives, and I can't help them if they're dead.'

There was a quiet integrity to this woman she liked. She understood that her priority was to treat the person right in front of her. She couldn't save the world, and whatever she was doing seemed to work. Stephanie Lakehurst had accepted her sexuality and was moving forward with her life.

'I admire your passion. Doesn't leave much energy for a home life, does it?' Kim asked. There was not one clue about any attachments in her narrative or her workspace.

'Would you like a rod to fish with, Inspector?' Megan asked with a wry smile.

Kim shrugged. That was as subtle as she got.

Megan sighed. 'My hours are too long for a dog, I'm not keen on cats, I've never been keen on anything that has to live in a cage and I lost the love of my life in my teens. Now is there anything else you'd like to know?'

'Thanks for that. May I ask you one more question?'

'Go ahead,' she said wearily.

'Knowing what you know about Celia Gardner, do you think she's capable of murder?'

'Absolutely yes,' Megan said, reaching for a mug that was already empty.

'Why so certain?' Kim asked.

'She has a lot to protect.'

'The business?' Bryant asked.

Megan shook her head. 'Much more than that. The programme cannot fail. If it does, her whole life is built on a lie.'

And that was a hell of a lot to lose, Kim thought as she thanked the woman for her time.

SIXTY-FOUR

'You know, I just don't believe this,' Penn said, shaking his head.

'Yep, I always said Lynne was out of your league but hey ho,' Stacey quipped, enjoying being able to joke with him about his newfound love life.

'Not that, although I think you have a good point. I can't find anything on Celia Gardner that's not connected to Change.'

'Not so strange really,' Stacey said. 'Not everyone can be found on Google.'

'Says the woman who can find out anything with a few keystrokes.'

'Want me to have a look?' she offered.

'No, I'm perfectly capable.'

'You've not just searched under Gardner, have you?' Stacey asked, just to make sure.

'Yes, Stace, cos this is my first day on the job and I don't understand that's her married name. Obviously, I've searched under her maiden name.'

'You know, Penn, if I didn't know any better, I'd say you're not getting any—'

'Delivery,' said a cheery voice from the doorway.

'Percy, your timing is impeccable,' Penn said as the techie put the box on the spare desk.

'One laptop, one phone, one suicide note. Who wants to give me their autograph?'

Penn wheeled across the room and signed the chain of evidence forms.

'Thanks, Percy.'

'*Ciao, bambinos*,' he said, waving as he went out the door.

'Strange guy,' Penn said, wheeling back.

'Oh, the irony.'

Penn chuckled.

'Listen, do you wanna get started on that lot?' she asked, nodding towards the box, 'and I'll do more digging on Celia Gardner.'

'You saying I'm shit at this?' he asked.

'As you're the highest-ranking officer in the room, I would never be so bold as to tell you outright that your skills lie in other areas.'

'Okay, swap,' he conceded.

Stacey immediately began tapping as he grabbed and opened the box.

Sensing that she might be annoying Penn a bit, she chose to search for the marriage certificate and the maiden name herself.

Despite Penn's claims, she did a full search on the name Celia Thatcher. Eight pages down and just about every article had ruled out the first name of Celia and was about the late ex-prime minister, or one of her children. Unfortunately, Google didn't understand the concept of 'not that Thatcher'. She drummed her fingers on the table. She could see why Penn had hit a wall. There was nothing anywhere for Celia before she'd married Victor in her mid-twenties. No school report, no college courses, no university degree. It didn't make any sense.

Unless that wasn't the name she'd been using.

Stacey ate a second shop-bought muffin while searching deed poll records.

Nothing.

There had been no formal name change either from or to Thatcher, which meant she'd used her real name on her marriage certificate but had gone by another name throughout her higher education.

Why?

What had happened before her higher education years?

She put in the search 'Celia Thatcher teenager'.

The search results were in the lower millions, but an article on the third page caught her eye. It was the word 'teenager' being included that had brought it higher up in the search results.

She opened it as Penn's phone rang.

'Shut the front door,' Stacey gasped, reaching for the phone. 'I need to call the boss right now.'

'Give her a message from me,' Penn said, ending the call. 'The warrant just came through. She's now free to search the clinic.'

SIXTY-FIVE

Inspector Plant pulled up beside Bryant's car and handed her the warrant through the window.

She was parked at the end of the lane just out of sight of the clinic.

More squad cars were pulling up behind them.

She read the terms of the warrant.

'Shit. Treatment rooms and offices only. No common areas, no patient quarters and no questioning of patients. Right to privacy to be observed.'

Kim had hoped to have open access to the whole site and the people. She'd have liked to talk to some of the current patients.

'How do you want to play it?' Inspector Plant asked.

'Give us five minutes to serve the warrant. We'll be heading for the third floor. The second floor is out of bounds because it's residential, so you focus on the ground floor, admin and back-of-house areas.'

'Got it,' he said as Bryant started the car and headed towards the property.

'You gonna speak to Celia about her past?'

'Oh yeah but not until we've taken a good look round.'

The building came into view, and Kim was struck by how inoffensive it was. It was hard to imagine the horrors that had been described.

Kim got out of the car and strode into the reception.

Jessica greeted her with an open smile. 'Hello again, Inspector. How may—'

'We have a warrant,' Kim said, pushing the document through the gap underneath the glass partition.

'Okay, but is that really necessary? I'd have happily let you in again.'

'We're not here for the guided tour this time. The details are in the warrant.'

Jessica glanced over the document and reached for the phone.

'Who are you calling?' Kim asked.

'It appears this document prefers you not to have contact with our patients so I need to have them directed to their rooms. It'll take just a minute and you can listen. I really don't know what you think we're hiding.'

Kim said nothing as Jessica hit two buttons on the phone.

'Eric, can you confine all patients to their rooms? The police are here to conduct a search.'

Kim couldn't hear Eric's response.

'Thanks,' she said, hanging up.

Jessica pressed the button to allow them through.

'Eric will be here in a minute,' she said as the rest of the police cars pulled onto the drive. Jessica frowned. 'Is this some kind of raid?'

'We just have to be thorough,' Kim said as Inspector Plant and a constable entered the reception.

'Inspector Plant and his team will be focussing on this level, including your parents' office,' Kim said. 'That could definitely be classed as admin.'

'My parents are in a meeting with a prospective client.'

Damn it, that was a grey area. The warrant insisted on privacy, and she wasn't going to have anything happen that some clever defence lawyer could use if they found anything incriminating.

Kim shook her head at Inspector Plant to indicate that the office was off limits for now. 'But have someone close by,' she advised.

Her colleague nodded his understanding. They would make sure nothing was removed.

If the meeting was finished once she was done upstairs, she'd take care of that room herself.

The side door opened and Eric stepped in with a tight smile. 'At your service, Inspector.'

For some unfathomable reason, Kim had a knot forming in her stomach. This was how warrants were supposed to be executed – no fuss, no histrionics, no attempt at refusal. And yet something felt a little bit off.

'We'd like to take a look around the third floor,' she advised.

'No problem – follow me.'

The feeling in her stomach got worse as Eric held the door open for her.

'We'll take the back stairs. They bypass the second floor where the patients are. I'd rather your presence didn't unnerve them.' He offered her a smile as he paused on the first landing. 'They've been told we have pest control in for an ant problem.'

She listened for sounds of glibness but heard none. He appeared to be as open and honest as his sister.

'So, you're the business brain of the family?' Kim asked conversationally as they hit the second landing.

'I enjoy the numbers. My sister enjoys the people.'

'And the controversial nature of the business doesn't bother you?' Kim asked as he opened a fire door that led them onto the third floor.

'I don't see it as controversial at all, Inspector. Early forays into cosmetic procedures like nose jobs and breast enlargements were all met with distaste and distrust. People were vilified for wanting to improve or enhance their appearance. In this day and age, we have the freedom and the resources to change anything about ourselves that we don't like or aren't happy with. Why should our sexuality be any different if we have the knowledge and tools? Why shouldn't we help people lead the life they want for themselves?'

Kim wondered if Eric was responsible for writing the clinic's promotional material. If not, he should be. After speaking to these people with their steadfast, unwavering faith in the process, she found herself half convinced.

'But does it actually work?' Kim asked. 'Are you not just causing people to hate themselves?'

'Inspector, the people who come to us for help already hate themselves. They don't want that lifestyle. No one is forced to come here, and our waiting list has us booked solid until the middle of next year.'

The knowledge of that saddened her deeply.

'And you only take willing patients?'

'Of course,' he said, looking genuinely bemused. 'What would be the point otherwise? Have you ever had to make a difficult lifestyle change?'

'I gave up smoking,' Bryant chimed in.

'Ooh, tough. Did you want to?' Eric asked.

'Yes.'

'How would you have managed if you hadn't wanted to?'

'I'd have failed.'

'But that's a habit,' Kim argued. 'A bad one, an addiction, but something formed after birth. It's not part of your genetic make-up.'

'Most smokers would disagree on the simplicity of your

statement but let's try again. Name something else that's part of your genetic make-up?'

'Eye colour.'

'Can be changed if you don't like it. An eye surgeon can cut open your cornea and put in a coloured silicone implant. There is surgery available for any physical attribute about yourself you'd like to change. There is psychiatry and psychology to aid psychological and mental-health issues, and we can help with sexuality.' He smiled at the look on her face. 'I can see I'm not going to convince you so I'll just leave you to your search. Take the staircase back down to reception, although I'm not sure what you could possibly want up here. This floor is never used.'

'Thank you, Eric,' she said as he headed back through the fire door.

As soon as it closed, she turned to her colleague. 'Hey, numpty, in future, if you're gonna side with the enemy, keep your mouth shut.'

'He asked a question,' Bryant answered.

'You're not falling for this bullshit, are you?'

'No, but I can understand why desperate, vulnerable people do. He makes a good argument to the people who want to listen.'

She couldn't disagree. Every time she met these people she felt as though she was being schooled.

'Okay, you take the left and I'll take the right,' Kim said, observing the long hallway that seemed to run the length of the house.

'You do realise that—'

'Yeah, but let's do it anyway,' she interrupted, knowing what he was going to say. It had all been too easy. There had been no protest, no argument, no hostility.

Silently, they worked their way along the corridor, opening and entering every room. They reached the end of the hallway together, and Kim knew the frustration was showing on her face.

This was supposed to be the nerve centre, the hub, the torture chamber. There was no evidence that anyone had been up here for months.

'Guv, I think we've been fed—'

'Stuff, Bryant,' she said as they walked back along the corridor together.

'Gonna need more than that to offer a response.'

'What do you do with empty rooms?' Kim asked.

'Fill 'em with stuff you don't need. Get your crap out of the way.'

'Exactly. Why are some of these rooms not filled with stuff that's built up over the years?'

'Good point,' he conceded.

'Something else,' she said, pausing at the top of the staircase. 'How many empty rooms up here?'

Bryant looked back. 'Twelve.'

'And a waiting list that stretches into next year. Wouldn't you convert these empty rooms? Maximise your capacity? It is a business after all.'

Kim headed down the stairs. Either the people here had put the last twenty-four hours to good use and cleared the whole floor, or Stephanie and Megan were feeding them a pack of lies. She wasn't sure which option unsettled her more.

SIXTY-SIX

'Anything?' Kim asked Inspector Plant at the bottom of the stairs.

'Not unless you count a restaurant-quality kitchen, gourmet menu, pleasant dining room and an 85-inch TV a new form of torture.'

'Keep looking,' she said as Jessica appeared from the reception.

'Mum's free, if you want to speak to her.'

Oh, did she ever, Kim thought as she gave the ever-chirpy Jessica a nod.

They followed her to the end of the hall, back to the door marked 'private'. Jessica opened the door to reveal Celia alone, behind the desk.

She removed her glasses and smiled. 'We weren't expecting to see you again so soon.'

Weren't you? Kim wondered.

'Though I'm not sure what you could be looking for. We showed you everything, willingly, yesterday.'

Kim ignored the slight rebuke in her tone, as though all she'd had to do was ask.

Celia indicated for them to step over to the sofa area as she came around the desk.

'There have been serious allegations regarding some of your treatment methods,' Kim said.

'By whom?' Celia asked, taking a seat.

'Not something we're going to share at this point; but I would like to ask you about Gabriel Denton.'

'Our accountant?' Celia asked as her eyebrows drew together.

'An anonymous letter was placed into the belongings of Gabriel Denton.'

Celia's face crumpled in confusion. 'A letter? Saying what?'

'That your treatment of people here is inhumane; that you beat, starve, torture and rape patients within the parameters of your conversion therapy.'

Celia's mouth fell open in surprise. 'That is completely and utterly preposterous. We're not monsters here. Do you really think that if we treated people this way, you wouldn't have heard of this before now?' she asked, quickly regaining her composure.

'Apparently your legal team makes sure that doesn't happen,' Kim countered.

Celia shook her head. Back in control despite the accusations that had just been levelled against her. 'Our legal team is good, Inspector, but they're not able to prevent atrocities on that level coming out. Surely you know that?'

Kim noted the way Celia always brought the question back to her rather than directly answering it.

'But any sniff of bad press would be bad for business, wouldn't it?'

'Of course, and we're very lucky to have the type of success rate that prevents that from happening. That's the reason for the lack of bad press, not the actions of our legal team.'

'You're saying nothing like that goes on here under the guise of treatment?'

'I think I've already answered that question.'

Not really, Kim thought. She hadn't yet heard any outright denial.

'So you had no idea about the letter?' Kim asked.

Celia shook her head. 'Of course not.'

Kim suspected that she'd be pulling out all the stops to find out who wrote it. If she didn't know it was Jerry, Kim wasn't going to point her in that direction. 'Because, coincidentally, Gabriel Denton hasn't been seen since Monday morning.'

The deep frown was back again. 'What does that have to do with anyone here? You're going to have to spell this one out for me, Inspector.'

Kim was happy to oblige. 'There's no chance that you got wind of this incriminating letter and silenced Gabriel Denton so that he couldn't pass on the information?'

'Yes, we definitely did that. And we're also responsible for the Jack the Ripper deaths and the Zodiac murders. Is there anything else you'd like to try and pin on us, or do you realise how ridiculous these accusations sound?' Celia asked, her eyes blazing.

'Where is Gabriel Denton?' Kim pushed.

'I have absolutely no idea, but his disappearance has nothing to do with us. We are a treatment facility. We help people who are—'

'Unhappy with their sexuality,' Kim finished for her. 'Yes, we know all that. Does the name Liam Sachs mean anything to you?'

Her face showed nothing. 'I'm sorry but I'm not prepared to answer that. All of our patients are entitled to privacy, and unless your court states otherwise, I'm not saying any more.'

'But we know that both Jamie Mills and Sarah Laing spent time—'

'The deaths of these young people is indeed a tragedy but not one you can link with the service we provide here.'

Kim seriously hoped something was going to turn up on the search because she was getting nothing incriminating from this woman.

'It's not your first brush with tragedy, is it, Celia?' Kim asked.

Celia maintained eye contact but offered nothing as she waited for whatever was coming next.

'I would imagine you were pretty traumatised by the murder of your mother.'

'It was a long time ago, Inspector, and has nothing to do with what we're discussing now.'

'I think it shows great strength of character that you were able to process the horror and make a good life for yourself. You were how old when you found her?' Kim didn't add that the woman had been found with her skull caved in from multiple blows with a suspected hammer.

'Sixteen,' Celia answered, giving nothing away.

'You must have been terrified.'

'Of course.'

'I understand that robbery was the motive. Your mum's purse was missing from her handbag?'

Celia nodded.

'And they never caught the man responsible, did they?'

'No.'

'That must have been painful. Not even being able to see justice done to the person who had murdered your mum?'

'Very, but I've had to learn to live with it.'

Kim wondered what it would take to elicit some real emotion from this woman. They were talking about what was arguably the worst time of her life and she wouldn't let the emotion out.

'No father?' Kim asked.

'Not that I knew.'

'So you went to live with…?'

'My aunt Elise. A good strong woman.'

Kim was unsure why Celia had chosen to qualify that.

'Was she the one who sent you here?' Kim asked.

Celia nodded. 'And I thank God she did,' she said, allowing her face to soften. 'She changed my life for the better and set me on the right road.'

Celia seemed more open to talking about that aspect of her life.

'Had you experimented?'

'God, no,' Celia said, placing distaste on her face just a split second later than Kim would have expected.

'You told her you had feelings for other girls?'

'My mum had already told her. I didn't know that, but my aunt helped guide me in the right direction.'

Kim was confused. 'But if you'd never had any involvement with another girl, how did you know so certainly that you wanted to change?'

'I knew enough. I knew that these relationships are often born in secrecy. They develop in the dark, away from disapproving eyes. That very intimacy and furtiveness gives the whole thing oxygen, life. It breeds a bond that's all-inclusive, that is all-consuming but excludes everyone else. It is dark and hidden and intense. It is destructive and cannot survive the light of day.'

Kim was speechless.

Celia continued. 'My aunt saved me before I made a huge mistake, before I acted on any twisted impulses. I was given the opportunity to change, make my own choices on who I wanted to be and the life I wanted to live. My life is out in the open, beyond scrutiny, not subjected to prejudice, disgust, insults. I live a normal, wholesome life with a wonderful husband and two beautiful children. Now is there anything else you'd like to know?'

Kim shook her head, having learned more than she thought she would. For a woman who had never entered into a same-sex relationship, she sure knew a lot about how they worked.

SIXTY-SEVEN

'Pretty big thing to come to terms with, don't you think?' Penn asked, taking another mouthful of pastry.

'Not sure I'd even have survived it,' Stacey answered, knowing exactly what he was talking about.

After uncovering the horrific murder of Celia's mother and passing on the details to the boss, Stacey had shouted them both lunch from the canteen. She'd left half of her generously portioned spaghetti bolognese, but he was still working on his steak pie and gravy. The details were clearly still fresh in both of their minds.

'I mean, we know the motive was robbery but, even so, four blows to the head was particularly brutal,' Stacey noted. 'Pathologist concluded that the first blow would likely have been enough to kill her but not immediately.'

'She probably started making a noise and the burglar panicked and hit her a few more times to shut her up,' Penn said, pushing his plate to the side. The memory of the post-mortem photos had wiped out the rest of his appetite. The injuries had been horrific, and her skull had been a smashed, bloodied mess.

'Celia came home to that,' Stacey said, shaking her head.

'Yeah, investigation determined that it was probably done by a hammer which was brought to the scene, but I don't know how you ever get that image out of your mind,' Penn said, remembering when his mother had passed. Jasper had begged to go to the chapel of rest to keep her company, but Penn had talked him out of it, not wishing for that to be the image of their mum that stayed in his brother's mind.

'Police report said that Celia ran next door screaming and crying for the neighbour to call the police, and the burglar was never found. She must have been terrified that they were going to come back,' Stacey said.

'Probably a good job she moved away with her aunt,' Penn said, rifling in the box of goodies that Percy had dropped off.

Stacey watched him as he took out an evidence bag.

'I absolutely knew you'd go for the suicide letter first,' Stacey said.

'There's something here, I just know it,' Penn said as Stacey reached into the box and took out Liam's phone.

'Read it again,' Stacey said, closing her eyes.

'What are you doing?' Penn asked.

'I hear inconsistencies better if I switch off other senses.'

'And folks around here call me weird,' Penn mumbled.

Stacey opened one eye. 'Get on with it.'

'"My darling Monica, I am so sorry to do this to you. You don't deserve this. You have been my devoted wife for six years now, but I cannot live with myself any longer.

'"Inside me are urges that I just can't control however much I try to ignore them. I am disgusted by myself and the thoughts that go through my mind. I cannot lie to you any longer, and I cannot put you or our child through the shame of what my indiscretions would bring as I am no longer able to keep these repulsive actions to myself. I am despicable for not being completely honest and for not having the willpower or determination to overcome the sickness inside me. You deserve much better than I can ever give you.

"'Please know that my heart is yours forever.

"'Goodbye, my love.'"

'Sounds okay,' Stacey said, opening her eyes. 'Monica confirmed it was his writing.'

'Absolutely, but if you were being forced to write a suicide note, wouldn't you try and leave some kind of clue?'

'Not if someone has a knife to your throat.'

'We don't know that he did have a knife to his throat.'

'We don't know that he didn't. What I'm saying is the poor guy is terrified, knowing he's gonna die and he's being told what to write, how does he think to leave a clue? Are you thinking of what you might try and do in the same situation?' she asked.

'Maybe.' He shrugged.

'You sure there's nothing on this?' Stacey asked, waving the phone around.

'Nothing obvious.'

'Hmm...' Stacey said, checking all the usual places. Penn was right, there was nothing. It was clean. Too clean.

Stacey went to the box and pulled out the laptop. She fired it up and put in the code from Ridgepoint to bypass the password screen.

She searched around his computer and found the same thing. Clean. No photos, no lists, no financial spreadsheets or scanned documents.

'Restored,' she said, feeling a rush of excitement.

'What?'

'Restored to factory settings,' Stacey said.

'That sounds like bad news.'

'It is because it means the information isn't readily available but doesn't mean it's gone.'

'But it's been wiped?' Penn insisted. 'It's as blank as it was when it left the factory, hence the phrase.'

'Bloody hell, Penn, do you always take a nap during our cybercrime refreshers?' she asked, chuckling.

'Most times,' he admitted.

Stacey could understand his boredom. The majority of police officers avoided cybercrime. It wasn't what they'd signed up for. But she loved the fact that humans made machines and yet they were still fallible. She loved finding a way through a locked door.

She rifled in her pen pot and threw him a pencil.

'A quick demonstration. Write your name on a piece of paper.'

He did so.

'Now rub it out,' she instructed.

He did.

'Can you see it?'

'Nope.'

'But it's still there. Not in the same form but the indent of the pencil is still in the paper. The only way to destroy it is to rip the paper up completely or set fire to it. It's the same with the hard drives. The factory reset removes apps, programs, photos, anything installed after it left the manufacturer. But it can't completely erase the data until it's overwritten with fresh data.

'You can get specialist software to perform complete data erasure or degauss to destroy the magnetic field on the—'

'Glazing over now, Stace,' Penn said, passing his hand in front of his eyes. 'The only question that matters is: do you know how to get to it?'

'Nope,' she answered honestly. 'But I think I know a man that can.'

SIXTY-EIGHT

Kim's meeting with Celia was still on her mind when they pulled up outside the Exodus premises.

Penn had uncovered some colourful history for Charles Stamoran's receptionist and guard dog, Lorraine Abbott, that, given the nature of the crimes, couldn't be ignored.

Bryant parked right next to the Jag so they'd know immediately inside that they were here.

Kim got out of the car and pressed on the intercom.

'Mr Stamoran is in a meeting,' Lorraine said curtly.

'Good, because it's you we came to see.'

'I'm afraid I'm busy.'

'No problem. Please attend Halesowen police station at your earliest convenience. Feel free to bring legal—' Her words were interrupted by the buzzing of the door.

'Was that supposed to scare me, Inspector?' Lorraine asked as Bryant closed the door behind them.

'It was intended to give you the idea that we want to speak to you either here or at the station. Your choice.'

Lorraine indicated towards the two chairs as if to say 'well now you have your way'.

'I'll stand thanks,' Kim said, moving closer to the reception desk. 'I'll get right to it, Lorraine. We're here about an altercation you had with your neighbour.'

She stuck her chin out. 'Go ahead. I've got nothing to hide. I beat her up, pleaded guilty, did my time. Nothing to hide.'

'And no regrets either?' Kim asked.

'Absolutely not. I gave her fair warning.'

'About the daffodils – sorry, pansies?' Bryant asked.

'No, to move house. I didn't want to live next door to her, and I was there first.'

Kim wondered if Lorraine had any clue how petulant she sounded, which was not attractive on a woman in her early thirties.

'And this was because she was gay?' Kim asked.

Lorraine nodded. 'Yep. I didn't like her. I don't like any queer folks, especially a woman living right next door. Her bedroom window looked onto my garden. She could have been perving on me any time.'

Kim wanted to laugh at the sheer stupidity of the woman. Sometimes it was hard to believe that women like Lorraine still existed.

'You were scared that she might find you attractive?' Bryant asked.

'Of course. They'll go for anyone, won't they?'

'I don't actually think that's how it works, but what if it had been a man's bedroom?' Kim asked.

Lorraine shrugged. 'I wouldn't really have thought too much about it. I mean it'd be natural for a bloke to have a gawp, wouldn't it?'

Oh, it was good to know the double standard still survived in bigoted and outdated views.

'I'm not sorry, if that's what you've come to ask. I'm glad I beat the shit out of her. It got her to move.'

Kim felt the rage build in her stomach for the victim of this hate crime. The violence was bad enough, but Kim could imagine the insults and abuse she'd received for having done nothing wrong. 'And you think that's okay?'

She shrugged. 'I mean, I wish I hadn't had to do eighteen months in the slammer for it, but it was worth the time.'

'You have no sympathy for your victim?'

'Nope, and if I'd lied about that, I'd have been out five months earlier, but I ain't gonna lie. I hate the queers. I don't mind the blacks, the Indians, the Romanians or the Jews. I just hate the queers.'

Kim thrust her fists into her front pockets before they acted on what she was feeling. 'Ever beat anyone else up?' she asked.

Lorraine shook her head. 'Nah, I keep it all online now. I abuse people over the internet. Way more fun and it doesn't bruise my knuckles.' She laughed at her own joke.

Kim and Bryant let her laughter hang in the air as Charles Stamoran appeared from behind.

'Everything okay?' he asked, placing his hands on Lorraine's shoulders; a wildly inappropriate action in the workplace unless...

The brief smile that passed over Lorraine's face confirmed the unless.

Despite the place they both worked, Kim had to wonder if Charles Stamoran knew just how foul his mistress was.

'Miss Abbott, would you mind telling us where you were in the early hours of Sunday morning?'

'Excuse me?' she said as colour flooded her face.

'And where were you on Monday evening?'

'You can't ask me—'

'And for a full set, where were you on Wednesday night?'

The smile on her face was a distant memory.

Bryant took out his notepad and pen. This enraged her even further.

'There's no way I'm going—'

'She was with me,' Charles said, giving her shoulders a squeeze.

'All three times?' Kim asked.

He nodded.

'All evenings?' Bryant said. 'I'm sure that's something we can check with your wife.'

The colour dropped from his face as Kim's phone began to ring.

She moved away from the desk.

'Go ahead, Stace.'

'Got a minute, boss? We think we might have found something.'

SIXTY-NINE

Kim couldn't step out of the Exodus offices quickly enough. Despite spending most of her day dealing with killers, thieves and other reprehensible characters, she rarely met anyone as despicable and repugnant as Lorraine Abbott.

She took a good deep breath of air outside.

'Okay, Stace, go ahead,' Kim said as Bryant joined her.

'We've got a link, boss, between Liam Sachs and Sarah Laing. Both were messaging someone called Jackal.'

'Through a dating app?' Kim asked, wondering what kind of name that was.

'Starts that way by the looks of it and then goes to phone messaging. No phone calls, just texts. Pretty raunchy and suggestive approach with Sarah.'

'Go on,' Kim said, feeling the tingle in her belly that they finally had a link between two of their victims.

'Jackal suggested to Sarah that the two of them meet at Norton Covert. They must have gone back to her flat afterwards.'

Of course – the Woodland Trust site was just a stone's throw from her home.

'And Liam?'

'Same. It was suggested to him that they meet in the woods by his home. The messages between the two suggest it was just going to be a sexual encounter.'

'Our killer seems to know enough about our victims to be able to suggest a place that's off the beaten track and remote enough so they won't be seen. And yet there was no evidence of sex noted during Liam's post-mortem,' Kim said.

Keats's report had reached her about an hour ago.

'What about Jamie?' Bryant asked.

'He's not on the dating sites and we don't have his phone.'

'But we found some stuff on his Facebook page, didn't we?' Kim interjected.

'The account has been taken over. All the settings have been changed. I can't get in there at all.'

'Damn. Okay, leave it with me,' she said, ending the call.

'Tesco's, Cradley Heath,' she said to Bryant as they got in the car. There was only one person she could imagine taking over Jamie's account.

Bryant pulled out of the car park and began to talk. 'Our killer isn't as stupid as we'd like him to be.'

'I know,' Kim agreed. 'He plans every crime meticulously. He sets the tone, he sets the date, time and location. He researches areas close to where they live and even takes the time to try and cover his tracks by attempting to make it appear they died by suicide.'

'I've been thinking about that, guv, and I'm not sure that's what he's doing.'

'Have you not been paying attention to how our victims have been found?'

'I have indeed. Our first victim, Jamie Mills, was reported in the press initially as a suicide but then changed to a murder investigation. I can understand that our killer might not have got the memo before killing Sarah, but a double murder investigation was all over the news before Liam was murdered. Why keep up the charade? He knows we're onto him and don't believe that our victims took their own lives, so why carry it on? Why not just stab them or something that takes less elaborate planning?'

'Do I get points for a correct answer?'

'Maybe,' he answered, heading towards Cradley Heath.

'He's staging them as suicides because he thinks that's how they should have died.'

'All the points,' Bryant said, turning into the supermarket car park. 'I think he wants them to appear to be so distraught by their sexuality it's not even worth living, leading them to their final act. That's what he wants the world to see and he doesn't even care.'

'Hmm...'

'Not even a *well done, Bryant, on your intuition and sensitivity?*' he asked.

'You know, in my college days I lived above a woman named Mrs Richards. She had three dogs. Two of them could do all sorts, shake a paw, roll over, beg, but not the fat bulldog. Only thing he could do was sit on command but he expected to be congratulated for it.'

'I'm not a fat bulldog,' Bryant protested.

'And I'm not Mrs Richards,' Kim said as he parked the car.

She got out and made for the entrance, having already spotted the old Mini parked roughly where it had been the other day.

She headed straight for the fishmonger, which was next to the deli.

'May we speak with River?' Kim asked the tall, balding man behind the counter.

'Who wants him?' he asked, sticking out his chin.

Kim sensed a smidge of protection in the man's tone.

Both she and Bryant showed their IDs at the same time.

He turned and called the boy's name.

River appeared from out back, and Kim would have walked right past him. The white coat was fastened up and appeared a full size too big for him. The hairnet covered a shock of dirty blonde hair. The pink was gone.

'Got a minute?' Kim asked.

River looked to his boss, who nodded and then glanced after him with concern as the boy came around the counter.

River beckoned them to the side of the cheese counter where a fire-exit door led to a back corridor. The stench of fish seemed to be ingrained in the breeze-block walls.

'Wass up?' he asked.

Kim realised he not only looked like a different person but was acting like a different person. The boy they'd seen on Wednesday had been a shining star, full of life and vitality. This person was faded, lifeless, invisible.

'River, have you taken over Jamie's social media?'

'Yeah, I closed it right down to include only people he knew personally and changed the visibility.'

'Why?'

He shrugged. 'I put a memorial post on and he wouldn't have liked the comments.'

'Like what?' Bryant asked.

River sighed heavily. 'Just things like "one less faggot in the world" and "one down three million to go" and that's just the ones that weren't filthy and obscene. There were too many. It wasn't what I wanted. I posted so his life could be remembered for the sweet, funny guy that he was.' River wiped at his eyes. 'But the ignorant pricks even had to spoil that.'

Kim felt her heart ache for this boy who had wanted to do something nice for his friend and it had been met with hostility and aggression. The freedoms were not the same regardless of how far we've come, Kim realised.

She pulled her mind back to the case even though a sense of

sadness was stealing over her at the transformation that had taken place in front of her in a few short days.

'River, were there any messages or posts that might help us?'

River balked. 'You think Jamie was in contact with his killer like some kind of psycho stalker bullshit?'

'We think the murderer may have made contact with Jamie and arranged to meet.'

'There was nothing in his messages, and he never said he was going to meet anyone. He would have told me,' River said, forcing back the tears.

'And there's nothing else you can remember him saying recently.'

River shook his head. 'Nothing recent. Last one he told me about was some guy called Panther wanting to hook up, but that was a couple of weeks ago.'

And Jamie wasn't known to rush these things, Kim thought.

'You're sure it's Panther?' she asked. 'Not Jackal?'

He shrugged. 'All the same, isn't it? It could have been. I was glittering my eye shadow at the time.'

Kim looked to her colleague. His expression said he agreed that they were dealing with the same person. Right now, they were three for three. She had what she had come for.

'Bryant, can you give us a minute?' she asked, nodding towards the door that led back into the store.

'Sure,' he said, leaving them alone.

'Is this where you strong-arm me for more information?' River asked, looking around. 'No witnesses.'

Kim laughed. 'Too many cop shows. No, River, this is where I ask you what happened to the guy we met the other day?'

River shrugged and looked down at his feet. 'It's exhausting, being yourself when there's so much hatred. Sometimes you just gotta toe the line. Don't be yourself, don't stand out. Do what you have to do but behind closed doors. Don't speak of it. Don't be proud of it.'

He lifted his head, tears streaming down his face as he continued. 'What's the point? Jamie's dead and even in death you gotta deal with the haters. How is death not enough?'

'Because some people have so much hate inside them it affects everything they do, everything they say,' Kim answered. 'It eats at them and makes them ugly. They feed off victory. Every little triumph gives them energy and power because then their hate has had effect. It's had an impact. It has triumphed.'

River was listening intently.

'How do others learn how to feel about themselves if they don't have examples, good examples. Don't you dare hide yourself under a bland hair colour and ordinary lashes. Don't you dare show yourself as less than who you've worked hard to become. For what reason? To mollify bigoted idiots with half your IQ. You've already said that even death isn't enough so why even try to please them?'

River's mouth fell open.

'So get that Facebook post back up and delete the shit. Make them disappear and celebrate the life of that young man the way he deserves.'

River nodded and wiped his eyes one last time.

She held the door open and watched as he sashayed back to the fish counter. He gave his boss a wink as he passed by. The tall guy burst out laughing.

He looked her way and gave her a smile.

She nodded and walked away.

She had to go trap herself a Jackal.

SEVENTY

'Okay, Stace, what can you tell me about this Jackal?' Kim asked once she was back in the car. She could feel the late afternoon slipping away from her and their progress today had been slow. Other than linking that name to their three victims, they had nothing. They had no clue who or where he was.

'I can tell you that he's very clever and adapts his methods to his target. He matches them and gives them everything they want. With Sarah he spent a couple of weeks chatting and getting to know her. They'd exchanged almost a hundred messages before Jackal suggested they meet. It was all very gentle and coaxing and a bit coy. It couldn't have been more different with Liam Sachs. It was right in there with sexual flattery, innuendo and an arrangement to meet up in less than twenty messages.'

'He basically becomes everything they're looking for,' Kim observed.

'Even though we can't get to any communication between him and Jamie, I'll bet he came over as a nervous, unsure, newly outed gay man.'

'Oh yeah,' Kim agreed. That would appeal to Jamie.

Someone he could relate to, someone he could talk to, someone to take things slow.

The manipulation of each of the victims was sickening.

'Thing is, boss,' Stacey continued, 'I'm currently working through the dating websites and his accounts are being closed. Thurst, gone. Open, gone. Fem, gone. 'HER— Ooh, hang on. He's still active on this one.'

'Why?' Kim asked, feeling the dread form in the pit of her stomach. His exit from the sites could have meant that his spree was over, leaving them to track him down without the risk of anyone else losing their life.

'Gimme one sec,' Stacey said, urgently pressing keys. 'This site is a bit trickier. And in lesser hands that might be a problem but... gotcha. Okay, he's only made one connection on this site. He's been talking to— Oh shit.'

'What?' Kim asked.

'His one connection is with Stephanie Lakehurst.'

'Shit,' Kim said as Bryant started the car. The girl had told them the previous day she had a date, finally, with someone she felt she could trust. Clearly, the Jackal had been everything Stephanie had needed too.

'Bryant, happy for you to put your foot down,' she said, knowing there were twenty-five miles and a good forty-five minutes between her and knowing Stephanie was safe.

'Try and get her on the phone, Stace, and if that doesn't work, call the local station and see if they can check on her any quicker than we can.'

'Will do, boss.'

'And if you reach her, tell her not to go on that date and to go sit with a neighbour until we get there.'

'Got it,' Stacey said, ending the call.

'Bryant, I swear if you don't put your foot down, I'll—' She was prevented from issuing her threat by the ringing of her phone. It was a number she didn't recognise.

'Stone,' she answered.

'Inspector, it's Charles Stamoran.'

She frowned but didn't put him on speakerphone. She wanted all of Bryant's focus on getting them to Much Wenlock as quickly as possible.

'How can I help you, Mr Stamoran?'

'I've been... err... thinking. I think I was mistaken when we spoke earlier.'

'Mistaken about what?' Kim asked, allowing her voice to drop a couple of degrees.

'I've checked my diary and I seem to have got confused with when we were actually working late, so there's no need to confirm anything with my wife.'

'Okay, Mr Stamoran, let's be clear. What dates are you saying you were not with Lorraine Abbott?'

'Any of them.'

Kim felt a chill steal around her. Was he changing his mind to prevent them checking with his wife?

'May I ask why you're retracting your alibi, Mr Stamoran?'

'I told you. I was confused. It's been a strange week, but I definitely wasn't with Lorraine on any of the dates mentioned.'

'That puts us in a difficult position with your colleague. Could you please ask her to give us a call to—'

'I can't. She's left. She has plans and, no, they don't include me,' he added to drive the point home.

'Thank you for the clarification,' she said, ending the call.

Right now, she didn't know what to believe.

'Want me to turn around?'

Kim considered rushing to Lorraine's address and confronting her.

'No, keep going,' she said, focussing on the road ahead.

They didn't know for sure that Lorraine was the Jackal, but they did know that Stephanie was the Jackal's next victim.

SEVENTY-ONE

Stephanie Lakehurst checked her appearance in the mirror for the tenth time. She had changed her outfit twice before settling on jeans with cut-out patches on the knees and a V-neck camouflage-patterned top under her petrol-blue leather jacket.

She had spent hours deliberating and analysing every decision for fear of how she might portray herself. Should she tease the quiff on her head to full height? Should she put a ring in her nose piercing or leave it bare? Should she wear the bulky, gadget-laden sports watch her mum had bought her for Christmas or the gold, dainty bangle one from her aunt, received on her twenty-first birthday? Delicate gold jewellery on her wrists and neck or meaty silver-plated curb chains? Should she wear her Tory Burch designer trainers that had been a present to herself, or the more comfortable ones that had lasted her years from Sports Direct? These decisions were important. What did every one of these choices say about her and her personality? Her mum always told her that you never got a second chance to make a first impression, and she still wasn't sure what first impression she wanted to make.

Did she want to appear gay or not? If she did, how gay did

she want to look? Would she scare off her date by looking either too gay or not gay enough? It was an absolute minefield, but time was moving on and she had to start making some decisions.

As she gelled the medium-height quiff into place, she marvelled at the progress she'd made. Spending time with Megan and actually understanding the reasons why she didn't want to stand out had helped the healing process. Megan had made her understand that as young children we see how people who look or act differently are bullied, marginalised, taunted. It prompts in us a fear of standing out, of being that person on the end of the taunts or being ostracised. Megan had explained how, as humans, we are programmed to want to belong so we hide parts of ourselves, we stifle self-expression, individuality so we can remain within the collective and that we don't challenge conformity. Megan had encouraged her to challenge everything, to start again, learn about that side of herself, accept it, embrace it.

With Megan's help she'd signed on to just one dating site and had been lucky to click with someone pretty quickly. Jackal was in the exact same position, except that she'd had a boyfriend for a short while before realising that she was lying to herself. She was also nervous about meeting for the first time, which took some of the nerves away from Stephanie's stomach.

They had been exchanging texts for weeks until Stephanie realised that chatting with Jackal was the last thing she did at night and first thing she did in the morning. Initially, she had dreaded the possibility of being asked to meet. Over time, the fear had turned to hope, and when Jackal had finally broached the subject, Stephanie had fist-pumped the air and enjoyed the stupid grin that had settled on her face.

As she chose the black sapphire nose stud, she remembered the day she'd entered the clinic. She had been full of hope that she would leave the place cleansed of what she'd felt were repulsive desires. Her own naiveté had been responsible for allowing her to think that her desires could be extracted, surgically removed like a harmful growth. She shook her head as she recalled that was pretty much how it had been sold to her.

As she chose the comfy trainers, she pushed away the guilt that she hadn't been completely honest with the police officer the previous day, although she hadn't actually lied. The officer had never mentioned Sarah's name, but she had seen it on the news. At worst, she had evaded the truth but not outright lied. She had known Sarah. She had eaten lunch with Sarah. She had been at Change at the same time as Sarah. She was the one who had followed Sarah to her room when she'd been brought back from three whole days on the third floor.

Eventually, Sarah had opened her door to tell Stephanie that she didn't want to talk about it. That she was fine. Sarah had closed the door and literally shut her out, but not before Stephanie had seen the empty, haunted look in her eyes as though she'd experienced something from which she would never return.

It had been a day later that Eric had informed them all at a group meeting that Sarah had completed her treatment and had left the clinic, cured and ready to begin a new life.

They had sat in their circle and cheered as though she'd just graduated a degree course, and Stephanie had masked the empty, hollow feeling in her stomach. It was an alien feeling but it was as though light cloud had obscured the sun. She'd realised just how much she'd enjoyed her time with Sarah. How much she'd looked forward to seeing her each day. It was the feelings she'd felt developing for Sarah that had made her realise that three weeks in and her treatment plan wasn't working.

She'd asked Jerry, the kitchen guy, if he'd seen Sarah before she'd left and he'd shook his head. Seeing the disappointment on her face and realising what that meant for her recovery programme, Jerry had revealed that Sarah had been raped while up on the third floor. At first Stephanie hadn't believed him but then she'd remembered the look on Sarah's face before she'd left.

For the first time in her life Stephanie had felt real fear and had been about to pack her bags and run for the hills when she'd been collected and escorted up to the third floor.

Even now she wasn't sure how many hours she'd spent in that chair, but it was enough to stop her body responding to anything they put on the screen. She remembered waking up in her bed exhausted, hurting and broken. When they told her she'd been cured and that it was time for her to go, she had packed her bags and left.

She'd arrived home and locked herself in her room for weeks. She hadn't wanted to see or speak to anyone. She'd hated herself more than ever. Not only had she still been gay but she had failed miserably at trying to correct herself. Eventually her mother had begged her to see Megan Shaw just one time and she'd agreed. And thank God she had.

Stephanie shuddered at the memories. She was thankful to have put some time and space between herself and her experience at the clinic. A part of her would always grieve for Sarah, but Megan had encouraged her not to dwell on the past and to focus on moving forward into a new life with a new attitude.

And that's exactly what she intended to do.

SEVENTY-TWO

It was almost four thirty by the time Bryant pulled into the street in Much Wenlock.

No contact had been made with Stephanie, and the local police were dealing with a three-car accident in Shrewsbury, leaving them no one spare to pay a house call on a woman that may or may not be missing.

Kim was opening the car door before the vehicle had stopped moving.

'Jeez, I thought my days of checking the kiddie locks were behind me,' Bryant said, bringing the car to a halt.

Kim jumped out and sprinted to the front door. She banged hard and waited.

Bryant went past her and tried the side gate. She heard the tell-tale rattling of the wood and latch.

'Locked,' he said, coming to stand beside her.

She knocked on the door again as the unease continued to weigh down on her.

Still no answer.

Bryant leaned down and opened the letter box. He listened and waited before straightening.

'It's silent. Either no one home or they can't get to the door,' he said.

'Damn it, Bryant. Where is she?'

'You wanna do the usual?'

Kim knew he was asking if she wanted to break the door down.

She knocked again even though her instinct told her they were wasting time.

'Hey, hey, hey, what's the noise all about?' asked a voice from the other side of the hedge. A man in his late sixties was regarding them with disapproval.

'We're police,' Bryant said, flashing his ID.

He appeared unimpressed. 'Doesn't matter who you are, does it? If there's no one home, you can bang all you like and disturb the rest of the street, but—'

'How do you know no one is home?' Kim asked, moving towards the hedge.

'Barry goes for a drink straight from work on a Friday, and Carole works the late afternoon shift at the museum on the high street opposite the square.'

Kim hadn't even known the place had a museum. 'What about Stephanie?'

'What do you want with Steph?' he asked, narrowing his gaze.

'I'd like to know where she is,' Kim snapped, feeling the minutes slip away.

'Has she done something wrong? Is she in danger?' he asked.

Kim turned away and knocked the door again. This man wanted nothing more than to satisfy his own curiosity.

Demonstrating a superior level of patience, Bryant responded. 'We'd certainly like to make sure she's safe and well.'

'She looked okay when she went out about twenty minutes

ago,' he offered. 'Looked very nice, in fact, wearing jeans and a smart blue jacket.'

'Did she get into a car?' Bryant asked, making more progress with his easy manner than she would ever have managed.

The man shook his head. 'Don't think so.'

'Which way did she go?' Kim asked, feeling a surge of hope if she was travelling on foot.

'Turned right out of the gate but don't know where she went after that.'

'Okay, thanks for your help,' Kim said, heading for the car and taking out her phone.

SEVENTY-THREE

'Stace, we're here. The neighbour saw her go out on foot twenty minutes ago,' Kim said when the constable answered the phone. 'Get on to her social media. I want to know the last thing she posted.'

'She's got no Twitter,' Stacey said. 'Hang on while I check Facebook.'

A few seconds dragged by while she logged in.

'Nope, her last post was... Hang on, Penn might have something.'

'Speaker,' Kim said.

'On speaker now, boss,' Stacey said, sounding as though she'd moved into a tunnel.

'Penn?'

'Got a post on Insta two hours ago. Two outfits and a question. She asks, "What works best for getting ruined?"'

'Ruined?' Kim asked.

'Drunk,' Bryant said, as though she needed the translation.

'Pub,' Stacey added, already tapping away. 'In that immediate area we've got The Fox, The Talbot, The George and—'

'But that would only be a meeting place,' Kim said, feeling

the frustration build. 'None of the other meetings have taken place in such public places.'

'If she's on foot there's not much else in walking distance,' Stacey offered, tapping away on her keyboard.

'Or not a pub at all,' Penn said.

'Go on, Penn.'

'Ruined, ruins. Wenlock Priory is just a couple of minutes away.'

Jamie had been hanged in a park.

Liam had met the Jackal in the woods.

Sarah had met her attacker at a nature spot.

The priory sounded much more plausible.

'Thanks, guys,' Kim said, ending the call.

'I've been there,' Bryant said, starting up the engine. He pulled away from the kerb. 'It literally is just down the road, but if I remember, it's a pretty decent size.'

He turned right out of the street and then took another right off the main road. They passed a few stone-built cottages before the road turned into single track.

Bryant pulled into the car park.

There were two cars parked, and Kim could see immediately that a blue Toyota was parked close to a narrow gap in the hedge where you could access the site without going through the main entrance and ticket point.

Bryant nodded towards the opening. 'Shall we just...?'

Kim shook her head. 'Go into the shop. If anyone has been through, I want a description in case they get away.'

'On it, guv,' he said, heading towards the building.

She took a moment to appraise the aerial view of the site on a directional board that had a green dot saying 'you are here'. Much as she wanted to dart through the hole in the hedge and sprint down to the ruins, she needed to get a rough lay of the land.

She glanced over the narrative which told her Wenlock

Priory was a ruined twelfth-century monastery on the site of an earlier seventh-century monastery. Wenlock Abbey was a privately owned house, but the rest of the priory was open to the public.

From the enlarged photo on the board she could see that the whole site was a maze of ruins formed in a cruciform shape, with the priory church, sacristy and lady chapel at the far north of the site. Attached to that was the chapel house which then led on to the farmery hall and farmery chapel and the dorter range. To the right was the south-east range, and to the west was the cloister garth and frater. The whole site was peppered with ornately sculptured topiary.

Bryant was right. It was a sizeable area to search on foot when you were in a hurry and darkness was threatening to fall.

So where the hell was she supposed to start?

SEVENTY-FOUR

The bell sounded above Bryant's head as he opened the door into the visitor's centre.

He walked amongst tables filled with local history books and key rings to a middle-aged woman frowning at him from behind the reception desk. The place hadn't changed a bit since he and Jenny had brought Laura when she was ten years old. Unfortunately, it had been a very hot day, she'd seen the sign for ice cream on the way in and couldn't focus on anything to do with the ruins. A quick walk around and within fifteen minutes they'd been back in the car with dripping 99ers.

'I'm sorry, sir, we're closed,' the woman said, tapping the opening times board in front of her. 'Last admission is half an hour before—'

'Sorry to interrupt, Brenda,' he said, reading her name tag. 'I don't want to access the site but I need to know who has been through in the last hour or so.' He showed his ID to qualify why he was asking.

'Err... there was a young couple with a toddler but they left a few minutes ago. Child was fussing something awful cos they hadn't really got her wrapped up enough, and if you want the truth she was a bit big for that buggy but—'

'Anyone else?' Bryant pushed.

'Just one young lady who went through not more than ten minutes ago.'

Bryant's stomach turned. Looked like Penn might have called it right. 'Black hair, up here?' he asked, putting his hand an inch above his forehead.

Brenda nodded. 'That's the one. About five foot five,' she confirmed.

'You're positive she was alone and no one has been through since?' he asked, looking around the shop.

'Definitely on her own.'

He nodded towards the camera in the corner. 'Can I view the system?'

'Of course, but I haven't moved from this till for the last hour and that's the only camera we've got. Ain't nobody gonna try and pinch the ruins,' she said and waited for an appreciation of her little joke.

Bryant didn't laugh. Yes, he could understand that the focus was probably on the till but that wasn't helping him right now. Whoever Stephanie was meeting had accessed the site without paying and didn't want to be seen.

'Nothing outside?' he asked, clutching at straws.

She shook her head.

'You know you've got a gap in the hedge which allows anyone direct access to the ruins from the car park?' he asked.

'I've also got one groundskeeper instead of three who says he'll get to it when he has the time. Look, if someone is that desperate to view the ruins, I'm sure English Heritage can wear the—'

'It's a security issue,' Bryant snapped, losing patience.

'Is everything okay, officer?' she asked as her eyebrows drew together.

'Not really. Can you call the police?' he asked.

'But you are the—'

'Please, just do it,' he said, heading towards the door. He sprinted across the car park, taking out his phone. The detective constable answered almost immediately. 'Stace, get backup on the way.'

'From here?' she asked, clearly checking she'd heard him correctly. They all knew it was a forty-minute drive.

'Just in case,' he answered.

The local police were busy and might not be able to free anyone up for a while. It didn't hurt to have other help on the way.

'We know Stephanie went through the ticket shop,' he explained as he reached the gap in the hedge. 'But we don't know who with.'

'On it, Bryant.'

'And check out ownership of these cars,' he added. He read off the make, model and registration numbers of the two vehicles still parked on the car park. One probably belonged to Brenda and the other was likely going to belong to their murderer.

'Got it. Let me get backup moving towards you and I'll call you back with the details,' she said, ending the call.

He put his phone away and surveyed the view. There was no sign of the guv. Surely, after the last time, she wouldn't have been stupid enough to put herself at risk.

There was a young girl in danger, he thought, answering his own question.

He took a step forward before a blinding pain ripped through his head and the world turned black around him.

SEVENTY-FIVE

Kim headed down towards the ruins, her eyes darting around the vast space as she approached. She was making for the south transept of the church. Its eastern wall had an arcade of three arches which opened into the chapels. The south wall had two blank arches with lancet windows above that stretched up into the sky. In addition to the church itself, there were remains of the nave, library and chapter house to search.

Bryant should be with her any minute but she couldn't hang around waiting for him. The seed of anxiety in the pit of her stomach was growing into nausea which she swallowed down. She shook her hands to loosen up the tension that was stiffening her fingers. It was her idiocy in going it alone that had already almost cost her her life.

Where the hell was he? she wondered, looking behind. He should have been with her by now.

'For God's sake, woman, sort yourself out,' she growled to herself as she moved forward slowly. She was a police officer. This was what she was paid to do. She didn't relish searching alone, but whoever was here could get Stephanie to the car without anyone seeing a thing and then they'd have no clue where she was.

Kim had found herself warming to the young woman. Despite her prickly attitude, there was a humour and warmth just ready to come out. She'd been through the mill but had come out the other side with help from Megan and was prepared to give love a chance. And just look at what she was going to get for her trouble. The first person she'd found the courage to meet was likely going to try and kill her. But as long as she was alive, she could recover, Kim told herself as she edged around the side of the topiary bushes that filled the cloister garden which sat against the infirmary wing.

She passed an octagonal structure embellished with carvings of Christ and the apostles that looked eerie in the fading light that was playing havoc with her senses, causing her to see shadows everywhere. She passed a bush sculpted into the shape of two swans. The shadow of their long necks looked like arms that were going to reach out and grab her. She shuddered and stepped out of its range.

Come on, Bryant, she willed silently. Having someone else with her would stop her getting so spooked. She'd stop seeing danger and torment in grass and sculpted animals.

She moved around the south-west side of the ruin, keeping her back to the stone and pausing every couple of seconds to listen intently. Her heart started to pound in her chest. What if she'd missed them and they'd bypassed Bryant somehow? Stephanie could be on her way to just about anywhere.

Time was slipping away from her and she knew it. She wasn't sure this was what Woody had meant when he'd said, 'take it slowly', and she was trying to follow instructions after what had happened the last time, but she wasn't willing to risk the life of a young girl because she was a bit jumpy.

Another shadow moving through the ruins on the other side of the priory church drew her eye.

Her breath caught in her throat. Only this shadow was wearing a blue jacket.

Bryant, where the hell are you? she cried silently. The undulations in the grassy mounds prevented her seeing back up to the car park. She took out her phone and scrolled to his number. She put the phone to her ear and listened as it rang and rang until voicemail kicked in.

'Shit,' she whispered as she put the phone back in her pocket.

If she didn't move soon, she'd lose track of where that blue jacket had gone. They could circle back around the library and the west wall and head back up to the car park.

'Damn it,' she cursed, knowing she had no choice. If she'd been seen it wouldn't be long until they were hunting her instead of the other way round.

She shook her head with resignation before heading off in the direction where she'd seen the blue jacket disappear.

SEVENTY-SIX

'Location now, Pete?' Stacey asked from the doorway of the squad room.

The CID office was located just off the control room so she was able to get real-time updates on the progress of the support team she'd requested.

'Heading into Six Ashes,' Pete answered.

Stacey groaned. They were still a good half hour away from Much Wenlock. Two squad cars had been dispatched. It was at times like this she wished she could clear the whole road and give the officers a straight run with no regard for the speed limit.

She leaned against the door frame and folded her arms as though her presence would make the backup team get there faster.

'What did Bryant say when you told him about the cars?' Penn asked, not looking up from the suicide note.

'He didn't answer. I left a message. Should have guessed that the Honda Accord had false plates,' Stacey said. They wouldn't have been that lucky. The number plates belonged to a Volkswagen Polo that had been scrapped in Kidderminster three weeks ago. The other car belonged to Brenda Hooper, who had worked at Wenlock Priory ruins for eleven years.

'Where are they now, Pete?' she called over to the controller.

'Heading out of Six Ashes,' he said with an eye-roll. Yes, she knew it had only been a couple of minutes since she'd last asked but it felt so much longer.

She turned her attention to her colleague. 'Why do you keep looking at that letter?'

Penn sighed heavily and frowned. 'You know when you feel like you're missing something obvious?'

'Yep. I've had a similar feeling with Gabriel Denton. It was there until we made the link to the clinic, but now I'm just hoping that the boss finds out where he is.'

'You're not expecting him to be alive, are you?' Penn asked.

Stacey hesitated but shook her head. 'And that's a conversation I don't want to have. Beth hated me enough for saying Gabriel might have connected with someone else, so when I tell her we think he's dead, I'm gonna run for the—'

'Wait just one minute,' Penn said, closing his eyes and opening them again. 'Come here and take a look at this.'

She stepped away from the door and peered over his shoulder. Her eyes scanned the contents of the letter she'd already seen.

My darling Monica,

I am so sorry to do this to you. You don't deserve this. You have been my devoted wife for six years now, but I cannot live with myself any longer.

Inside me are urges that I Just can't control however much I try to ignore them. I am disgusted by myself and the thoughts that go through my mind. I cannot lie to you any longer, and I cannot put you or our child through the shame of what my indiscretions would bring as I am no longer able to keep these repulsive actions to myself. I am despicable for not being completely honest and for not having the willpower or determination to overcome the sickness inside me. You deserve much better than I can Ever give you.

Please know that my heart is yours forever.

Goodbye, my love.

She shrugged. 'It's the same letter you already—'

'Stace, get the boss on the phone. I think I know who we're looking for.'

SEVENTY-SEVEN

Kim worked her way slowly through the chapter house, her back moving against the ornate interlocking arches on the stone columns. A grotesque head had been carved into the doorway. Now was not the time to appreciate the irony that she was passing through the location the monks would have met to conduct business and administer punishments for disobedience.

She switched her phone to silent as she approached the window where she'd seen the blue coat disappear.

Bryant, hurry up, she thought as she moved slowly along the stonework to the next doorway.

As she drew closer, she heard the low hum of voices.

Thank God. Voices meant conversation, which meant still alive.

She carefully took another step.

'I never knew you felt this way about me,' Stephanie said.

Kim held her breath and waited for the response. It was low and she couldn't make out who it belonged to.

'But you hid your feelings so well,' Stephanie said with wonder in her voice. Kim's heart ached for the deception she was being subjected to.

Kim leaned in closer to hear the response.

'I could hardly tell you, could I?'

Kim was stunned.

She knew exactly who that voice belonged to, and the fake warmth in it chilled her to the bone.

She stepped into the doorway to see Stephanie against the wall, pinned into position.

'Step away from her, Jessica,' Kim said, moving forward.

The light flirtatiousness died in the woman's eyes as her hand darted into her pocket.

Stephanie cried out as Jessica brought a knife close to Stephanie's face. 'One step, Inspector, and she'll get it.'

This woman was unrecognisable as the chirpy, friendly person who had shown them around the clinic. Now she looked older, meaner, harder, and she had a weapon in her hand.

Kim stood still as Stephanie looked from her to Jessica.

'I... Inspector, p... please tell me what's going on?'

'Jessica isn't here to connect with you. She's here to kill you,' Kim said, not taking her eyes from Jessica's face.

Stephanie started to shake her head. Jessica tightened her grip and brought the knife closer to her face, making it impossible for Kim to consider rushing her. Ten feet separated them, and if she missed, that knife was going to bury itself somewhere inside the girl being held against the wall, frozen by shock.

Even with the glinting proof an inch away from her cheek, Stephanie protested, 'No... no... she's...'

'She's the person who's been calling herself Jackal,' Kim insisted. 'And she's killed at least three other people. Whatever she's said to you is a lie. She traps people into—'

'Tests, Inspector, please get it right,' Jessica said, rolling her eyes.

Kim took the opportunity to make eye contact with Stephanie and shake her head. She hoped the girl understood not to make any sudden moves. While Jessica was talking, she wasn't thinking about using the knife. She hoped Stephanie had understood the message, but with the numb look in her eyes it was hard to tell.

'I test people to see if they're cured,' Jessica continued. 'And if not, they die.'

Kim was taken aback by the simplicity of her logic.

'You're saying that Jamie, Sarah and Liam deserved to die because they gave in to temptation?'

'Absolutely. They weren't cured. They hadn't worked hard enough. Our programme works for the people that put in the effort.'

'So if they'd ignored your messages they'd still be alive?' Kim asked.

'Well, obviously,' she said with an attitude that Kim couldn't understand.

'So you tricked Sarah into meeting you. You communicated with her and won her trust. You pretended to be everything she wanted?' Kim asked.

'I pretended to be a girl and that was enough. Sarah couldn't meet me quick enough. It was disgusting. She was so eager to flaunt her new toy, her newly embraced sexuality. She believed me when I told her I'd developed feelings for her while she was at the clinic.' She shook her head. 'As if. It's disgusting and foul. We tried to help her and the failure was totally down to her, just like Jamie and Liam, who both fell for the same trick. It's pathetic and they all deserved to die.'

'How the hell can failing at something warrant someone's death?' Kim asked, even though they hadn't failed at anything. In Jessica's skewed moral judgement they had.

'You're not getting it, are you?' Jessica asked, barely perturbed at having been caught. It was almost as though she expected Kim to jump on board with her logic any second.

'Explain.'

'The clinic is everything. It always has been. It's my mother's life work. We live it both inside and outside of work. It's what we do. It's who we are.'

'It's what binds you as a family?' Kim asked.

'Of course it does. We all agree that these relationships are toxic. They damage people. They are obsessive, exclusive, harmful, damaging. We do everything we can to save people, help them towards a better life, and this is how they repay us.'

She shot a look of pure hatred at Stephanie, who looked away, but Kim could tell that she was listening to every word Jessica said.

'That's your mother speaking, not you,' Kim said, watching the knife. She'd heard almost the exact same words come out of Celia's mouth hours ago.

'It's all of us. All our lives we've been told how important it is, the good work we do, the lives we've changed. My mother is a visionary. She turned the place into a sanctuary, a place where—'

'You shock people,' Kim interrupted. 'You beat them and starve them and rape them. You don't heal people, Jessica, you break them, you scar them. That's not a sanctuary, that's worse than a prison camp.'

Jessica frowned and looked genuinely saddened.

Kim had a sudden realisation. 'Oh my god, if you can't beat them, join them,' she said, playing for time. Every second counted towards Bryant finding them. She had to keep Jessica's attention without inciting her to use the knife. 'You've competed against the clinic your whole life. It's always received more attention than you. Your mother's mission to cure gay people was her firstborn, her passion, and you've had to get on board to get any attention at all.'

'N... no... no, that's not it at all. You're twisting everything.'

'You're a photo bomber,' Kim said, finally understanding. 'You're the person who jumps in front of the camera when someone is looking at the landscape. It's the only way you can be seen.'

Jessica's face was beginning to harden.

'You're doing this for attention, for approval. Painting a picture or writing a good story probably never got more than a passing glance. I'll bet she never attended one of your sports days. She was always busy at the clinic. You want your mother to notice you and—'

'Rubbish, Inspector,' she said, straightening, and tightening her grip on the knife. 'That's not why we do it.'

Kim realised that there was one word there that she had forgotten to consider. And from the smile growing on Jessica's face, that mistake was about to cost her very dear.

SEVENTY-EIGHT

Kim caught the plural a nanosecond too late as she felt a foot in her back and she fell to the ground. In the same instant, Jessica moved the knife to the base of Stephanie's throat.

A small cry escaped from her lips as she seemed to realise that the danger was real.

Kim looked up into the eyes of Eric, and finally everything became clear. They were a tag team depending on the gender of the person they were trying to trap. And it had always made more sense that two people were involved in the murder of Jamie Mills, as it would have been hard for one person to pull his dead weight up to the branch.

Eric must have been waiting in the car for Jessica to come back with Stephanie so they could somehow stage her murder to look like suicide.

The car. Bryant.

'Where's my—?'

'Keep still,' Eric said, placing his foot in the small of her back. The pain shot down through both of her legs.

'Don't worry about your partner. He's not coming and neither is anyone else.'

What the hell had he done to Bryant?

'I'm warning you...'

'You're in no position to warn anyone of anything,' he said, putting more weight through his foot and pressing down on her back.

Kim cried out in pain.

'What now?' Eric asked his sister. 'We need to finish her off and take care of this one as well.'

'Did you bring the rope down?' Jessica asked.

He nodded and looked to the ground.

'Okay, tie her up. By the time they find her body we'll be gone, but we need to be quick.'

Kim understood the panic in both of their voices and the need for speed. The plan to lure Stephanie away to wherever they'd planned to kill her had been precise with very little wiggle room on the timing. The priory was closing any minute and two cars were still in the car park. Someone would come looking. Kim couldn't move beneath the weight of Eric's foot. The pin in her right hip prevented her from throwing herself around on the ground. She felt the frustration building within her. She just needed more time.

'You're wrong you know,' Stephanie said quietly.

'Shut up,' Jessica snapped. 'We don't have time for—'

'Your schedule not mine,' Stephanie said. 'You're gonna have to drag me kicking and screaming anywhere or kill me right here, but before you do, you have to know you're wrong. Doesn't matter what you do to me cos you're all still gonna be wrong. Same-sex relationships are not all like that; neither are straight ones. It depends on the people not the gender, you idiots. Love of any kind is okay as long as you're not hurting anyone else. You pair of tosspots. I'm gay and killing me ain't gonna make it less so.'

Kim felt the emotion rise in her throat. For some reason she was proud of the girl and her speech.

'Whatever,' Jessica said, grabbing Stephanie's arm and pushing her forward. She held the knife in full view for security as she continued, 'I'll get this one to the car while you sort her out.'

Kim felt her hands being pulled behind her back.

As Stephanie was pulled past her, Kim saw her chance and threw out her left leg to kick Eric. She missed by an inch.

'Ooh, you're a little fighter, aren't you?' he said, sitting on her behind while he tied the rope around her ankles.

'Eric, you're not gonna get away with this,' Kim said, trying to wriggle around beneath him.

'Been doing okay so far, and with you out of the picture, there's no reason—'

'Hurry up, Eric,' Jessica called, holding on to Stephanie just a few feet away from them.

'My team will have worked this out by now so you've got no chance—'

'Shut up,' he said, trying to keep her in position to fix the rope.

'You'd like that, wouldn't you, Eric? You wanted all three of them to shut up, didn't you? Neither of you wanted them bad-mouthing Mommy. How did you put on such an act?' she asked, wriggling around and feeling the fabric of the rope brush her ankles.

'Eric, for God's sake, tie her up,' Jessica called out.

'Keep fucking still or...'

Kim could feel Eric's agitation. She was squirming and bucking, and his sister was needling him to go quicker.

'How did you pretend to be gay so effectively, Eric?' Kim asked. 'You must have been pretty damn good at convincing both Jamie and Liam that you were into it. Are you sure you're not—'

'Shut up. I mean it,' he said, yanking at her legs to keep them still.

'Eric, sort it,' Jessica called out.

Bryant, hurry the hell up, she thought.

'Poor Sarah got the short straw cos your sister sure isn't—'

'Leave Sarah out of this,' Eric spat, kicking her in the knee.

'Why should... oh my God... it's you,' she said as the last few pieces fell into place. 'You raped her?'

A twist of the ankle was the reward for her discovery.

'Don't listen to her, Eric,' Jessica urged.

'I won't tell you again. Shut your damn mouth.'

'You raped her. You tried to turn her straight by raping her?' Kim said as the nausea rose in her stomach.

'It wasn't rape,' he said, confirming her suspicions.

'Eric,' Jessica bellowed.

'I don't believe you, Eric. Something bad happened to Sarah that—' Kim stopped speaking as she felt the rope being secured around her ankles.

Without warning, her vision began to swim. Her mouth turned dry and her heart began to beat its way out of her chest. Beads of sweat appeared on her forehead. The sensation of the binding around her ankles brought the panic surging all around her body and took her back to a place which she was still trying hard to leave behind.

'You're gonna die, bitch.'

'I've been waiting years for this, bitch.'

Punch, kick, kick, kick, punch, kick.

'I'm gonna break every one of your bones, bitch.'

Kick, punch, kick, punch, punch, kick.

'I'm not gonna stop until the last breath leaves your body.'

Kick, punch, fear, helplessness, pain, fear, kick, defeat, death.

'Noooo,' she screamed, convulsing and bucking. The pain ripped through her body but she didn't care. She had put space between herself and a stunned Eric which she capitalised on.

She sprang up and kicked him in between the legs. He folded to the ground and she towered over him. Spittle flew from her mouth as she screamed in his face, 'You will not fucking tie me up again, you—'

Eric's expression brought her back to herself. Terror and confusion paralysed his features.

She grabbed his arm and threw him onto his front and sat in the small of his back. She dug her knees into his ribs. Hard. *This is Eric. This is Eric*, she repeated to herself over and over again. *Get control. This is Eric.*

She took long deep breaths to get the air into her lungs and clear her head.

Stephanie was fighting her every inch of the way, digging her heels into the soft grass, but Jessica was determined to move her along. The expression on her face said she intended to salvage something from the situation and that something was Stephanie's life. If she let go of Stephanie to help her brother, there was a chance she would be overpowered, knife or no knife.

'Hey, hear that?' Stephanie asked, looking to the top of the site. Jessica followed her gaze.

Stephanie took the opportunity to knock the knife from Jessica's hand and then push her to the side. Jessica fell to the ground and Stephanie dived on top of her. For a moment Kim couldn't see where one girl ended and the other began as a mass of limbs flailed around at the foot of a topiary robin.

Stephanie emerged triumphant with a good grip of Jessica's hair.

'Ow. Ow. Ow,' Jessica cried, trying to get her hair back as Stephanie pulled her down to the ground. She positioned her like her brother and sat on her back to keep her down while still holding on to her hair.

'Get off me, you filthy piece of...' Jessica didn't finish her sentence as she tried to writhe free.

'Keep still,' Stephanie said, flexing her knees into Jessica's side.

Kim's own prisoner appeared to have seen the commotion at the top of the site and had conceded defeat.

She nudged him with her knees. 'Where's Gabriel Denton?'

'Wh-What?' he spluttered into the grass.

'Your accountant. What have you done with him?'

'Why would we hurt Gabriel? He's not gay.'

Denial until the end, she thought. They'd both be asked again under caution. She was sure she heard the beginning of muffled sobbing beneath her.

Kim glanced at Stephanie. They were no more than ten feet apart, each sitting exactly the same on the back of a prisoner.

'You okay?'

Stephanie nodded as they both looked to the top of the hill where green-and-black uniforms were heading down towards them.

Kim was relieved to see that the person leading the charge was her good friend Bryant.

SEVENTY-NINE

'You sure you're okay?' Kim asked her colleague. The bleeding had stopped from the cut to the back of his head but a sizeable lump was already forming.

'I'm fine. Are you?'

She nodded as Jessica and Eric were placed into separate squad cars. 'I am now.'

The support that had arrived first had been their own, and the prisoners were being transported back to Halesowen.

'And don't rush,' she called out to one of the officers getting into the driver's seat. She didn't want them informing Celia before they got to do it. They were only a couple of minutes away from the clinic.

'What a pair, eh?' Bryant said as the first car pulled away.

'What a dangerous pair you mean?' Kim responded, because who knew when they were ever going to stop their murder spree? The files were full of ex-patients for them to contact and tempt, test, whatever you wanted to call it.

Kim headed towards Stephanie, who was huddled beside the lady from the gift shop, who appeared to be named Brenda.

'You okay?' she asked.

'I th… think so,' Stephanie said as her body gave a slight tremble.

The lady put a comforting arm around her shoulders. The adrenaline-fuelled bravado had passed and her body was now allowing her to accept the gravity of what she'd just been through.

'I j… just feel so s… stupid,' she said, shaking her head and looking to the ground.

'For what?' Kim asked.

'Being suckered in. They just played with me and I fell for it. I was an idiot.'

'You weren't an idiot, and you weren't the only person to fall for it. They didn't just message you randomly. They knew you already and then they mirrored you.'

Stephanie raised her head and shook it, not understanding.

'It's a powerful technique for putting someone at ease. I'll bet they pretended to be just like you. Hesitant, unsure, nervous?'

Stephanie nodded.

'It makes you feel safe, like the person can be trusted because they're just like you. Except they're now on their way to a life sentence in prison and you're not dead, so they're not quite as good as they thought they were.'

Stephanie chuckled and then shivered again.

'I know you're still feeling the shock, but I'm gonna need you to go to Halesowen to make a statement. That last car over there will—'

'I'll take her,' Brenda said, squeezing her tighter. 'I know her mum and I'll stay until she gets there.'

'Thank you. That's very kind of you. Is that okay with you, Stephanie?' Kim asked.

The girl nodded.

'And listen, everything you said to Jessica down there about love is absolutely bang on. If you don't quite believe it yet, just keep telling yourself, because you're amazing and it'll be a very lucky woman who gets you. Got it?'

Stephanie smiled and nodded.

'Take care of her, Brenda,' Kim said, moving away.

'Bloody hell, guv, did you spend your time off on an empathy crash course?' Bryant asked as they headed towards the car.

'You want another lump to match the one you've got?' she asked, holding out her hand.

'What?' he asked.

'Car keys.'

'Why?'

'You've got a lump on your head the size of a small mountain. I'm not trusting you to drive. Give me the keys.'

He did as she asked.

She got in the car and adjusted the seat.

'Ring Stacey,' she said, handing him her phone.

He dialled and put it on loudspeaker as she drove out of the car park.

'Everyone okay, boss?' Stacey offered as a greeting.

Bryant had made a quick call while she'd been cautioning Jessica and Eric.

'Other than Bryant growing another head we're fine. Listen up, they're both on their way and so is Stephanie. Penn, make sure she's comfortable and take her statement. They're both playing dumb about Gabriel Denton, so Stace I need you to go see Beth and tell her the truth of what we suspect has happened to her husband. We'll try again during formal questioning.'

'Okay, boss.'

'Before you do that, Stace, I need you to call Megan Shaw and ask her to come to the clinic. There are some people there that are going to need her help.'

'Right away, boss,' Stacey said, ending the call.

'What are we gonna do that'll need the psychologist's help?' Bryant asked. 'I thought we were going to advise the parents.'

'We are, Bryant. And while we're there, we're gonna carry out a much-needed community service.'

'Huh?'

'We're gonna shut the damn place down.'

EIGHTY

It was almost seven by the time they pulled up outside the clinic.

'You know, I'd forgotten how much fun it was letting you drive,' Bryant said, uncurling his fingers from the roof handle.

She had to admit that it felt good to see that look of abject terror on Bryant's face again. She'd missed it. He'd had control of his own steering wheel for far too long.

She locked the car and headed towards the clinic entrance. A security officer sat behind the desk. The place had switched into night-time mode.

'Celia Gardner please,' Kim said as they both held up their IDs.

'One second,' he said, reaching for the phone.

He spoke for a few seconds before ending the call. He buzzed the door open. 'The Gardners are in the office. Apparently you know where it is.'

'We do, thank you,' Kim said, entering the reception area for the second time that day. Her body was bruised and exhausted but this had to be seen through to the end, and this clinic could not be shut down one minute too soon for her liking.

'A colleague of ours, Megan Shaw, is on her way,' she said to the officer as she passed. 'Please send her in the right direction.'

He nodded his understanding and picked up his Stephen King novel before they were out the door.

'Must be long nights,' Bryant observed as Kim headed for the office at the end of the hallway.

She knocked and was instructed to enter.

'Didn't expect to see you again so soon, Inspector,' Celia said, wiping her hands on a napkin.

'Good evening, officers,' Victor called from his desk.

Both of their workspaces were littered with takeaway boxes. The aroma of Chinese food and pizza filled the air. Friday night dinner spent working at the desk; so normal, so ordinary, so about to be destroyed.

Kim took a seat as Celia came from behind her desk. The woman sat on the casual sofas, drawing Kim's attention to the unopened boxes of takeaway. Meals for her children when they returned from wherever they'd gone. Too old to control but never too old to feed.

'I'm not sure what more I can help you with unless you now want my bra size and inside leg measurement.'

Kim said nothing as she took a seat.

'Sorry, just a bit of Friday night humour. End of the week and all that. Please, ask your questions.'

'We haven't come with questions, Celia. We have answers. Mr Gardner, would you mind joining us?'

While she waited, Kim tried to analyse why the anger in her mind wasn't coming out of her mouth. She quickly realised what it was. The takeaway boxes had winded her. Just the simple act of a caring mother ordering food for children that were not coming home.

The married couple sat together and waited eagerly.

'We're here about Jessica and Eric.'

The colour left both of their faces as they clutched each other's hands.

'Are they okay?' Celia said first.

Kim nodded. 'There's been no accident, and they're both fit and well.'

The sighs of relief were audible as they both thought there was nothing worse that she could say. And they were right. Almost.

Celia frowned. 'So, what... who... why...?'

'I'm sorry for what I'm about to tell you both but your children have been arrested for murder; three counts: against Jamie Mills, Sarah—'

'Preposterous,' Victor exploded, letting go of his wife's hand and jumping to his feet. 'Have you lost your mind?'

'... Laing, Liam Sachs,' she continued. 'And one charge of attempted murder against Stephanie Lakehurst.'

Victor was glaring down at her, but Celia continued to regard her in silent shock.

'Is this some kind of a joke, Inspector?' she finally asked as Victor reached for his phone.

Kim shook her head as Victor pressed the call button and looked at her in an 'I'll show you' kind of way.

She heard Jessica's voicemail kick in. He ended the call and tried again.

'They won't be able to answer, Mr Gardner. They don't have their phones. They are under arrest for the murder of—'

'I'm not listening to this hogwash for another minute. I don't know what you're playing at, Inspector, but believe me when I say I'll see you in court for bogus charges before my children set one foot into a courtroom. You've obviously framed them because you don't like us or what we do here.' He smiled triumphantly as if he'd just discovered the answer. 'That's it, isn't it? This will never even get to court. You've made a mistake trying to frame this family, and by the time I'm finished, I'll have your badge, your reputation and—'

'They're both on their way to Halesowen police station,' Bryant said, stopping his tirade.

Victor looked to his wife for either guidance or permission.

'Go. Get Donald and get there as quickly as you can.'

Kim could hear the tremor in her voice.

Victor grabbed his jacket, gave Kim a filthy look and left the room.

'They didn't do this, Inspector,' Celia said as the door slammed behind her husband. 'I don't care how it looks or what you think you know, but my children didn't do this. Neither of them are capable of hurting anyone. They didn't do it, I tell you.'

'They did, Celia,' Kim said, quietly but definitely. 'There is no doubt in our minds.'

Celia shook her head and was clearly fighting back the tears.

'We have three victims all linked to this clinic: Jamie Mills, Sarah Laing and Liam Sachs. All three spent time here attempting to change their sexuality. All three failed.'

'So what does that have to do with Jess and Eric?'

'Have you heard the term "honey trapping"?' Kim asked.

Celia nodded.

'That's kind of what Jessica and Eric have been doing. They've been making contact with ex-patients, pretending to be gay and tempting them into clandestine meetings. The ones that resisted are still alive. The ones that responded are dead.'

'Why would these people agree to meet Jess or Eric? That doesn't make any—'

'They used a code name for all the accounts. The victims didn't know who they were messaging.'

'So it could have been anyone behind that fake account. You

have no way of proving it was Jess and Eric. You've framed them for this. My husband was right.'

'He might have been if we hadn't caught them in the act just over an hour ago. They were in the process of kidnapping Stephanie Lakehurst.'

'Stephanie?'

Kim nodded. 'Another ten minutes and she'd have been victim number four.'

'I d... don't believe you,' she said but with less conviction.

'It's true, Celia. Jessica admitted it, all of it, and she even told me why.'

Celia was shaking her head in denial as though her body was telling her it's what she was supposed to do as a mother, but she was listening.

'Everything about this family is tied up in this clinic. You brought it to life, and your entire family lives it and breathes it. They believe in it wholeheartedly. They believe in you. You've drummed your beliefs into them so well over the years about same-sex relationships that they dare not have any different opinion. They feel that your love for them is tied up with their support and belief in this, your first and favourite child.'

'You're saying this is my fault?'

Kim thought hard before nodding.

'Yes, Celia, it is. You haven't given them the chance to grow their own beliefs or opinions on homosexuality. You've fed them their opinion their whole lives. I don't for a minute think you intended this outcome. Of the things I think you're guilty of, murder isn't one of them, but think about it, if it wasn't for the strength of your convictions, your absolute faith in being able to change sexuality, three people would still be alive and your children wouldn't be facing the next thirty years in prison. They did it for you, Celia. They were destroying the evidence of your failure.'

Celia lowered her head into her hands and wept.

Kim exchanged a glance with Bryant, whose expression held the same level of sympathy as hers. Yes, she was a woman in pain, but how many people had suffered because of her ideology, her treatment methods? No. On the sympathy front Kim was all out.

And things were about to get worse. She'd already taken away two of her children and she was about to take away the third and, arguably, most important child of them all.

'We're closing you down, Celia.'

The woman's head shot up. 'What?'

'We have the murders of three former patients carried out by two staff members who happen to be your children. Reopening will be for the courts to decide, but for now my priority is safeguarding the patients you have here now. We've drafted in—' Kim stopped speaking as a knock sounded on the door.

'Ah, speaking of which. Come in,' Kim called out.

Megan Shaw stepped into the room and closed the door behind her.

'Celia, I'd like you to meet...' Kim's words trailed away as she realised Celia knew who she was looking at.

Neither woman was looking at anyone else in the room.

Kim caught her breath at the emotion that travelled between them. Anger, hurt, love, desire, passion and regret.

The electricity in the room jolted Kim into understanding.

Kim realised that Megan had never actually answered the question about meeting Celia in her youth. She had lost the love of her life in her teens. Kim had assumed the woman had died, but that wasn't the kind of loss she'd meant.

'Oh my God, it was you two, wasn't it?' Kim asked. 'You two killed Celia's mother.'

Megan nodded without breaking her gaze away from Celia.

'The jig is up Ceecee. We've had long enough.'

Celia swallowed and said nothing.

'I missed the train, Ceecee, I missed the bloody train.'

Tears spilled out of Celia's eyes and rolled over her cheeks.

Kim caught Bryant's eye and nodded towards the door in the corner that led to a toilet and kitchen. The murder of Celia's mother had been a West Mercia case and they needed to be informed.

'Can you explain?' Kim asked as Bryant broke the force field between them.

'Ceecee's mother caught us kissing when we were sixteen years old,' Megan explained. 'She ordered Ceecee to break up with me, and she pretended to.'

'She said if she ever caught us again she'd send me away so that we'd never see each other again,' Celia added.

Megan stepped back in. 'We couldn't let that happen. We loved each other so we made the plan. To us it was as simple as getting her out of the way so we could be together. We didn't bargain on the blood, the sound, the realisation that we'd taken a life.'

Megan paled as the memory returned.

'Despite what we'd done, we still loved each other. Ceecee was sent to live with her aunt. I managed to get her address and sent a note giving a date and time to meet. There were no mobile phones then and we now lived over forty miles apart. On the day we were to meet, I missed my train. I got the times mixed up and I missed it. There was no way to let her know.'

'I thought she'd dumped me,' Celia continued. 'After all we'd been through, I could barely breathe at the thought of it. The pain was unbearable. I couldn't function. My life was over and I just wanted the agony to stop. I was trying to come to terms with what we'd done and then I'd lost the person I'd done it for.'

'Ceecee's aunt found out about us and put her in this—'

'I begged her to bring me here, Meg,' Celia protested. 'She told me about it and I pleaded with her to let me come.'

Megan tried to hide the disappointment that flitted across her face.

'And I'm glad I did,' Celia said, pushing out her chin as though she was sixteen again. 'I've lived a happy, normal life. I have beautiful children, and I'll never regret the decision I made.'

Kim wondered if Celia had forgotten what had happened in the last hour of her life. Her beautiful children had murdered at least three people.

Sadness washed over Megan's face as she shook her head. 'If that's your truth, Ceecee, I'm not going to try and change your mind.'

Megan turned towards Kim. 'I'm ready, Inspector, for whatever needs to happen next.'

Bryant appeared back in the room and nodded. They were on their way.

She stood.

'Megan Shaw, Celia Gardner, I am arresting you both for the murder of Erin Thatcher. You do not have to say anything. But it may harm your defence if you do not mention when questioned something which you later rely on in court. Anything you do say may be given in evidence. Do you both understand?'

Both women nodded.

Kim looked at them both individually, even though they could barely look at each other.

Megan had used her guilt from the terrible crime she'd committed to do good things. She had counselled and advised hundreds of confused teenagers and young adults. Stephanie had been given the courage to accept herself and maybe find love by this woman.

Celia had been in love, deeply in love, enough to murder her own mother for threatening that love and had then totally rebelled against her own feelings and desires.

How many lives had been lost or ruined? What had been

the cost of being forced to end a relationship because it didn't fit with convention? What could have been saved if they'd been allowed to stay together?

She sighed heavily. She couldn't remember a time when cautioning any suspect had brought her a level of sadness worse than what she was feeling now.

EIGHTY-ONE

Stacey knocked the door to Beth Denton's home. She had no idea if she felt better or worse about telling the woman they thought her husband was dead or in love with someone else. And quite frankly she wasn't sure how the reaction would compare either.

Beth opened the door on the second knock and made little effort to hide her frustration.

'Really, officer, back so soon?'

'May I come in?' Stacey asked, ignoring the woman's irritation. She was soon going to be feeling a whole lot worse.

Before entering, she nodded to the driver of the squad car that she'd be just a few minutes.

Stacey followed Beth to the kitchen, where she resumed rinsing dishes and putting them in the dishwasher. She scrubbed particularly hard at a tomato-based stain on a casserole dish, and Stacey had to wonder if she was visualising her face at the bottom of the bowl.

'Beth, can you sit down?'

She stilled. 'Have you found him?'

'That's what I want to discuss.'

She waited until the woman was seated. This was her last task at the end of a very long day before being able to go home to Devon's home-made special chow mein. It was her absolute favourite, but with the news she was having to deliver to Beth, she could wait just a little bit longer.

'So?' Beth said, pulling in her chair. 'Just spit it out.'

'We believe Gabriel may have been harmed by one of his clients,' Stacey said, doing exactly what she'd asked.

'Harmed?'

'The clients he worked for last week run a clinic that carries out questionable treatment on gay people. Someone there tried to tell the world what was going on by smuggling out a letter with your husband.'

'But you have the letter,' she said.

'We believe they think he read it and so knew what they were doing.' Stacey took a breath. 'People from that clinic have this evening been arrested for murder.'

Beth's hand covered her mouth but not before a startled cry escaped.

'They will be questioned extensively about Gabriel, but so far they're admitting nothing.'

'You think they've hurt him? Or worse?'

Stacey opened her hands. 'It certainly looks that way, but right now we can't say for sure.'

Beth seemed to get the gist of what she was saying. 'Are you telling me that I might never know for sure what happened to my husband?'

'We won't ever stop trying to find out,' Stacey assured her. 'Gabriel's details will remain on the missing persons list until—'

'Until you find his body is what you're telling me?'

Stacey had no answer. She really was beginning to wonder if another officer would have handled this situation a whole lot better than she had.

'I'll never give up looking for him, even if you do.'

'Beth, I wish—'

'Please don't be offended but I'd really like you to leave. I have a lot to process and quite frankly you're just a reminder that I have no resolution.'

'Call me if there's anything you need,' Stacey said, heading to the door.

'Thank you for your kind words, officer, but I think we both know that from this point on I'm on my own.'

The front door closed behind her.

Stacey walked slowly down the path. It had been a good day. They had caught bad people and yet she'd rarely felt as shitty as this in her life.

She feared even Devon's home-made special chow mein wasn't going to cheer her tonight.

EIGHTY-TWO

The muscles are contracting in my arms. They've been tightly pulled behind my back. My legs are straight out in front of me, tied at the ankles. The slightest movement rubs against the blistering sores. I can't see beyond the darkness. My mouth is dry, my throat is sore. I feel ulcers on my lips and tongue.

I think I know where I am.

The drugs don't feel as strong today, but around me it's silent. I hear nothing. There's been no sound for hours or days. I'm not sure any more. I want to cry. I feel stupid, but I want to let it all out – the fear, the sadness, the hate. I want to bawl it all out of me, but I hold the tears back, still praying that this is some kind of nightmare and that soon I'll wake up. If I feel the hot salty tears rolling over my cheeks, I'll have to accept that this is real. I try to pretend it's not.

There's a noise. It's familiar – a low humming sound.

The light goes on and it's real. My suspicion is true.

I am in my own cellar and it's my own wife who stands before me. She's smiling.

'Oh, sweetheart, you're never going to believe what's happened now. They actually think you're dead.'

I let the hate fill my eyes and growl through the gag.

'Don't be silly, darling. You know I can't take it out quite yet. I have to be sure they're gone. Then you can have this nice cup of tea. Anyway, as I was saying, my plan exceeded my own expectations. First, they come and tell me that you've gone away to get your head sorted. That's all I wanted. In a couple of weeks, I would have called them and told them that you'd contacted me and asked for a divorce. But now they're not even looking for you. How cool is that? We're never going to be disturbed again.'

My heart drops into my stomach. My last hope dashed. How can a man just disappear? I know exactly how. I know that my wife has gradually isolated me from my family and friends until I had no one. Over the years I've wondered if Craig had actually been as guilty as I'd been led to believe, but I'd fought away the doubts, feeling disloyal to my wife for even letting the thoughts into my head.

'We don't need anyone else, do we, my love?' she asks, sitting on the stool four feet away from me.

'You may have thought so for ten minutes when that slut at work threw herself at you, but I think you see now that she was just trying to break us up, get between us; but we'd never allow that, would we?'

I should have seen the signs years ago. Any friends we made she found a reason to dislike within days. If we got talking to another couple at a restaurant, we would never go there again. The migraines when there was a work social event, the onset of anxiety attacks when I said I wanted a hobby outside of the house.

'I'm so glad I asked you to fetch that money out the bank. That really put the icing on the cake. You really thought I wanted to go get a new car?'

Yes, I really had thought that. She begged me to take the day off and go car shopping with her. I regretted that I wouldn't get to see Wendy, but I was already feeling guilty for my emotions even though I haven't done anything wrong.

I returned from fetching the money and was hit with something heavy as I walked in the door. When I woke, I was down here, tied up and drugged in a space I'd recently cleaned out.

'I wonder if your work whore has got the message yet?'

The thought of Wendy brings fresh sorrow to my heart. We clicked. I looked forward to our lunches together. I sent her a text. My wife checked my phone.

And now I'm pretty sure I'll never see her again. I don't know how long I've been down here, but I don't think I'm going anywhere. To everyone else I'm dead, and now I wish I was.

'So it's just us again. Just like it's always been. We don't need...' Her words trail away as a noise sounds at the top of the stairs.

Suddenly there is a woman, a black woman with a satchel, surveying the scene with horror. I don't know what's real any more. Is she a dream?

My wife's face turns vicious.

'You can't just come down here without—'

'Oh yes I can, Mrs Denton, when I fear for someone's safety. And after seeing you load the dishwasher, I remembered you were doing the same thing this morning. Too many plates, cups, saucepans for one person, and you told me yourself you have no family or friends. You knew he was growing away from you. You've managed to isolate him over the years and get rid of anyone he was close to so that it was just the two of you. Your failure to conceive a child prompted you to pull him even closer. That was bearable as long as you had each other. Just the two of you, but then you saw his text message to Wendy and that was the final straw. You knew you were losing him.'

As she speaks, she looks at me and then back at my wife.

'How could you treat him like this?'

'He's my husband,' Beth spits. 'No one is taking him away from me.'

'No, but we'll be taking you away from him.'

The woman steps further into the space to reveal a police officer behind her.

'Take her upstairs and cuff her,' the woman says.

My wife makes all kinds of protest but the officer is having none of it.

When they're gone, the woman kneels on the cold ground beside me. I still don't trust that she's real.

'Gabriel, my name is DC Stacey Wood and I've been looking for you.'

She's been looking. Someone has been looking. The emotion gathers in my throat.

She takes the gag from my mouth. 'It's okay, Gabe, you're safe now,' she says, touching my arm.

Again the tears want to come, and this time I make no effort to stop them.

EIGHTY-THREE

'Well, that was a week and a half,' Kim said to her brother's headstone. She'd come every Sunday morning since she'd got out of hospital, seeking the same answer every time.

The week had exhausted her and not just physically. From the very first minute of re-entering the workplace, she'd had to hold her tongue, stifle her irritation and stare at a living, breathing reminder of what had happened to her. In addition, she'd watched as he'd started to mess up yet another investigation. And if that hadn't been enough, he'd tried to jump her in the station car park.

Go slowly, Woody had said. Chance would have been a fine thing.

Her first real task had been to visit Jamie's parents. The anger still rose within her when she thought of their bigotry and how that had affected their son. She had not graced them with a personal update. She had delegated, unable to be in their company again without the real risk of violence or a formal complaint.

She had taken the time to visit Sarah's parents, especially as

Sarah's child had been the key to unravelling it all and getting the charges finalised.

Kim had taken over the questioning of Eric on Saturday morning when both siblings had been firm 'no comment' interviewees on the back of advice from the clinic's notorious legal team.

She had explained to Eric that she was using the DNA sample provided to run against the DNA of Sarah Laing's child. The news that Sarah had borne a child had stunned him into opening his mouth, leaving Kim in no doubt that it would come back a positive match. She had taken advantage of his confusion and had shot rapid-fire questions at him until he tripped himself up.

He blamed his sister for starting it all, and she blamed him. After silence came self-preservation. Eric wouldn't admit to the rape of Sarah and there was no way they could prove it. Kim had her own thoughts on the subject, but as it was her opinion, she chose not to share it with Sarah's parents. The child never needed to carry that baggage.

The hardest house call of the previous day had been to Liam Sachs's wife, Monica, who hadn't known a thing about his double life.

While cross-referencing the dates, they had found that Liam's stay at the clinic had been at the same time he was supposed to have been on an unavoidable work trip around Asia. It had happened suddenly when their child was seven months old.

Monica understood that Liam had wanted to be the best husband and father he could be and that he had loved them both very much. Monica had collapsed with a mixture of grief and pride when Kim had explained that even during his last few minutes alive, he had tried to point them in the right direction. As Penn had spotted in the suicide note, Liam had used two capital letters where they shouldn't have been. He'd capitalised a J and an E, trying to communicate that the killers were Jess and Eric.

Kim had asked Woody to get the legal team to look over the NDAs signed by the patients. She hoped they could find a way to break the imposed silence, so that every person who had spent time there was free to tell their story. She hoped that one day even John Dermot would be able to accept Jack's story as his own, recover from that knowledge and find the strength to be the person he wanted to be.

Surprisingly, the person that had the biggest slice of her sympathy was Victor Gardner, a confused, broken man who had apologised to her in the police station reception the day before. She hadn't known why he was sitting there: not one member of his family was going to be coming home any time soon. Bryant had called him a taxi just before midnight.

Her thoughts went to Celia and Megan. Oh, what a waste. They had killed to be together and then thrown it all away because Megan had missed her train. Celia had spent her whole life running away from what they'd done, and Megan had spent her life trying to make up for it. Both had offered a full confession. Without Megan's help, they had called on every psychologist and counsellor they had worked with to offer support to the current patients at the clinic. The place had been closed, and Kim hoped it never opened again.

A full search had been conducted of the patients' floor once the building was empty. There was one room at the end of the hallway, a guest suite not being used because of a plumbing problem. That was where they'd found the real chair used for aversion therapy as well as the restraints used for a multitude of treatment methods. Other equipment found had included leather belts and whips and bottles filled with noxious substances also used in the so-called aversion therapy. It appeared that even though they'd given nothing away during their guided tour, the family had decided to play it safe and the torture equipment had been removed within two hours of them leaving the premises. It was no surprise that they'd been so accommodating during the execution of the search warrant once they'd seen that patients' quarters were out of bounds.

Her employee of the week had to go to Stacey. No question. Without her keen observation and intuition, Gabriel Denton would still be tied up on his cellar floor. Kim shuddered at the thought. Stacey had taken the liberty of ringing both Gabriel's brother and his colleague. Wendy had arrived at the hospital within minutes, and although he'd not been able to say much due to an infection from the filthy gag, his eyes said he was pleased to see her.

Stacey had stayed with him long enough to see Craig arrive and to witness the emotional reunion that had taken place between them. Once he was out of hospital and had made his statement, he was going to Bristol to stay with his brother for a while.

And herself? Yes, the week had been exhausting, but it had also been exhilarating. She had been back amongst her team doing the job she loved. Of course she wasn't fully recovered. She wasn't that stupid. The fact had been made clear to her when Eric had tried to tie her up, but there was progress. She'd done as Frost suggested, although that admission would never leave her mouth. There was no improvement yet, but it was early days and she'd give it a fair chance.

There would be times when the ordeal came back to haunt her, but she had to start putting it behind her, which she would do once she'd spoken to the man who was currently parking his Astra Estate beside her Ninja.

He stepped out of the car and locked it.

She looked around the cemetery. 'Who the bloody hell is gonna nick it?'

'Habit,' he said, coming to stand beside her. He nodded to the headstone. 'Hey, Mikey, she been bending your ear again?'

'Yep,' she answered. 'I talk to him. I tell him what a nightmare my partner is. And other stuff. I ask him one question every week.'

'Tell me,' he urged.

She took a breath. It wasn't easy trusting another person with the innermost workings of her mind. She wouldn't have shared with a therapist, definitely not Frost and not even Ted. Only her one true friend. 'You'd think the nightmares would be about the pain, the beating, the fear, wouldn't you?' she asked him. 'You'd think they'd be about Symes?'

'Of course,' Bryant answered. 'I'd be surprised if that face didn't haunt your dreams every night.'

'Never. Not once has it been about Symes,' Kim said, nodding towards Mikey's grave. 'It's about him. I died, Bryant, and he wasn't there. He wasn't there,' she said, looking away.

'He will be,' Bryant said firmly. 'It wasn't your time. If he'd been there, you would have gone towards him. He knows that, but it wasn't your time. When it is your time, he'll be there.'

'Do you think so?' she asked, wanting to believe him.

'I absolutely think so but not yet. You've still got criminals to catch.'

Kim hoped he was right, and she was pleased to have finally said the words aloud, but that wasn't why she'd asked him to meet her.

She moved away from the grave and stood at the back of his car.

'Remember the other day when we stopped and had that chat in the lay-by?'

'For the record, may I clarify that we're talking about the time when you actually apologised to me?'

'Yep, but don't get too smug about it cos there was something I had to say that day as well but decided it could wait.'

'Okay.'

She turned to face him and met his gaze. 'Why did you lie to me?'

'About what?'

'About saving my life. Leanne couldn't have done it. Chest compressions with a dislocated shoulder? Really? It was you, so why did you lie?'

He broke her gaze and looked down at the ground. 'Thought it might be awkward with you being the boss but being eternally grateful and thankful to me, like, forever.'

Kim burst out laughing. 'You might get a mug of Colombian Gold but that's about it. Anyway, thanks, and just be sure I'd have haunted the bloody life out of you if you'd failed to bring me back.'

'Don't doubt it for a minute.'

'Right, glad we got that sorted. Come on, meet me back at mine.'

'Huh?'

'You're helping me clear all the exercise shit out of my garage.'

'And why would I want to do that?'

'Cos that's what friends do for each other, Alan. That's what friends do.'

A LETTER FROM ANGELA

First of all, I want to say a huge thank you for choosing to read *Hidden Scars*, the seventeenth instalment of the Kim Stone series, and to many of you for sticking with Kim Stone and her team since the very beginning.

And if you'd like to keep up to date with all my latest releases, just sign up at the website link below.

www.bookouture.com/angela-marsons

From the moment I heard the term 'conversion therapy' I knew I wanted to explore the concept. The more I thought about the idea, the more I wondered how deeply runs the belief that changing one's sexuality is possible. Alongside the subject of conversion therapy, I wanted to explore the motivations behind what makes us want to change at all. In an age where surgery is available to change/improve/enhance almost every physical aspect of ourselves, what drives us towards change rather than acceptance?

Additionally, it was difficult to write Kim's return to work after her near-death experience at the hands of the killer Symes. Any expert would know that she wasn't ready to return to work, but as usual she has put the experience into a box and hidden it from view.

On a lighter note, it was fun to finally reveal Bryant's first name right at the end.

I thoroughly enjoyed writing *Hidden Scars*, and if you

enjoyed it, I would be forever grateful if you'd write a review. I'd love to hear what you think, and it can also help other readers discover one of my books for the first time. Or maybe you can recommend it to your friends and family...

I'd love to hear from you – so please get in touch on my Facebook or Goodreads page, Twitter or through my website.

Thank you so much for your support – it is hugely appreciated.

Angela Marsons

www.angelamarsons-books.com

 facebook.com/angelamarsonsauthor

ACKNOWLEDGEMENTS

It's no surprise that my first and most humongous THANK YOU goes to my partner in both life and crime, Julie. After wrestling with a problem for a good couple of days, I called her for a meeting and within ten minutes I was back at my desk with enthusiasm and a clear direction. As I work through every first draft, I do so with the confidence that there is someone that will gently guide me back to the vision that I originally had in my head. She is equally as invested in the characters and story-lines as I am, and she holds my hand throughout the process on every single journey.

Thank you to my mum and dad who continue to spread the word proudly to anyone who will listen. And to my sister Lyn, her husband Clive and my nephews Matthew and Christopher for their support too.

Thank you to Amanda and Steve Nicol who support us in so many ways, and to Kyle Nicol for book spotting my books everywhere he goes.

I would like to thank the growing team at Bookouture for their continued enthusiasm for Kim Stone and her stories.

Special thanks to my editor, Claire Bord. I sometimes wonder if this poor woman walks away from our 'ideas' briefing shaking her head in despair, wondering what idea I might come up with next. If she ever has doubts about my intentions, she doesn't voice them and allows me the creative freedom to explore every crazy idea that comes into my head and then meets the result with unending passion, which makes every publication as fresh and exciting as the first.

To Kim Nash (Mama Bear), who works tirelessly to promote our books and protect us from the world. To Noelle Holten, who has limitless enthusiasm and passion for our work, and to Sarah Hardy and Jess Readett, who also champion our books at every opportunity.

A special thanks must go to Janette Currie, who has copy-edited the Kim Stone books from the very beginning. Her knowledge of the stories has ensured a continuity for which I'm extremely grateful. Also need a special mention for Henry Steadman who is responsible for the fabulous book covers which I absolutely love.

Thank you to the fantastic Kim Slater who has been an incredible support and friend to me for many years now who, despite writing outstanding novels herself, always finds time for a chat. Massive thanks to Emma Tallon who keeps me going with funny stories and endless support. Also to the fabulous Renita D'Silva and Caroline Mitchell, both writers that I follow and read voraciously and without whom this journey would be impossible. Huge thanks to the growing family of Bookouture authors who continue to amuse, encourage and inspire me on a daily basis.

Thank you to Cornell Charles Stamoran who won the chance to be a named character following an auction in support of Aid for Ukraine. Your generosity is truly appreciated.

My eternal gratitude goes to all the wonderful bloggers and reviewers who have taken the time to get to know Kim Stone and follow her story. These wonderful people shout loudly and share generously not because it is their job but because it is their passion. I will never tire of thanking this community for their support of both myself and my books. Thank you all so much.

Massive thanks to all my fabulous readers, especially the

ones that have taken time out of their busy day to visit me on my website, Facebook page, Goodreads or Twitter.